PENGUIN

Junk

Melvin Burgess was born in 1954 and was brought up in Sussex and Berkshire. After leaving school he moved to Bristol, where he was generally unemployed, with occasional jobs, mainly in the building industry. He wrote, on and off, unsuccessfully. His first book, *The Cry of the Wolf*, was published in 1990.

Melvin Burgess writes full time and lives in Manchester with his wife and their children.

JUNK

Melvin Burgess

PENGUIN BOOKS

PENGUIN BOOKS

Published by the Penguin Group
Penguin Books Ltd, 27 Wrights Lane, London W8 5TZ, England
Penguin Putnam Inc., 375 Hudson Street, New York, New York 10014, USA
Penguin Books Australia Ltd, Ringwood, Victoria, Australia
Penguin Books Canada Ltd, 10 Alcorn Avenue, Toronto, Ontario, Canada M4V 3B2
Penguin Books (NZ) Ltd, Private Bag 102902, NSMC, Auckland, New Zealand

On the worldwide web at: www.penguin.com

Penguin Books Ltd, Registered Offices: Harmondsworth, Middlesex, England

First published by Andersen Press Limited 1996
Published in Penguin Books 1997
Reissued in Penguin Books 1999
3 5 7 9 10 8 6 4 2

Penguin Film and TV tie-edition first published 1999

Text copyright © Melvin Burgess, 1996
All rights reserved

The moral right of the author has been asserted

Made and printed in England by Clays Ltd, St Ives plc

British Library Cataloguing in Publication Data
A CIP catalogue record for this book is available from the British Library

ISBN 0–141–30557–6

For Gilly

Acknowledgements

Anarchy in the UK © 1978 Rotten Music Ltd., Warner/Chappell Music Ltd., London W1Y 3FA is reproduced by kind permission of International Music Publications Ltd.

Girls Just Wanna Have Fun written by Robert Hazard. Lyrics reproduced by kind permission of Sony Music Publishing.

Ever Fallen in Love written by Peter Shelley. Lyrics reproduced by kind permission of Complete Music Ltd.

Promises written by Peter Shelley and Steve Diggle. Lyrics reproduced by kind permission of Complete Music Ltd. and Notting Hill Music Ltd.

The Beast written by Peter Perrett. Lyrics reproduced by kind permission of Complete Music Ltd.

Another Girl, Another Planet written by Peter Perrett. Lyrics reproduced by kind permission of Complete Music Ltd.

Author's Note

This book is set roughly in the early and middle 1980s, when I myself was living in Bristol. All the major events have happened, are happening and will no doubt continue to happen. I saw many of them myself and heard about many more. As for the people here ... some are pure invention, some are seeded from real people and then fictionalised, some are fictitious with bits of real people stirred in. The only proper portrait is Richard, one of the nicest and strangest people I've ever met, who is beyond praise or prosecution, bless him. He died on the motorway some years ago.

The book isn't fact; it isn't even faction. But it's all true, every word.

1

A boy and a girl were spending the night together in the back seat of a Volvo estate car. The car was in a garage. It was pitch black.

'I'm hungry,' complained the girl.

The boy turned on a torch and peered inside a grey canvas rucksack behind him. 'There's an apple.'

'Nah. Any crisps left?'

'Nope.'

Gemma sighed and leaned back in the car. She pulled a blanket over herself. 'It's cold,' she said.

'Barry'll be here soon,' Tar said. He watched her closely in the torchlight, frowning anxiously. 'Sorry you came?' he asked.

Gemma looked over and smiled. 'Nah.'

Tar snuggled up against her. Gemma stroked his head. 'You better save the batteries,' she said in a minute.

Tar turned off the torch. At once it was so black you couldn't see your own hand. Surrounded by the smell of damp concrete, oil and petrol, they carried on their conversation cuddling in the dark.

Tar said, 'Come with me.'

'What?' She was amazed, surprised. It had never occurred to her ... He could feel her staring at him even though it was too dark to see anything. In the darkness, Tar blushed deeply.

'You must be crazy,' said Gemma.

'Why?'

'What have I got to run away from?'

'Wait till you get home ...' The two laughed. Gemma had been banned a week before from seeing Tar. Her parents had no idea where she was that night, but they had a pretty good idea whom she was with.

'It'd be something to do,' said Tar in a minute. 'You're always saying how bored you are.'

'That's true.' Gemma was the most bored person she knew. Sitting in class she sometimes felt dizzy with it, that she'd pop or faint or something if it didn't stop. She felt she'd do anything just to have a life.

Still ...

'What about school and that?'

'You can go to school any time.'

'I can run away any time in my life.'

Gemma would have liked to. She wanted to. But ... What for? She didn't love Tar, she only liked him. Her parents, and her father in particular, were totally ghastly but he didn't knock her around. Not yet anyhow.

Was being bored a reason for running away to the city at fourteen years old?

Gemma said, 'I don't think so, Tar.'

Tar lay still in her lap. She knew what he must be feeling because she'd seen it on his face so many times. Tar's heart was painted on his face.

Gemma bent down close. 'I'm sorry,' she whispered.

Tar had a reason, plenty of reasons. The latest were painted on his face, too. His upper lip swelled over his teeth like a fat plum. His left eye was black, blue, yellow and red. Gemma had to be careful not to touch his wounds when she stroked his face.

There was a noise at a small door behind them. Tar and Gemma ducked down out of sight behind the seats.

'It's only me ...'

'Bloody hell – you nearly killed me,' hissed Gemma angrily.

'Sorry. Here, put that torch on so's I can see where I'm going ...'

Tar shone the beam over to a plump blond boy carrying a plastic bag. He grinned and came over.

'I suppose we ought to have a secret knock or something,' he said. 'Here ...' He handed over the bag. Gemma poked inside.

'It's only rolls and cheese. They'd have missed anything else,' apologised Barry.

'Didn't you get any butter?' complained Gemma.

'No. But I got some pickle ...' Barry handed over a pot from his coat pocket.

'Branston. Brilliant!' Gemma began tearing up the rolls and chunks of cheese. Barry had forgotten a knife; she had to spread the pickle with her finger.

Barry watched Tar's face by the torchlight. 'Christ! He really laid into you this time, didn't he?'

'Looks like a bowl of rotten fruit, doesn't it?' said Gemma. 'Not that you'd want to eat it ...'

They laughed.

'You haven't been turning the light on, by the way, have you?' asked Barry anxiously. 'Only ...'

'We said we wouldn't, didn't we?'' demanded Gemma.

'... only they might see it through the cracks in the garage door.'

'I told you ...'

'All right.'

Gemma stuffed a roll leaking pickle into her mouth. 'Wan won?' she asked Tar thickly.

'Yeah, please ...' he beamed.

There was a pause while Gemma pulled another roll in half.

'When are you going?' Barry wanted to know.

'Tomorrow,' said Tar.

'Got everything?'

Tar leaned over the front seat and patted his rucksack. It wasn't that full.

Barry nodded. He watched Tar eating for a second and then he blurted out, 'But what about your mum?'

Tar looked stricken.

Gemma glared. 'His mum's gonna be all right. She'll probably clear off herself once Tar's gone. She's only been staying because of him anyway; she's said that thousands of times, hasn't she?'

Tar nodded slowly, like a tormented tortoise. Gemma glared at Barry and mouthed, 'Shut up!'

'Right.' Barry nodded energetically. 'Best thing you could do for her, clear off. She won't have anything to tie her to the old bastard then.'

'That's what I'm hoping,' said Tar.

It got very cold in the garage later on. Gemma and Tar snuggled up together and wrapped the blankets around them. They kissed. Gemma didn't stop him when his hand glided under her top, but when she felt his hand sliding down her tummy she slapped his fingers lightly.

'Naughty,' she said.

'Why not?' asked Tar in surprise.

'Not here ...'

She didn't mind him touching her there. But she was worried about spending the night together ...

'I just don't want it to go any further.'

'You might never see me again after tonight,' said Tar cunningly.

Gemma shook her head.

'It won't go any further, then.'

'All right.'

2
Gemma

My parents are incompetent. They haven't got a clue. They think being a parent is like being an engineer or something – you do this, you do that, and this is the result you get at the other end.

Someone ought to give parents lessons before they allow them to breed.

That night in the garage, we never did anything. I mean, I wanted to sleep with him. It would have a been a nice way to say goodbye, and poor Tar could've done with a nice goodbye, really. That's to say, if I'd done it before, it would have been a nice way to say goodbye, but I don't know if the first time is the right way to say goodbye. But I might have done it anyway – for me, for him. It wasn't for either of us I didn't.

I only didn't do it for my parents. I wanted to be able to say, Look ... this was my boyfriend. He was in some really nasty trouble, he was really upset, he was hurt, he'd been beat up by his dad for the nth time, he was running away and I spent the night with him because he needed some company.

And I think he might be in love with me.

But there was no sex, we never did that. It was just ... being close.

Is that human or what?

The only thing I regret is that I put my dad before Tar. I won't make that mistake twice.

When I got home the next day, all hell broke loose.

My dad was wagging up and down the room. 'There must be limits ... there must be rules!'

Mum was sitting on the edge of the chair with no lips trying not to cry.

'We all have to follow the rules, Gemma. When I forbid something I expect you to obey me ...'

I tried to smile at my mum but she looked the other way.

Then he came out with this real beauty. Listen to this: 'Her reputation is a girl's greatest asset ...'

Stone Age!

'What about her GCEs?' I said. 'What about her ability to put her lipstick on properly?'

My mum tried to bring the conversation into the real world.

'Darling, you're too young –' she began.

'She'll have to learn!'

'What are we going to do, Gemma? Your father's right, there have to be rules. Surely you can see that?'

'Where's David?' my father said. That's Tar. I christened him Tar, because he was always telling me off for smoking.

'You'll get tar in your lungs,' he kept saying.

'Ring up his house and find out,' I told my dad.

'I have. He's not come home. But his father's promised to give him what for when he does.'

I nearly said, He'll have a long wait, then. But I bit my tongue. 'He already has,' I told him. 'He beat him up again the night before last.'

Dad snorted. 'He got into another fight, you mean.'

Tar's dad's a teacher at one of the local high schools. You can see the way my dad's brain works. Teacher = good. Bad relationship with Tar = Tar's fault.

'He hits the bottle,' I told him. 'Go round and see him next time. You'll smell it. That's the sort of influence we young people have to look up to,' I said.

'Don't try and be clever with me!'

'Look ... Tar was upset. He just needed someone to stay with him. But there was no sex. Honest. All right?'

There was a pause in which my dad looked at me. You could see how furious he was. As if me being responsible was some sort of threat to his authority.

Then he said, 'Liar.'

The whole room went cold. My mother was furious, I reckon. She glared at him. I mean, I don't know if she believed me, but she wanted to. I don't know what he believed. He just wanted to hurt me, I reckon.

He did. But I didn't let him see that. I just said, 'I believe every word you say, too,' or something, and made for the door. Of course that wasn't good enough for him and he dragged me back and started up again but I'd had enough. I just lost it.

'Just ... drop down dead!' I screamed and I ran out of the room.

I locked myself in my room and tried to take the planet over with music.

THEN WHEN HE SEES YOU IN THE COLD MORNING LIGHT
HE SAYS DAUGHTER WHAT YOU GONNA DO WITH YOUR L-I-IFE?
OH DADDY DEAR YOU KNOW YOU'RE STILL NUMBER ONE
BUT GIRLS JUST WANNA HAVE FU-UN
OH GIRLS JUST WANNA HAVE FUN
THAT'S ALL THEY REALLY WA-A-A-A-ANT ...

I played that over and over and over but I expect it was lost on my dad. He never listens to the lyrics.

The difference between Tar's dad and my dad is that Tar's dad is basically a reasonable bloke who forgets to be reasonable, even if it is in rather a big way. Whereas my dad's basically an unreasonable bloke who never forgets just how much you can get away with by *appearing* to be reasonable.

He came up afterwards and apologised and for a bit I thought the whole thing was going to be settled in a friendly way. I should have guessed what was going on when he started on about how he'd been big enough to admit when he was wrong. Now it was my turn.

Well, I wasn't wrong. I'd have been a real cold bitch not to keep Tar company on his last day in Minely. I was beginning to think the only thing I'd done wrong was refusing to sleep with him. But I know when to open my mouth as well as when to keep it shut. Dad's easy enough to handle. The trouble is he enrages me so much I forget to do it sometimes.

I decided it was time to do sugar-sugar. I apologised, whimpered, flung my arms around him and gave him a hug and a kiss.

'You're still my number one, Daddy,' I told him. And he went as pink as a cherry. I had him right there, in the palm of my hand.

That was when my mum popped round the door like something out of a pantomime.

'Have you two made friends now?' she asked as if she didn't know. She must have been hiding behind the door waiting for her cue the whole time. I hate being manipulated.

'Oh, yes,' said my dad. 'Er, we were just discussing what to do next, weren't we, Gemma?'

Now, my dad tends to be the business end of this parenting. Like, my mum points him at me when she wants me to jump. It was fairly easy to disarm the old man on his

8

own but once my mum came round the corner ...

Out it all came.

No going out during the week. Homework inspection every evening. Privileges withdrawn. ('What privileges? Breathing? Using the bathroom?') Tar, forbidden. Tar's friends, forbidden – that was code for the 'louts that hang out on the seafront ...' Friday and Saturday nights out, back by nine o'clock.

'Oh, can't we make it half past nine, please?'

'If you promise to make it half past nine *sharp* – okay,' replied my mother.

I was trying to be sarcastic.

Job, packed in.

I was waiting for that one. The job was supposed to be the cause of my downfall.

I was trying to be cool. I was dripping sarcasm, dripping. I wasn't even going to bother arguing. But I was livid. So was Mum. I could see Dad looking a bit injured, as if this was all going too far. But Mum had really made her mind up.

I opened my mouth to say something clever but nothing came out – just a sort of bleat.

'Just till you get back on course,' said Mum, getting up and smoothing down her skirt.

'You just think that I can't be trusted but I did everything I could to make it blah-blahity ... boo-hoo-hoo.'

I should have kept it shut. I never got to the end of the sentence. I was bawling. I rushed out of the room, but I didn't have anywhere to go because they were sitting on my bed. Dad called out, 'Gemma!'

Mum said, 'Leave her ...'

I rushed downstairs like a wet sponge at a hundred miles an hour. I hid in the kitchen trying to hold my breath.

Then Mum and Dad came back downstairs and I rushed back up and locked myself in my room.

'Bastards, BASTARDS, B A S T A R D S ! ' I screamed.
There was an understanding silence.

After a bit I calmed down and I decided to play it cool and hope that the whole thing would blow over. I didn't go out in the week ... well, there was no Tar, was there? The rest of the gang were still hanging out on the beach on the seafront, but I could do without that for a few days. But at the weekend I went to work. I wasn't going to miss that.

I had a nice little job serving tea to tourists. Actually, looking back, it wasn't a nice little job at all, it was slave labour. And only in a place as terminal as Minely-on-Sea could serving people tea be deemed exciting. But I thought it was the bees' nuts, and anyway it was some money in my pocket.

No one said anything to me. They let me swan off out of the house and never even asked where I was going.

When I finally got to Auntie Joan's Tea Room, there was another girl setting out places by the window. Then Auntie Joan came stalking out and ... 'Oh ... it's Gemma ... what a surprise.'

'I work here,' I reminded her.

Auntie Joan peered over her specs at me. She's not my auntie ... she's not anyone's auntie as far as I know. She named herself after her own tea room.

'I hear you've been a bit naughty, Gemma,' she said nicely.

I said, 'Eh?' Well, what's it to do with her? So long as I don't stick my tongue down my boyfriend's throat while the customers are scoffing scones ...

'Your father got in touch,' she murmured, looking all coyly at me.

I didn't say a word. I just waited.

'And I'm afraid there's no work for you here any more ...'

She didn't even have the decency to look embarrassed.

Need I say? Need I say how *livid* I was? The old bastard had rung up and terminated my job for me.

He had no business.

He had no right!

And as for her, the hypocritical old bat, who did she think she was?

'Since when have you been inspector of the Moral Police?' I asked.

'No need for that,' she snapped pertly. 'I'm sorry, but I can't take responsibility for employing a girl over and above the wishes of her parents.' And she swirled round and trotted out.

I turned round and glared at the other girl, who blushed furiously and tried to hide behind the saucers. I expect she thought I'd been holding one-woman orgies in the kitchen while the kettle boiled.

The humiliation was unbelievable.

'See if I want to work in an establishment where the strawberry jam tastes of FISH!' I yelled at the top of my lungs, and I stormed out. That made her wince. In a moment of badly judged intimacy, she'd admitted to me that she made her homemade jams in the same pan that she used to boil up fish scraps for the cat. All Minely would know about *that* before the day was out.

I walked down to the sea and wept and wept and raged and wept. My life, such as it was, was in tatters. As for that old bag Mrs Auntie Joan – she'd loved every minute of it. There was a myth amongst the local traders that all the trouble in Minely was caused by the local kids. If someone bent a car aerial or turned over a wastebin on the seafront, they'd all gather together like gulls and mutter darkly about Youths and no discipline and how the young people were ruining Minely. Of course they were quite happy to welcome any number of out-of-town thugs. They could run around the town vomiting, screeching and kicking wastebins over as long as they liked, and it was just youthful high spirits.

Basically anyone who had a fiver in their pocket was Mother Theresa of Calcutta as far as the local traders were concerned.

Minely was all geared up for tourists. If the local traders had their way, the place would have been closed down in the winter and the native population sent to Scarborough or Siberia or somewhere like that. But that's another story.

Furious as I was at Mrs Auntie Joan, it was like a mild spring day compared with the soul-deep rage burning for my loving parents.

I didn't go back that day. In fact, I stayed away all weekend as a protest.

Response: banned from going out of the house at weekends.

My next plot was to stay out until ten each night during the week. They couldn't keep me off school in the name of discipline, surely? They got round that by my dad picking me up from school. My God! Everyone knew what was going on. He actually came into the class to get me! I thought I was going to die of humiliation.

This was getting really out of hand. I could see my mother was having second thoughts, but by this time Dad was going on all burners. I heard them arguing one night and I like to think she was trying to get him to slow down, but by that time his authority was at stake and you might as well have tried to stop the Pope blessing babies. Of course Mum didn't have a leg to stand on because she'd started the whole thing off.

My mum is the philosopher in the family.

'The love is there, Gemma,' she explained to me. 'The generosity is there. The compromise. I don't like treating you like a child. All you have to do is show us you can follow a few simple rules and we can resume a proper family life. You can get a new job and stay out at weekends again. We just need to see some responsibility. That's all we ask.'

My parents needed to be taught a lesson.

Don't tell me. You've had this horrendous argument with your parents. Life is abominable. Why should you put up with this? you think. Why indeed? Why not leave home instead? It's easy, it's cheap. And it gets your point across beautifully.

Only it's not easy, is it? That is to say, it might be easy and it might be hard, but how do you know? You're only a kid, you've got things to learn. It isn't as though you can walk into a shop and ask for a handbook.

Well, here it is – what you've all been waiting for:

GEMMA BROGAN'S
PRACTICAL HANDBOOK TO RUNNING AWAY
FROM HOME
A step-by-step guide for radical malcontents

1 You will need: Clothes – woolly vest, long underwear, plenty of keep-warm stuff. Plenty of underwear and other personal items. A waterproof coat. A sleeping-bag. A pencil and paper. Money. Your father's bank card and pin number.
2 Your wits. You'll need 'em.
3 Think about it. What are your mum and dad going to do? Try to get you back, of course. It'll be police. It'll be, Oh, my God, my little girl has been abducted. It'll be, Maybe some dreadful pervert is at her right now. Maybe she's lying murdered in a binliner in the town rubbish tip THIS VERY SECOND! It never occurs to them that little Lucinda got so fed up with Mumsy and Dadsy that she

actually left of her own accord. So ... if you don't want every copper in the land on your tail and pictures of little you shining out of all the national newspapers, you tell your mum and dad *exactly* what you're doing. (Of course, maybe you *want* your piccy in the local rag. Not me. I was leaving home.)

4 This is where the pencil and paper comes in. You write them a note explaining that you're going away so that they can expect to see very little of you in the immediate future. Wish them luck, tell them no hard feelings and that you hope they will understand. Alternatively you can ask them how they can bear to live with themselves after they've made your young life so unbearable that you've had to go away into the hard world, etc. etc. But beware! This will undermine your credibility.

5 Book your coach ticket using your father's Visa card.

6 Take the money and run.

If you want to make really sure, you write or telephone and tell them how well fed you are and how many woolly vests you're wearing. (This is where the warm underwear comes in.) That way, when they ask the police to help them get their property back, the police say, 'Two woolly vests she's got on, has she? Took a sleeping-bag, hmm?' Because, you see, while the police might care a whole load about you while you're dead, they ain't going to spend a penny more than they have to on you while you're still alive.

Actually – this is a secret – I'm only going away for a bit. I'll know when I get there. Couple of weeks. A month, maybe.

Mum and Dad don't know that, though.

Tar rang me on Tuesday. My parents had gone to play squash. I started telling him and suddenly I was smiling all over my face. That's when I knew I was really going to do it. Before ... you know, I meant to but there was this thought that maybe I was just kidding myself. But when I began grinning, I knew. He was smiling too. I could hear his face stretching even over the phone.

I felt a bit guilty too because ... he wants me so much and ... People are always talking about love like it's something everyday. People say they love their parents, but what does that mean? Not exactly intoxicating, is it? I hate mine sometimes but I don't suppose I feel any less for them than anyone else. All I know is this: if there is such a thing as being in love, I may not be there yet but when I do I'm going to be INFATUATED. All over the place. I'll do anything for him. You name it. Whatever.

But in the meantime, I intend to make the most of my freedom.

Tar's so sweet. He's the sort of person who makes you want to be close to him. And he's had such a hard time, and no one deserves a hard time less than Tar. He's the sort of person you'd pick to be in love with. Knowing me I'll fall for some real shit with earrings and a loud voice. Just my luck.

So it was ... maybe a bit unfair on him. On the other hand, I liked him more than anyone and I fancied him something rotten. After the phone call I started to think about spending days with him with no one to say do this, do that ... and I just felt SOOOO good about it. Holding his hand in the dark. Sleeping with him, talking to him when there was no one else there. Looking after him because, poor Tar, he needs someone. He wants someone. He wants me.

Sometimes when we were hiding behind the breakers with the crowd, he'd hold me so tight, I'd think he's not just holding me, he's holding on to me, like I'm stopping him from falling off. I'd see him looking at me and his eyes were so full of ... I dunno. Like he was about to cry. And, it's stupid, I know, but I think maybe he's hurting because he loves me and I don't love him, and this great lump used to come up into my throat and I'd hold him tight and try and squeeze him as tight as I could and try as hard as I could to fall in love with him the way he loved me.

And then other times I'd think, it's just the way his face is that makes him look like that.

3
Tar

Me and Gemma.

You'd never have believed it. I didn't to start off. When she first turned up on the beach I thought I wasn't going to like her. It was Saturday night. We'd built a big fire opposite the old factory sheds about half a mile out of town. It was a good big fire. We'd found a huge lump of wood, part of an old boat. Me and Kenny dragged it up the beach. It was tarred and it had copper nails in it. The copper turned the fire green. It was magic.

Gemma was wild about it. She gets so excited by things – that's one of the things I like about her. She was excited by the fire, by meeting us for the first time, by the sound of the sea in the dark, by the night ...

Minely's the most awful dump. No one's got any time for the locals. You wander round in your own town feeling like an outsider and then ... you find this bunch of people your own age sitting half a mile out of town by this magic fire drinking and smoking and doing their own thing. I remember when I discovered the beach life. It's great.

She was beautiful but she was going on and on, rattling away about how wonderful this was, and how wonderful that was. She was getting drunk and stoned, and I thought, Doesn't she ever get tired of her own voice?

But I stayed and she stayed and in the end there were only about five or six of us left.

That's the time I usually went home. The later it got, the more people got paired off until in the end, if you were sitting there on your own, you turned into a gooseberry. I usually tried to leave before that happened, but that night, I was there and Gemma was there and all the others were paired off, and I thought, Oh, no ...

Because in that situation I always feel as though I ought to try and make a move but I didn't dare. And I didn't want to just go and leave because everyone would know I was scared to talk to her. You'd have to be a lot more sure of yourself than I am to pull a girl like her.

She came and sat next to me and started talking ...

There were these long silences. I was anxious she'd be fed up but she didn't seem to mind. Then she started asking me about myself ... and I told her about home and Mum and Dad. I felt like ... stupid, you know? Because everyone knows about my problems and here I was talking about them to this beautiful girl. I thought she must just be dead bored by it. But she kept asking me about things in a quiet voice, not like the voice she used when she was hooting and yelling earlier. I told her everything. Everything – too much. I kept looking at her, thinking, Why are you asking all these questions? What have you got to do with me?

Then she started talking to someone else and I thought, Oh well ... and the next thing I knew I could feel her fingers tickling my hand. I couldn't believe it, I thought it was some mistake. We held hands. Then I picked up all my courage and I put my arm round her waist and she leaned into me. And I just smiled. I was so pleased. I couldn't kiss her, I was smiling so much.

'Ow!' she said, when I banged her mouth with my teeth.

I told her, 'I'm so happy.'

'Good,' she said. 'Good.'

When I rang her up that Tuesday after I left home and she told me she was coming to see me, my face went like it did that first night. I was grinning like an idiot. People were smiling at me as I walked away from the telephone box. It was great.

I'd been feeling pretty down – being away from home, being on my own. Now I felt great. I wanted to make that moment last as long as I could. Like in a film – you know how they play a song or some music and a particular feeling stretches out – like that. I should have been in a boat floating down the river or in a hot-air balloon with someone playing a guitar, but there I was in the middle of this tatty old Bristol street and I knew that any second something'd happen and I'd be feeling dreadful again. I had to *do* something.

Then I thought, I'll go for a walk in the park ... Yeah. There'd be toddlers on the roundabouts, people walking their dogs. It was late spring. The daffodils were still out, there were trees in bloom. People would be feeding the ducks and the pigeons. I could have an ice cream. I had my Walkman with me so I could even have some music if I wanted.

I could feel that moment lifting up, ready to jump into the air ...

I put my hand in my pocket. I don't know why. I had a quid. And I thought, Shit! because I'd already left it too late and I could feel that good feeling going down the drain already.

The thing was, if I spent my money on ice cream I'd have to go into town and beg in the pedestrian precinct – the Dust Bowl, they call it – so I could get something to eat that night. And begging is so grim. There's no way you can do it nicely. You just put your head down between your knees and you hold your hand out and try to pretend it's not happening.

It was so stupid. As if I had to have money to feel good about Gemma coming to see me! I knew it was going to happen, I knew there was just too much shit about to let me feel good for more than a second. The moment gathered itself up and jumped up into the air ... and I was left on the ground watching it go ....

And then I noticed the dandelions.

They were on the grass verges along the road. It was a solid mass of yellow, bright, golden yellow. I'd been standing there thinking about daffodils somewhere else and all the time here were the dandelions – wild dandelions, not put there for me to look at but there because they wanted to be there. All along the grubby street it was ablaze with yellow and everyone was walking up and down without even noticing them.

I must have walked past them a dozen times. I walk about without seeing, sometimes.

I know it sounds stupid, but it was like, the flowers had come out for Gemma.

I stood there for a bit and I felt like I was soaking up that colour. I love yellow. It's the colour of sunlight. When all this is over and I get myself sorted out, I want to go to art college. I want to be a painter or a designer. I really think I'm good enough.

I stood there staring at it, and I had an idea for a painting. A dandelion – just one huge bright dandelion. The background was all black and the dandelion was all the bright yellows and oranges, every petal a long yellow triangle. It would be a big painting. I was going to do it and put it on the wall of the squat for Gemma when she came.

And that big happy moment came swooping down, and I reached up a hand and caught hold of it and off I went. I picked a big bunch of dandelions and went off back to the squat. I felt great again.

I say squat. It was more of a derry really, but I'd been trying to clear it out a bit the past day or two.

The first couple of nights I slept out in doorways. The very first night I tried to go to sleep in my bag in the doorway of a small supermarket but it was too cold. I ended up wandering about all night. Towards morning I saw people crowded together in a subway, all wrapped up in cardboard boxes, and I thought, That's how you do it! And I wandered about some more till I found some cardboard in stacks outside a shop waiting for the binmen I wrapped myself up in that, and that was better. But you still keep waking up all night. You never seem to get a decent night's sleep on the street.

I slept like that for a couple of nights, but I didn't like it on the street. The thing is, you're in public. People can see you all the time, even when you're asleep. Sometimes at night you wake up and the police are shining a torch into your face. I hated that – the thought of people examining you while you're asleep, all those strangers. I began to feel like something in a zoo. So when I found this row of derry houses, I thought, Right. This is gonna be home.

I found a little room with a door still on it. The first night I kept getting woken up by people banging in. It was pitch black so they couldn't see me till I called out. It happened about five times that night. I was really scared the first few times, but after a bit I realised it was just people looking for a place to sleep. I shouted out, 'It's taken,' and they left.

The next day I made up a little sign: 'Do Not Disturb.' And I wrote, 'Property of Hotel d'Erelict' in little letters underneath.

Everyone had to find their way about with matches or a torch, so they all saw my sign and I never got bothered after that. Just a couple of times some drunks came charging in without seeing my notice. Sometimes they thought it was so funny they'd wake me up.

'Will you leave your boots outside for cleaning?' someone yelled. And, 'Will Sir be requiring his breakfast in bed?' That sort of thing. That was okay.

It was out of the open but it was a right mess in there. People had dumped binbags full of rubbish, waste paper, old clothes, even rubble. I slept on top of it for a few nights. I suppose I was feeling depressed. I was thinking a lot about my mum.

Then I thought, Get on with it.

First of all I scooped all the rubbish into binbags and carried it out round the back. I pinched the binbags from someone's dustbin. I found a broken broom in a skip and gave it a good brush down. It was still a tip, but at least it was a brushed tip.

Since then I'd been collecting bits and pieces – a few wooden crates, a bit of carpet someone chucked out. I couldn't make it too nice because someone would have nicked stuff or wrecked it. But I'd tried to make it mine. That's why I was so pleased when I had this idea for a picture. I'd wanted to do a picture. I'd brought my pencils with me but I hadn't got round to it yet, and now I had this great idea for Gemma.

It was about two miles back to the squat. On the way I had to go past Joe Scholl's tobacconist. I thought I'd go in and have a Twix. Have a treat. I completely forgot about the begging. You do. You just forget, you buy a bar of chocolate and then you think, Oh, no ...

Joe Scholl's a nice man. He'd given me a few quid a couple of times in the past few days. I think he gave quite a bit of money to the people on the street.

'You look full of the joys today, David,' he said, eyeing my dandelions over the counter.

'Yeah. My girlfriend's coming to stay,' I told him. I think I only went in there so I could tell someone the news.

'Hence the bouquet, eh?' he said, nodding at the dandelions.

'Yeah,' I laughed. I took a Twix bar and dug in my pocket for the money. He didn't laugh, but then he never did. He always kept his face completely straight, except his eyebrows were permanently up in the air. You hardly ever saw him move his face, even when he was cracking you up with laughter. Deadpan.

'That's good news then.' He didn't take my money. He just looked at me. 'Leaving her folks like you did, is she?' he wanted to know.

I looked at him. 'Yeah ...'

'How old is she, then, David?'

I didn't dare tell him how old she really was. I said, 'Sixteen.' That's how old I'd told him I was. I started eating the Twix to hide my embarrassment.

'Nice.' He stood there with his hands hanging by his sides watching me. 'Where you putting her up, then?' I was beginning to feel miserable again. 'Honeymoon suite in the Hotel Derry?'

'Yeah ...' I put the money back in my pocket.

'Thank you, Skolly, for the free Twix bar.'

'Oh! Yeah ... I'm really sorry. I was thinking ...'

'That's all right. Not a nice place for a young lady, though, is it, David?'

I just hadn't thought. He was right! Albany Road was all right for me but not for Gemma. You get all sorts in there – tramps, alcoholics, junkies. Most of them are all right but some of them ... Once or twice I've seen the alkies with women with them, but you never see any young women in there. The girls all sleep out in doorways, in public ...

I never thought why.

'Here...' I held out the money again, but he waved it away. 'Don't be daft.'

I was about to put it back in my pocket but then I had second thoughts. 'No, take it. Or I won't be able to keep coming in.'

'Ah ...'

'You'll think I'm begging.'

'A time and a place for everything, eh, David? I take your point.' He leaned across and took my money. 'I'll give it back to you later on, okay?'

I laughed. He was so funny. His face was funny. He was quite fat and bald, and he always looked as if you'd just given him a mildly unpleasant surprise, as if you'd told him the price of chocolate had just gone up or something.

'Life is a complicated business,' he said. Another customer came in and he turned to them. I nodded and started for the door, but he called out, 'Hang on a minute ...'

I stood and waited while he sold a newspaper. I felt dreadful again. I hadn't thought. I was being selfish. I couldn't ask Gemma to come and live like this with me!

'She's not coming to stay. She's just visiting,' I began when the customer left.

'What you doing tonight?'

'Well, nothing ...'

'Be here at six o'clock. I've got someone to see. We might be able to sort something out for you.'

'Really?'

'I've gotta see someone, all right? You be here at six. I might just tell you to clear off home.'

'Thanks, Mr Scholl!'

'Mr Scholl.' He rolled his eyes briefly. 'Skolly.'

'Thanks, Skolly.'

'Go on, piss off.'

I practically skipped down the road. Everything was working out! Gemma coming, Skolly taking me on. Well, I say that, but of course not everything was going to work out. There was one thing that never was going to – and that was the really big one.

My mum.

I'd made myself this promise not to ring up for a whole month. The trouble was, I kept thinking I'd feel better if I spoke to her; but I knew it wasn't true. I'd left her a note when I went but that was ages ago. It was Gemma's idea not to ring her for a bit. She said my mum'd just make me feel really bad, maybe she'd even talk me into coming back. But things were going so well I was thinking maybe I could cope with it. I'd only been away a couple of weeks, but it was the longest I'd ever been away from her.

I knew I shouldn't ring. Gemma was right. You don't know my mum, she can make you do *anything*. I'm more scared of her than I am of Dad, really.

In the end I thought, See what happens tonight with Mr Scholl. I mean, if he got me sorted out with somewhere to live, everything would be okay and I could think about getting in touch with Mum. If not, well, that'd be different. That'd be a disaster. I'd have to ring up Gemma and tell her not to come. Because Skolly was right. You couldn't ask Gemma to come and live in a place like Albany Road.

The dandelion didn't come out like I wanted. The colours were too pale. I wanted these really deep yellows and the black like velvet behind it. You can't do that sort of thing with pencil crayons. Pastel sticks would've done it. I had a set at home, I was really mad with myself for not bringing them. But they're so fragile I thought they'd get broken.

4
Skolly

He was there. Well, he would be, wouldn't he?

'Good evening, David.'

'Hello, Mr Skolly.'

I said, 'Just Skolly.' I headed off up the road and he came loping after me. He was a tall lad, a good six inches over my head.

'It's really nice of you to help me out ...'

'I haven't done anything yet.' Very polite boy. That's one of the things that made me take to him. He was bobbing along beside me, looking sincere. He had his leather jacket on and his rucksack on his back. You could tell he hadn't been on the streets for long because his rucksack was still fairly clean. Jeans, boots, long hair. He looked the same as he usually did. They all look the same as they usually do. They tend not to have an extensive wardrobe.

He was the first one I ever felt like helping, apart from doling out money and fags and chocolate. Most of the others are either depressed or stupid. They ought to be back at home with their mums and dads.

The first time I saw him I gave him a couple of quid and asked him what he thought he was playing at.

He just glanced up and touched the side of his face. I hadn't noticed the bruises. He didn't have to say any more, he looked so miserable. I nodded and gave him a couple of Mars bars on top of the money and his face changed. It startled me. His entire face changed. He beamed at me. I'd really made him happy, for a minute or two, anyway. That made me feel good. I like feeling good.

He didn't seem to have any front. You need all the front you can get in this old world. Look at me. I'm nearly all front. What you see is what you get. But this kid – you only had to look at him to know he'd believe whatever you wanted him to. You had the feeling that if you didn't hold his hand he'd get crushed in the stampede.

I proffered a packet of Bensons. 'Fag?'

'Thank you, but I don't smoke.'

'You will,' I told him. Practically everyone living rough smokes.

'You fill yourself up with tar,' he said. He got in front of me and peered into my face. 'There, it's turning your skin grey,' he told me.

I stopped short in the middle of the pavement. An old lady nearly collided with me from behind. 'Pack it in ...!'

I mean, there I was helping him out and he was telling me I was turning grey. He just grinned and I thought ... you bugger. He was teasing me. He had me going, too.

We carried on down Picton Street, and I thought, He's right, though. My old dad's eighty-two, he smokes like a chimney and he's the colour of fag ash.

I smoke cigars meself. When I was younger I always tried to have a fag hanging out of the corner of my mouth by way of advertisement. As a tobacconist, if I don't smoke, who will? You see a lot of tobacconists these days – particularly the Asians, I may say – who never smoke anything. That's not right. How can you respect your customers if you think it's stupid to smoke? How can you know what you're selling 'em? I reckon I could tell a Benson from a Regal blindfold, from smell alone. Or I used to, anyway.

I gave up fags, I was smoking too many. A cigar is the

ideal smoke for a tobacconist because you can always have one in your gob, but it keeps going out. That way, you're still smoking even when you're not, if you see what I mean.

'How about a Mars bar, then?'

He took that. I always keep a pocketful of chocolate bars, again on account of being a tobacconist. I eat them, too. Consequently I'm fat and permanently short of breath, but at least I'm not a hypocrite.

And I'm well informed, too. I read the newspapers.

Richard was waiting in the shop for us. George Dole's old electrical shop, that is. He'd squatted it a few weeks before.

'Hello, Skolly.' He beamed at me. Or rather, he beamed at the door behind me. He's a strange person, Richard. Very friendly but – he's always smiling but he never actually seems to look straight at you, for some reason.

He's like me, Richard is, a bit of an act. 'Here's the lad I was telling you about.' I gave David a little shove in the back and he stumbled towards the door. Richard held his hand out.

'Always delighted to meet a new candidate for the squatting movement,' he said.

'Thanks, thanks ...' said David.

I made to go. Richard was disappointed.

'Aren't you going to join us, Skolly?'

'I've got a home of me own, thanks.'

'No, for tea. I'm making burgers especially for you.'

'Burgers?'

Every time he saw me he was inviting me round to eat some disgusting mess of beans or sprouted seeds or yoghurt.

'Especially for you,' repeated Richard, grinning at the street opposite.

I paused. The missis was away visiting the brood in Taunton. I had been planning on going down the pub, but then the pub was open all night. Richard only wanted to convert me, but unlike some I could mention, I've never lost my curiosity. Besides, let him try and convert me. It might amuse me.

I pushed David in front of me and followed them up the stairs to the flat above the shop.

When I first found out that George Dole's old electrical shop had been squatted, I was quite upset. George used to be a friend of mine until his heart did for him — that was about eighteen months before. I don't like squatters. What's to stop 'em working and paying rent? And they're such a scabby bunch. They like to think they belong to the underworld, but most of the crooks I know *work* for a living ...

I first had my suspicions that this was different from the usual type of squat because this little notice appeared on the front door, announcing that the place was squatted and that the police had been informed. It just goes to show what this country's come to if the villains go and tell the police what they're doing, so they can be left alone to get on with it. I mean, can you imagine it with any other sort of crime? A little notice going up: 'This bank will be robbed tomorrow at 11 am,' and the police touching their helmets and saying, 'All in order, sir, let us know if you have any problems ...'

After a few days the usual lot appeared — scabby-looking yoofs with boots two sizes too big and Mohican haircuts scurrying in and out the door like so many rats. I thought to myself, There's more to this than that lot. But when I saw Richard come out, I knew at once it must be him.

Richard had the earring and the short hair. He had what you might call a slight Mohican — his crew cut was longer on the middle of his head than at the sides. But he was a lot older than the others, in his mid-twenties, maybe, whereas the rat yoofs were sixteen, seventeen. I was standing in the doorway of my shop watching the street go by when he emerged, smiling to himself. He locked the door behind him and walked off, still smiling a half gormless grin at the wind, at the buildings ... I dunno, just at being Richard, I expect.

I left the missis in charge of the shop and collared him.

I was concerned, you see. There was stock left in that shop. George Dole never had any relatives as far as I was aware, but someone must have owned it.

I was prepared to be angry. I poked him in the stomach and I said, 'I don't know why you bothered leaving home.' But he just opened his mouth and smiled even wider.

'I'm always happy to have relations with the neighbours,' he said. 'Is there anything I can do for you?'

'Maybe.' I told him about the electrical stuff. He invited me in for a cup of tea. Well, I was taken aback. I thought squatters were so busy smoking pot and watching the dirt grow on top of the fridge, they never had anything to do with anyone.

'You understand my concern,' I told him as he opened the door.

'Naturally. I have no respect for theft,' he announced proudly, which made me bristle a bit. I've done a bit of thieving in my own time. Of course I never told him that.

I was impressed. All the electrical stuff had been packed in boxes, neatly labelled and carried out and stored in a little room behind the shop.

'I must admit I did help myself to a house fuse when I was getting the electric on,' he said. 'But I've already replaced that.' And he looked at the door and beamed in pleasure.

'But you don't mind nicking someone's house, though,' I told him.

'Not if it's standing empty and there's people sleeping on the streets. Of course, property is a rather strange concept for me ...'

I thought I was going to get a lecture but he shut up and went to put the kettle on.

30

Now if it had been me, I'd have had that gear out and sold it before you could count to three. But Richard was moral. He really thought that squatting a shop and not nicking the stock was going to change society. That was why he was so delighted to have me round for tea. He thought that if he got enough people like me on his side, Parliament would fall tomorrow.

It transpired he worked in a bicycle shop on the Ashley Road but he made it his business in his spare time opening up squats for the kids round about. He'd break in, set up the electrics, post the little notices, inform the police, stay there a few nights until it became clear whether or not they were going to get any trouble. Then he'd go home for a few nights until the next one came up.

I had extreme doubts about eating anything in any squat. This one was perfectly disgusting. The place had deteriorated beyond all credence since I'd had tea with Richard that time.

'You don't expect me to eat in here, do you?' I said. I rubbed my toe into the grease on the floor. 'I wouldn't unwrap a bar of chocolate in here.'

Richard was tying on an enormous white apron; it was as clean as the rest of the place was dirty.

'Don't worry, Skolly. I've brought everything in, even the pan to cook on. I won't feed you beetle-burgers.'

'Do they all live like this?'

'This one is particularly bad,' he confessed. He looked terribly unhappy about it. I could see one or two of the locals glancing at each other uncomfortably. 'It gives squatting a bad name,' said Richard in a loud voice. The yoofs pulled faces and one of them walked out.

I settled myself down in an armchair at the side of the kitchen table and waited.

David was standing in a corner with his eyes popping out

of his head, trying to take everything in at once. He couldn't take his eyes off Richard. I'd told him on the way what Richard did. He obviously thought Richard ought to be the next Prime Minister.

'I think what you're doing is fantastic,' he blurted out. Blushing, God bless him.

'Thank you,' said Richard, beaming out of the window. 'In that case you'll be delighted to hear that we're going to open a new squat tonight. Virgin territory.' For a second the poor kid looked terrified and I thought he was going to bottle out. But then he started frowning and nodding in a determined fashion. I thought, Ahhhhhhhh, sweet ... Because for half the kids squatting is just a large form of vandalism. But poor old David had never broken the law in his life, you could tell by just looking at him.

There were a couple of yoofs rather older than the rat pack I'd seen going in and out of the shop. Richard introduced them to David as his new housemates. 'This is Vonny, this is Jerry,' he said. 'They're anarchists,' he announced to the kitchen light switch, and grinned so much I thought his teeth were going to fall out. That remark was for my benefit. I could see him watching me out of the corner of my eye to see what reaction he was getting. The bloke looked embarrassed. Vonny nodded and shook my hand politely and offered me a drink.

I accepted a can of cold beer.

David went to help Richard with the burgers and pretty soon the two of them were deep in confab about Squatting, Anarchism, the Right of the Individual to Break the Law, and various other forms of cobblers.

The burgers were quite nice actually. Richard took great care that mine never touched the surroundings, which I appreciated. I had two.

'Not bad for homemade,' I told him.

'As good as a McDonald's?' he wanted to know.

'Not a bad flavour, but a tendency to fall to pieces in your bun gives them a lower mark,' I replied.

'But then I expect Macs use meat in theirs,' he announced, beaming at the ceiling.

'And what did you use, Richard?' I enquired.

'Oh, soya protein. I'm a vegan, didn't you know?' He was over the moon that he'd made me eat that stuff. He was actually giggling and guffawing to himself. I suppose he thought I was on my way to anarchy, now that I'd eaten beanburgers. I wouldn't mind, but I don't look any good in earrings and my bald patch prohibits a Mohican.

I didn't have the heart to tell him my missis uses soya quite regularly.

I don't know how I managed to end up going out with them that night. Richard was as pleased as punch. He said it was because I'd provide perfect cover, but of course he thought I was turning into one of them.

You might ask, with some reason, what's a Tory like me doing helping the squatters? A proper Tory mind, not one of your watered-down, middle-of-the-road ones. If I had my way, all the darkies'd get sent back home. Why not? They have their culture, we have ours. If you knew the number of people I do who've turned round and found themselves stuck in the middle of the Carib-bloody-bean and it was Bristol City twenty years ago, so would you. And cut down on the social security and all that.

But, politics aside, we all break the law. Coppers break it, judges break it, businessmen break it, you break it, I break it. Just because I'm patriotic doesn't mean I'm an idiot. How do I break it, I hear you ask? It's wise not to know too much, my friend. That is to say, it's wise to know as much as you can, but it's wiser to keep everyone else in ignorance.

The only thing I've got against squatting is that it's legal. I mean, be fair, there ought to be a law against it. There's a law against everything else. If you want to break the law, fair play. The very least you can expect is a fair chance of getting caught.

It was a very nice terraced house just a couple of streets away at the Montpellier end of St Paul's. Nice big garden, whacking great big rooms. Bigger than my place it was. It'd been boarded up a while, you could see where the local kids had got in and smashed a few windows and stuff.

Actually I felt quite like an old hand. They were sneaking about, peering over walls and setting lookouts up and down the road, while Richard tried to find a way in. I was sauntering around with my hands in my pockets. David made me laugh, trying to hide behind a dustbin. Talk about attracting attention! I mean, what would you think if you saw someone hiding behind a dustbin at nine o'clock at night? I stood next to him and I said, 'What are you doing down there?' He must have felt a right berk.

'I think you better keep your head down, Skolly,' hissed Richard.

'If I can't blag my way out of this, I'm better off dead,' I told him. He went down a bit in my estimation that night. It wasn't professional. Now, whenever I did a job, the thing was to look like you were where you were supposed to be right up until the last minute. But of course, these anarchists were all dressed like mad squatters. I looked like a tobacconist and therefore stood a chance of getting away with it.

I was nervous, mind. I hadn't done anything like it for years. Christ knows what the missis would say if I got caught.

Richard was taking so long to open the window that I went over to give him a hand, but he got a bit panicky.

'You're going to get us caught, Skolly,' he hissed irritably. 'Keep your head down.'

'I've only come to lend a few tips ...' But he wasn't having it. He called the girl, Vonny, to come and take care of me. She tried to make me squat down behind a hedge, but I wasn't squatting for no one. It never occurred to any of them that I'd forced open more windows than the rest of them put together.

Finally Richard got the window up. There was a bit of a panic as someone came down the road. Even I had to hide behind a telephone box just up the street. Whoever it was trotted past and never saw the open window with the boards off, or they didn't care. Then we all climbed in one after the other. I was severely out of breath and almost flattened Richard as he pulled me up over the window-sill. Then he fixed the boards so it looked like they were still attached, and we were in.

Inside it was pitch black. They were all talking in whispers. Richard started handing out torches.

'Don't let anyone see any light from the street,' he hissed. He began allocating jobs – helping with the electric, making sure the windows were sealed, checking the gas, seeing if they could get the back door opened. I lit a fag and peered out from behind the boarding on to the street.

'Would you mind not smoking in front of the windows?' asked Richard severely.

'What's up, we're in, aren't we?'

'It's best to lie low for a couple of days until we're established,' he told me. 'The longer we're here before they find out, the better the chances of staying.'

He went off to get the lekky on. I went upstairs to finish my fag on the landing.

Who'd have thought it, me breaking and entering a house with nothing in it to nick? I wandered around a bit but there really was nothing there. It just goes to show the changing face of crime. No one ever used to think of stealing whole houses ... and without even having to move them, either.

Jerry was running about sticking bottles with candles in them on the stairs and in all the rooms. Richard soon got the lekky on but we weren't allowed to put the lights on in case someone saw us. He and Jerry started running in and out of the back door filling the place up with boxes and suitcases and bags. The idea was to get established as quickly as possible. It was a lot more difficult to eject them if they had a houseful of stuff in there with them.

I thought, time to clear off.

I went to see how David was getting on and to say goodbye. He was down in the basement kitchen with Vonny. Someone had brought in a cardboard box full of cooking things – pans, plates, cutlery, a bit of flour and a bit of cooking oil, that sort of thing. They'd got the gas cooker going and he was making a cup of tea.

The whole place looked very nice by candlelight. I thought, They've only been in here half an hour and it's half a home already.

There was an old chair by the work surface. I sat down.

'Well, David.'

'This is fantastic, Mr Skolly.'

'Skolly.'

'I'd never have found anywhere like this on my own. And the people are ...'

I think he blushed a bit.

'They're not people, they're anarchists,' I corrected him.

'They're all really interesting ...'

'Would you like a cup of tea, Skolly?' the girl wanted to know. She was a right sight. Shaven head, scrawny neck like a plucked goose. You couldn't see what shape she was under the ... I dunno ... sacks or something, she was wearing. But I'm willing to believe it was all very nice under there. I should be so lucky.

'No thanks, I've got to be off.'

'How about some of this, then?' It was Richard. He was offering me a joint. I looked at it out of the corner of my eye.

I was tempted.

'I haven't done that for twenty years,' I said.

'Bring back your lost youth,' urged Richard.

I accepted the joint and took a drag. It felt nice. 'Used to smoke masses of this stuff in the Navy,' I told him. I was in the Merchant for five years when I was a lad.

Richard beamed. 'Part of our great British tradition of drug taking,' he said.

I took a few lungfuls before passing it on.

I have rarely regretted anything so much in my life. I used to quite like it when I was a lad. I don't know whether this was stronger or I was weaker. I broke out in a cold sweat. I started hearing things ... people coming down the stairs. I got this really strange impression that my missis was going to come in and catch me sitting in this smoky den with these kids. She'd go mad if she knew. Even though I knew she was miles away visiting Doreen ...

I wondered what was going on for a second, before I realised it was that joint. Just my luck, I thought. My heart was going like ten tons of coal falling off the back of a lorry. I just closed my eyes. I heard Richard asking me if I was okay, but I pretended to be asleep. I don't know what he must have thought. I felt like a right prat.

By the time I felt fit to open my eyes and have a look around, Jerry, Vonny and David were all sitting on the floor smoking more of the obnoxious things. Richard had disappeared. It felt like the whole room was crawling with little worms. Horrible. They all had cups of tea. So did I, it was by my chair, half cold.

I saw the girl nudging Jerry to look at me and they all laughed.

'Ha bloody ha,' I said. I was somewhat annoyed. I didn't come there to be laughed at by a bunch of paper anarchists. It doesn't mean anything to call them anarchists, anyway. You might as well call my wallpaper the Politburo.

I waited a bit, watching them. They were all right, I guess ... better than the lot in George Dole's shop. From the way Richard was with these two I figured they were more like his friends. They were treating David very nicely, listening when he had something to say, talking seriously to him. They must have been eighteen and nineteen, and he couldn't have been more than ... I dunno, fourteen, fifteen.

I got up and brushed my trousers down.

'Well, David, what do you think of the place then? Des. res. or what?'

'Oh ...' David jumped up like I was the Queen Mum. 'Thanks, Skolly, it's really great ...' He gestured to the yoofs on the floor and smiled shyly.

'Here ...' I tossed him a packet of fags. 'You can use them for joints with your new mates.' I'd noticed he was smoking one himself. He seemed to be enjoying it.

He took the fags and looked at them doubtfully. He was still wondering what to do when Richard appeared.

'Just booking another customer,' I told Richard, who duly laughed, but he didn't look too happy. He doesn't mind them rotting their brains with pot but he disapproved of smoking well enough.

I made another attempt to leave. Richard led me up the stairs. 'You can be the first man out the new front door,' he said. He opened the door. I was still crawling with that pot. The fresh air smelt so good, I almost skipped out of the house. As I stood on the path a woman I knew, Mary Dollery, was walking past. I smiled at her.

'Good evening, Mary.' You could see her looking at me and then at Richard. Then she scuttled off down the road like a crab on two legs.

'If you see any more likely candidates, do let me know,' beamed Richard.

'I don't see many deserving cases,' I told him.

'Oh, the streets are full of them,' said Richard sadly. As far as he's concerned, if you ain't got it, you deserve it, and if you have got it, you've ripped someone off.

'That bloody joint nearly killed me,' I told him severely.

'Oh!' He was distressed. 'I didn't mean to.'

'I thought my missis was coming out of the floor at me. It was a nightmare.'

Richard laughed. 'It was rather strong. I only got it this evening.' He beamed at the house opposite and then frowned as he remembered I'd had a bad time. 'Sorry about that.'

'That's all right. I've learned my lesson.' I said that so he knew he'd blown me becoming an anarchist. He looked miserable. Another step back from the New World Order.

I gave him a Twix bar and said goodbye.

'Oh, no, I can't ... there's animal fats in these,' he said.

'Try smoking it,' I told him. 'It gets you off.'

He was killing himself laughing.

I didn't see much of David after that, not for ages. He disappeared off the street, so I suppose they were taking care of him. He was a capable sort of bloke, I reckon, despite appearances. You felt he'd always find someone who had time for him.

I might have gone round and had a look once or twice, but I fell out with Richard shortly after that. Some acquaintances of mine to whom I owed a favour got to hear about all that electrical stuff in George Dole's old place. There was some good stuff – hifis, tellies, videos – quite a few quid's worth. Actually I mentioned it to them. I'm sure Richard had done his best to convince those horrible kids not to touch it, but let's face it, you'd have to be a Richard to leave that lot alone.

Anyway, these friends of mine decided to do a bit of liberating themselves. One of those kids came down and found them in the middle of it and got himself knocked around a bit. Nothing too serious, but he lost a couple of teeth. Richard was extremely upset. He met me on the street and told me what had happened. He was nearly in tears. I perhaps foolishly indicated that I knew something about it.

Well, it was wasn't like it was an old lady. The kid was on someone else's property. What's the point in getting sanctimonious about someone else doing a bit? I can't stand that sort of hypocrisy. You get it on both sides, mind – I know plenty of villains who'll sit around and moan about squatters all night. As far as I was concerned that kid got taught a useful lesson. They live in Never-never land, half of them. Bit of contact with the real world, do him a power of good.

But as I say, Richard was extremely upset. I don't know what he thought I ought to have done. Tell the police? Give him notice what night the lads were going round? The stuff would have walked, don't tell me. Give my mates up for swatting a brat? Nah. But he went right off me after that. The prejudice wasn't on my side. Being a friend isn't enough for people like that, see. You have to be on the right side ...

I got a decent new video out of that job.

5
Tar

It was the best luck I ever had in my life.

It wasn't just the house, it was the people. They were just so amazing. Right from the start. Especially Richard. Right early on, when they asked me how old I was, I just said, 'Sixteen,' without thinking about it. They were all sitting round drinking beer and smoking. After I'd said it I got all bothered because they were all so straight with each other ... and here was I telling stupid lies! So I plucked up my courage and blurted out, 'I'm not sixteen really. I'm only fourteen.'

'Oh, dear,' Richard said. He looked quite appalled. I was certain he was going to tell me I had to leave. But it turned out he was just shocked that my dad had been hitting me when I was just fourteen.

'That means he can't sign on,' pointed out Jerry.

'I've been begging. I want to find a job ...' I began.

But Richard – you'll never guess what he said.

'You'll just have to be a parasite off us for a couple of years.'

Actually I don't think Jerry liked it, but Vonny said quickly, 'One more won't make any difference.'

Could you believe that? Talk about landing on your feet! They really liked me, they wanted to take me on and it wasn't as though they were rich or anything; they were all signing on except Richard. He even offered to bring home bits of work from the bicycle shop.

I was *so* pleased. I mean ... they didn't even know me. I could have been in Bristol a hundred years and not found people like them.

Even Jerry came round. He was a bit different from the other two. But then he smiled and he said, 'Perhaps I can teach Tar some shoplifting techniques.' And he gave me a wink.

'Oh, I don't think that would be a good idea,' said Richard. 'If he gets caught he'll either get sent home or put into care, and we don't want that, do we?' he added, beaming at the fridge.

They started talking about how I could earn some money but I was suddenly thinking about Gemma. I just realised ... I'd found us a place to live! She could come to stay after all. And they'd help her like they were helping me and we'd have this amazing set of friends, more like a family, really, all here waiting for her.

Straight away I told them about her and ... well, it was a bit disappointing, because they weren't so keen.

It was partly my fault, because I wasn't sure whether she was coming for a visit or for good, but I was hoping she'd come for good and I wanted them to help me convince her. I told them about the problems she'd been having at home but ...

'The point is, Tar, you're asking a lot of her, aren't you?' said Jerry. 'She's got to give up her education, her parents, everything for you ...'

'It's not like that,' I said. But was it? I started to talk about her parents again, but Vonny said,

'I had arguments with my parents, too, but I didn't have to leave home.'

I felt incredibly glum. I so much wanted her to come with me but I hadn't looked at it like that before. I guess I'd been pretty selfish.

these terrible rows

cursing and swearing, or passed out on the floor

house would be a tip and Mum would be lolling about

cope, but he just got angry. He'd come back and the whole

of us ...

'He's only fourt...

'You can fall in love at any ...
always falling in love at fourteen.' And they ...

Later on I told them I wanted to ring up my mum, and you
know what? They all chipped in a quid each so I could have
a good long chat with her.

I know what you're thinking about me and my mum. Apron
strings. But it wasn't like that. I think it wasn't like that.

People think my dad is worse because he beats me up, but
Mum's worse really. He's easy; I just hate him. I hate him
because he lets things get into a mess and blames everyone
and won't do a thing to stop it, and because he treats me and
Mum like dirt. I guess I hate Mum too. The trouble with her
is, I love her as well.

Dad used to go to the pub and then drink all evening. He
was just a pisshead, though. Mum was at it all day. No one
knew – even Dad didn't know for ages. She just drank
enough to keep herself topped up. It was only when it got
worse and she was drunk when he came home that he started
to cotton on.

It used to be all right. I mean, it was awful but it wasn't
horrible. She was quite attractive when she was a bit tiddly –
sort of feathery and giggly. But later on it got worse and she
got ugly with it, falling over and weeping and moaning and
being sick.

Dad should have seen that she was ill, that she couldn't

They had ——— rows. Really terrible, black rows, screaming and threatening to kill one another and smashing things — really violent. Only at first they never touched one another, except by accident.

So I started helping out. I'd come back from school and do the shopping and cook tea, or I'd tidy the place a bit, just so it looked as though she'd done something, instead of lying in bed all morning and getting drunk in the afternoon, which is what really happened.

It was like, just me and Mum. We barely saw Dad; he was out in the morning and again in the evening. He didn't care so long as he got his dinner all right. She was always telling me how she didn't know how she'd cope without me. She made a real fuss of me. I liked it. It would have worked but ... my mum, she's such a shyster.

I mean, she didn't have to bother after that, see. At first I was just helping her. But ... I started coming home and she'd be lying dead drunk on the settee next to a pile of ironing or something and beg me to do it because Dad needed his shirts and he'd be furious if she hadn't done them. I didn't mind the work, but I knew she was just using me. The thing that really annoyed me was, when she was going out somewhere, or when someone was coming round, she managed to get it together then. The house would be cleaned then. The shopping would be in then. But if it was just me and Dad, she never lifted a finger.

It started to get me into trouble. One day I was sitting in maths trying to write a shopping list and Mr Webster the maths master caught me.

'Well, at least you can add up properly,' he said. I guess he knew what was going on because he smiled and gave it back to me. But he must have told the headmaster or someone and someone obviously got in touch with Mum and Dad at home.

I got home a couple of days later and they were both there waiting for me, dead drunk, both of them. They were furious. He was going on at me for doing her work and interfering and encouraging her to drink. He was going on at her for using me like a skivvy and interfering with my education, and she was screaming at him for getting between her and her son and telling me how much she relied on me and needed me while she was ill.

She was really drunk. She started clinging on to me. She does that. She wraps her arms round me and starts moaning and crying and tells me how much she loves me, and I have to help her stand up. It's horrible. And then ... Dad just really lost his temper. He was suddenly coming at both of us with his arms out and his eyes bulging. I thought he was going to kill her. She ducked behind me and I got it right on the side of the face. He knocked me flying. I was just getting up to see if Mum was okay when he came in with the boot ...

It was *me* he was after, all the time! I couldn't believe it. I couldn't understand it. He kicked me right round the room. Mum was lying next to the table while it was going on. I saw her find a can of lager and take a swig. Then she got up and flung herself at him and he left me alone after that and went running upstairs. I heard him charge out of the house a moment later and start up the car. Mum was dabbing at my cuts with a flannel. They made me spend a week off school but I was still bruised when I went in the next Monday. No one ever complained to my mum and dad again.

The thing I could never work out was what he was getting at *me* for. I mean, if it was Mum, that'd be normal. I'm not saying I wish it had been her, but I could have understood what was going on. So why me?

I still can't work it out.

Things improved for a bit but then it started up again. Dad really used to hate me doing the housework for some reason, so I used to try and get it done before he came home. That way he might think she had done it. So Mum left more and more of it to me, and she was getting drunk earlier and earlier and I felt guilty because I was giving her less to do. They were having more and more rows and I was getting beat up more often ...

That's why I left. The trouble is ... she depended on me. See? I kept thinking of the rows they must be having. I kept thinking about how angry he was going to get, how he'd tell her she'd driven me away ...

Vonny offered to come with me for the phone call, but I felt I had to do it on my own – I don't know why. It was a mistake, really. If only I'd followed what Gemma said – she understands people so much better than I do. But I found a phone box down the road and dialled the number. My heart was bursting. I said, 'Hello,' quietly so as not to shock her too much and ... it was like a shock coming down the phone.

She just said, 'David ...' Then she waited for me to explain myself.

I started to talk. I can't remember what – stuff about me being all right, about finding somewhere to live and everything being okay, and the people being okay and how I was eating enough and looking after myself. You know.

When I finished there was nothing. I could hear her smoking, that was all. Half the time my mother is falling about, or grabbing hold of me or the tablecloth or the wall or anything else that's nearby. But this time I felt that she was wide, wide awake, like a bird or a fish that never slept, listening to everything and waiting.

'I'm sorry I went away,' I said. 'I didn't mean to ... I didn't want to, I mean. And ... are you all right, Mum? Mum, say something, won't you?'

'I can't say much, Tar,' she said in a fairly ordinary voice. 'He's upstairs listening.' Then she dropped her voice to a harsh whisper and she said, 'He's started to beat me ...'

And the bottom just fell out of everything.

You know, I'd never thought of that. I'd never thought he might do that. But it was so obvious! It was only me being there that stopped him. It felt like someone had picked up the entire world about ten feet and then dropped it on a concrete floor. And it was all my fault.

She started then, the way she does. I'd thought she was stone cold sober at first, but she was as drunk as ever, really. It was night time after all.

'I've been so scared,' she said. 'Every night he gets so drunk and I never know what he'll do next. It's so lonely. I can't get the housework done, darling. I try ... you know what he's like ... so fussy, so angry when things aren't right. It's not his fault, I've been a bad wife and a bad mother. You shouldn't have left me, David, you know that, don't you?'

There was a pause. 'Yes,' I said. Well, what else could I say?

'You know how much I've relied on you ... and I've been trying so hard .... oh, darling, how could you ...?'

I could almost feel her sliding down the sofa on to the floor and dissolving, weeping. I felt that her tears would trickle out of the telephone and on to my hands.

'Listen, Mum ...' I could hear the sound of her sobs. 'Mum, just stop crying, please stop and we'll talk about it. Is it bad, Mum? Is he hitting you hard?'

'Darling, please come home, please ... He's been saying that I drove you away ...' And she was weeping and weeping and weeping ...

'All right, Mum, please stop ... look, I'll come home, I'll

come home. It's not forever. I'll come home.' I would have said anything, then. It was so terrible him saying that it was her who drove me away, because it wasn't true at all. It was him who drove me away. But ... it was true, too.

'I'll come home. All right?'

'When?'

'Soon. Mum, there's just a couple of things I have to do first.'

'You could do it now. You could walk away and catch a coach ...'

'I haven't got any money.'

I could hear her drawing a breath of cigarette smoke as she thought about it. 'Hitchhike,' she told me.

'I'll come as soon as I can.'

'And you haven't got any money? But I thought you said you were all right ... '

Then she was off about me looking after myself. She always worries about me. She always wants to know that I've eaten properly and that I'm wearing decent clothes. That sort of thing. She's a good mother really. Or she would be if she managed to get off the bottle.

Then she started asking me questions. I was scared about saying too much ... she was asking me about the people I was with, where I was, what my address was, what their names were. She said she wanted to thank them in some way, but I didn't trust her. She got angry because I wouldn't tell her.

'Don't you trust me, David? Don't you trust me?' she kept saying. And of course I didn't but I could never say, 'No, I don't trust you,' so I had to make excuses. It went on and on. The pips kept going but I stuffed more money in. I spent three quid talking to her. I only stopped when the money ran out and the phone went dead in mid-sentence.

I hate my mum more than my dad, because my dad only scares me but my mum makes me feel dirty and useless. She undoes everything I want to do with myself. I felt so shit when I went away from that box. I'd promised her to come home, I promised her everything I'd sworn I wouldn't promise. I knew I shouldn't have rung!

She always does it. She can make me do anything. She used to do it for fun sometimes, just to amuse herself. She did it in front of Gemma when Gemma came round to see me ... just talked and talked and made me go around the house doing stupid jobs for her until I got so anxious and confused I started dropping things and getting embarrassed. I saw my mum glance at Gemma. I knew what was going on. Gemma did too, I'm sure, although she never said anything. My mum was showing off.

But I'd promised her to go back and I can't break promises – not to Mum. Not to her of all people. Now I'd have to ring Gemma and tell her not to come. Now I'd have to go back home and the whole mess'd all just carry on forever ...

I was walking around for ages. I got back to the house hours later. It was late. I was hoping they'd all have gone to bed but the light was on in the basement. They'd all want to know how I'd got on.

I went away and walked around for a bit more, but the light was still on, so I thought, Oh, well, get it over with ...

When I'd finished no one said a word, but then Richard got up and gave me a big hug, then Vonny ... even Jerry got up and hugged me. It was ... it wasn't like they knew me so well or anything, and it felt a bit awkward at first because I'm not ... my family doesn't hug much. Sort of like it was medicine they were giving me. But then I forgot about that and clung hold of them and I had to try and try not to cry. It was so miserable.

Richard said, 'But of course you're not going, you know that, don't you?'

I was so surprised. I really didn't expect them to say that.

'No,' said Vonny. 'Gemma was right about that. Leaving home was the best thing you ever did.'

I said, 'But I promised ...'

'She made you – that's not a promise,' said Jerry.

'I don't think confessions under pressure count,' said Richard.

'But he's hitting her ...'

It went on for hours. I just didn't see any way I could leave her like that. They said all sorts of things to try and convince me. Vonny reckoned that now that he'd started hitting her, he'd keep doing it, so I couldn't stop it anyway. Richard was going on about how I wasn't responsible, which I knew anyway but it didn't help.

He said, 'She can't look after you and you can't look after her, can you?'

Everything they said was true. I'd thought all of it myself before. The trouble was it didn't make any difference. It didn't matter, none of it. What mattered was, he'd started beating her up since I went away and maybe I could stop him doing it by going back ...

6
Gemma

I told him, 'She's lying.'

'She wouldn't do that,' Tar said.

'Wouldn't she?' I said, but I hardly needed to, because we both knew she would. She'd tell him she'd been to bed with Prince Charles if it suited her. And expect him to believe it.

And he would.

'I told you not to ring her up. She's only saying it to make you feel guilty. Same as she always does.'

There was a long pause. I could almost hear him thinking down the phone. I held my breath. Then he said, 'I've done it again, haven't I?' And I almost crowed because I was scared stiff he'd come back, and where was I supposed to run away to then?

'I'm so stupid.'

'Nah, you're just too nice,' I said, and I would have covered him with kisses if I could.

To be honest I wasn't half as convinced as I made out. He beats Tar up and then when Tar goes he starts on his wife. It was quite logical, except that it was equally logical that she was lying about it.

'It seemed so typical of him to start on her ...' he said.

'That's why she said it. That's what she does, doesn't she?'

'Yeah ... I know.'

Tar and I made arrangements for Saturday. I think I can

say he was a much more cheerful boy by the time I put the phone down.

I pretty soon found out it was all true after all. Joanne Roberts told me. She lives round the corner from his mum and dad and she found out everything from her mum and dad. Jo said it was the best thing that had happened on their street for years.

She had a big fat lip. Joanne actually saw the lip when she was out shopping with it. She wore dark glasses but she couldn't hide the lip.

Of course, she could have done it falling down the stairs or walking into a wall. She'd done that before. But it sounded like a fair bet it was Mr Muscles wot done it. It seemed like he didn't waste much time, either. He walked straight in and thumped her one as soon as she showed him Tar's note and she ran straight off down the road to a friend of hers who told Joanne's mum all about it. She slept on the sofa and their cleaning lady said there was a pile of sick behind it in the morning.

I wasn't telling Tar that, though. Not yet, anyway. He only needed the slightest excuse to dash back and get beaten up for Mumsy.

I went round there once and she was *all over him*. I was surprised she didn't put her tongue in his ear and wiggle it about. Honestly. She was grabbing hold of him and pulling him on top of her and holding on to him like Young Love, except that she's about forty and all baggy and scrawny with her hair all over the place, like the Hag Woman of Minely. It quite put me off him for a bit. I'd smell her on him sometimes. She used to use gallons of perfume to try and drown out the booze, and she came out smelling like she drank the stuff. Maybe she did.

Poor Tar was ever so embarrassed but his dad was livid.

He was clanging around in the background pouring drinks for him and her, not forgetting to abuse her for drinking it, of course. I never heard language like it. His dad, actually, must have known she was only doing it to wind him up but he couldn't help getting angry about it. Not that he wanted to have her wet tongue in *his* ear ... but he didn't want her to even *pretend* to put it in anyone else's, especially not Tar's. And of course that's exactly why she did it.

It was all deeply crazy stuff and both Tar and his dad knew exactly what she was up to but they didn't seem able to help themselves. She had the old man knocking Tar about, when all he really wanted to do was land one on her.

It sounded as though he hadn't wasted much time waiting for his dreams to come true. And of course she wanted Tar to come back and carry on inserting his face in between his dad's fist and her own ugly mug.

I had no intention of letting him.

I tried to get round to have a look at his mum myself. I thought I'd go and knock on the door and pretend to be all sympathetic. Fat chance. My mum and dad would have fed me to the sharks first.

Since Tar ran off, things had been tighter than ever. Dad wasn't just picking me up from school. He'd started *taking* me there as well. He must have got time off work to do it, because I didn't get ready until about ten to nine. There were top-level meetings at school. I used to catch glimpses of the teachers keeping an eye on me when I went to the loo, that sort of thing. Of course it was All For My Own Good. They wanted every second of my life accounted for. I suppose they thought that the moment I had a spare minute, I'd be peeling my knickers off and diving into the boys' toilets ...

I tried telling them. 'I'M STILL A VIRGIN!' I screamed from the top of the stairs one day.

There was no reply.

I'd had the police round questioning me about Tar. Mum and Dad hated that. I think they hated me for it, bringing their home into disrepute or something. They'd even taken to locking the doors in the evening to stop me sneaking out. The stupidity of it, when you think ... I mean, I could have gone out of the windows or anything. And, of course, my weekends out hadn't been banned, not yet anyway, although I assumed that it was only a matter of time. Let's face it, if I was going to run off there wasn't much they could do about it, beyond tying me to the bannisters. As they were soon to find out.

They thought I was on drugs, too. I got accused of smoking and sniffing glue on the beach with the crowd.

'I expect that boyfriend of yours is dead by this time,' my father suggested, sounding as though it would be no bad thing. Tar, sniffing glue ... I ask you. Or me, for that matter. It's true some of the kids did it but all I'd ever done was smoke a bit of hash. Of course, they knew all about it. I don't know who told them but they knew all right.

My parents belonged to the Slippery Slope school of thought. They had no doubt at all that unless my life was made as miserable as possible, I'd be a junkie whore by midnight.

I made my plans. I went along with it, staying in, presenting my homework for the nightly check, waiting for my dad at the school gate to collect me. I was even dropping the sarcasm.

'I hope there's nothing behind this good behaviour, missy,' my mother told me. Talk about trust. I suppose I overdid the not being sarcastic. Sarcasm flows in my veins like blood. But it shows how much they thought of their darling daughter, that I couldn't even be good without arousing suspicion.

* * *

If things hadn't been falling to bits at home I could have arranged it better. I'd have pretended I was staying away with a friend for the weekend. I'd have left on Friday night and they wouldn't have even known until Monday morning. But there was nothing I could have said. If it involved going away for the weekend they'd *know* I was out having an orgy and beating up old ladies.

Still, I did pretty good. Saturday was the best day for it. They'd get furious at teatime when I was supposed to check in and start worrying at night when I didn't turn up. But in the end they'd get hoisted by their own paranoia. I reckoned they'd think I was staying the night with some boy. It wouldn't occur to them I was actually giving them the elbow. They'd start really worrying, I mean police worrying, about Sunday night. Monday morning, and they'd get a nice letter in the post from their loving daughter.

This is how I did it.

I hid my bag in a garden a few houses down on Friday night, so I wouldn't be seen walking out with it. Next morning, shower, breakfast ...

'Where are you going this weekend?' my dad demanded. He'd dropped any pretence of liking me over the past few weeks.

I shrugged. 'Down town, maybe.'

He snorted. My mum leaned across and held my arm. 'Stay out of trouble, Gemma,' she begged, but I didn't even bother looking at her. I thought, If you only knew.

I sneaked out about ten. Mum was upstairs and Dad was out at the supermarket. I walked out of the house and down the road to the coach station.

Oh, there was one little arrangement I forgot to tell you. On Friday I got my hands on Dad's Visa card and booked my ticket. I also helped myself to his bank card. He was always running about the house yelling, 'Where's my cards, where's my cards? If I can't find them I'll have to ring up and get them cancelled again ...' So even though he'd miss them some time over the weekend, he'd wait a few days for them to turn up before getting suspicious.

I have indicated that my parents are not overendowed in the head department. Dad left the number you need to type in the money machine written on the back of a mirror in the bedroom. He's not very good at remembering things. On the way to the station I dropped by the bank and got a hundred quid out. It was no sweat. In the town centre I posted the letter to my parents.

Then I stepped on the coach.

And the coach drove off.

And it was as simple as that.

Don't judge me. I don't have to justify myself to anyone. I didn't feel so great about some of the things I had to do but I didn't have any choice. Stealing off my folks ... well, it was either them or someone else. The way I looked at it, if they'd known ... I mean if they were able to put themselves in my place, which I know is ridiculous anyway, they'd have given it to me, I expect.

That letter I sent them – I tried to make it all right. Actually I wrote about six or seven letters. I hadn't realised how hard it was going to be until I sat down and tried to say, 'Look, I'm going.' I mean, what can you say? They used to love me when I was a kid but they hardly knew me any more and there was no way I could make them understand. Thanks for everything, goodbye, that's what it boils down to. And I love you. I said that. I didn't think it was true at the time but it made me cry anyway. I kept writing letters and tearing them up, writing them and tearing them up. I got it as good as I could but I had tear smudges on it and had to start again. I wasn't going to post my tears to them. I was going ... I was going and it didn't matter how many hearts I broke – mine, theirs, anyone's. In my mind I was already gone.

I sat on the coach and watched the town go by. I didn't say goodbye to the buildings and people of that place where I grew up, I just watched, I was happy to see them go. I didn't know then how long I was going for. Sometimes I thought – just for a week or two. Other times I thought, I'll never see this dump again. Thank God.

The coach trip took two hours. I was sitting there wetting my knickers all the way. Every time a police car came by I thought they were going to pull us over and arrest me and take me home. Of course nothing happened. When we got to Bristol I was goggle-eyed looking out of the windows trying to see everything. I was getting so wound up, I just wanted to dive into those busy streets and disappear like a little fish.

I was almost chewing my nails with frustration and excitement by the time we got to the coach station. I almost welcomed that feeling actually, because I didn't want to be cool about it. I was planning on giving Tar a welcome he'd remember for the rest of his life. I was going to really go for it, knock him off his feet. I wasn't going to be cool and swagger down the stairs and say, 'Hi ...' It was going to be full pelt, total happiness. Tar's had so much grief in his life. I wanted to make the poor sod feel so good. And I wanted him to make me feel good too.

I was thinking that all that excitement and frustration building up inside me was rocket fuel ...

I saw him out of the coach window, waiting for me. I ducked down. I didn't want to water myself down with little glances through the window. I kept my head down right up until I was on the last step down from the coach ... then I saw him.

I yelled, 'TAR!!!' and I dropped my bags on the steps and

I went off like a scalded cat, shrieking across the tarmac, screaming his name at the top of my voice. He looked quite alarmed. I got my arms round him and I hugged him and, oh, and I kissed him and I hugged him and I kissed him and I danced around and then I hugged and kissed him some more and, oh, and I squashed my boobs on his chest and slowly this enormous great smile crept across his face ...

'Oh, it's so GOOD to see you ... Oh, I've MISSED you, I've MISSED you ...' And I was pressing myself into him and pulling him against me and and and and – and I think it worked.

Actually, I didn't have to put it on that much. I was pretty near hysterical anyway. It wasn't just Tar I was kissing and hugging. It was ... being on my own, having an adventure. Yeah. It was life. A big, fat slice of life. I'd been so anxious sitting on the coach but as soon as I stepped off it all that just vanished. I was *thrilled*. Just walking down the road was brilliant. I felt like a kid. If I was with anyone except Tar I might have wanted to try and look a bit more cool about the whole thing, but that sort of thing's wasted on him. He's so cool anyway. I just wanted to infect him with Gemmaness. I reckon I did, too. He was walking along with his lips wrapped halfway round his head. I felt like I was blowing him along the road.

I made him walk me round a bit. We went through the town centre to the docks ... and I just fell in love with the place. It wasn't big and busy like you think a city's gonna be. No one was desperate about anything. There were weeds growing out of the walls and people weren't rushing. I cooled down and I started feeling really mellow. I mean, I was still high, but it was okay to be high. No one was bothered about stopping me; it didn't feel like I was going out of control. I remember thinking, I'm gonna like it here.

Tar was worried about getting home. 'They've cooked us a meal,' he kept saying. 'They're really nice people, it's rude ...' But I wasn't interested in them.

I don't love Tar, I've said that, but I didn't half fancy him that day. I kept catching sight of myself in the windows. I was very pink in the face and I was wearing all these russety coloured things – scarf and jumper and a skirt. I should have worn jeans and things but I'd dressed up.

It was all for him, see. I wanted to feel like he could have done anything he wanted with me and I'd have let him.

We got away from the docks and into the market and I suddenly leaned against the wall and pulled him on top of me. He's about a foot taller than me. I pulled him on me so he was leaning against me. I could see from his face what I was doing to him. Then he kissed me – a real long kiss like we were on our own in the middle of a forest or a desert and there was no one within a hundred miles and we could do anything we liked.

I said, 'Wow ...'

'Yeah, wow.'

I wanted him to touch me so much I think I'd have dragged him into a shop doorway but there were too many people about. But that was okay. There was always later on.

We got to the squat in the end. I was impressed, actually. I mean, he'd found a place to stay, got himself a bunch of people who weren't just prepared to put him up, they were even willing to *feed* him. He'd only been away two weeks and he had the whole of that side of it worked out. The only thing he didn't have was a scene ... you know, people to hang around with. Friends. You couldn't put Richard, Jerry and Vonny in that class. They were too old and too nice. To tell the truth I found it a bit put on. The girl, Vonny, came over and gave me a kiss and a hug, and I hugged her back and grinned, but she hardly knew me. And I didn't get the impression she approved of me all that much.

Richard was a bit weird, grinning all over the place, but he was fun. I think he was shy or something. Jerry was okay, he was fairly normal but even he was putting it on a bit. I felt like they could have been vampires in disguise for all I saw of the real them. You had the feeling they were nice because they'd decided it was the fashion to be nice. You could see them working out how to be nice. For all I knew they were probably no nicer than I am.

Now, if it'd been me, I'd have been sleeping in doorways and eating toenail clippings. But I'd have found a crowd to do it with, I expect. I guess I'm not all that interested in niceness. Sometimes people call me nice but that's just because I can make them feel happy. Inside, I just want to have a good time, enjoy myself.

I expect I'll get found out one day.

The first bad sign was that the meal Richard had made for us was drying out in the oven. Richard didn't care. When I said we'd been sightseeing he beamed at the ceiling as if it was the most exciting thing in the world and said, 'Oh, that's all right.' Vonny was a bit put out, though, even though she hadn't cooked it. Well, except she'd made an apple pie for pudding.

Over the apple pie Vonny said, 'How long are you staying with us, Gemma?' And there was this pause. I could feel them all looking at me.

I thought ... oho. Because it wasn't, do you think you'll like living here, but, how long ...

I just smiled and I said, 'I don't know. I just don't know ...' And I smiled and they smiled and Tar smiled.

Like I say ... they were all very nice.

Later on we went to the pub. It was good, sitting in there drinking half pints of lager. They had to sneak me and Tar in slightly, in case the barman refused to serve us.

They wanted to know if I'd heard anything about Tar's mum. So we talked about that for about an hour which made him utterly miserable. Mind you, they seemed to have a good time.

After a bit it turned out they were all anarchists. That took me back a bit. I mean, I don't know much about it, but aren't anarchists supposed to go around blowing people up, not hugging one another? It turned out they had this big plan for Sunday night. They were going to go out and superglue all the locks in the banks.

Richard got really beside himself about this. He kept putting his beer down and grinning wildly at the ceiling with the sheer delight of ruining the banks' trade for a day. I said, 'Don't banks have back doors, then?'

'Oh, we'll glue those up, too. And the night safes.' And he beamed all round the pub like a man who had been given a million pounds.

It was all arranged. Me and Tar were going along with them. I got quite excited about it. I thought, This is different. I always looked down at the vandals at home – you know, having a good time by smashing up the kiddies' playground. Great fun, eh? But this had a purpose and anyway, I'd have given anything to see the bank manager's face when his lock wouldn't open. We all had a good laugh about that.

I told them about my mum and dad and they seemed very sympathetic. Richard was quite distressed about it. 'My parents used to let me misbehave all I wanted,' he said, and he grinned in that mad way he had at the ceiling. 'I made plenty of use of the opportunity,' he added happily.

I was getting to like Richard.

We started swapping stories about mums and dads and how terrible they were. Tar was a bit quiet. Well, he would be, wouldn't he? But I was beginning to get the giggles. I'd had a vodka and orange on top of the lager and I was thinking how just at that very time my parents would be beginning to get utterly furious. It was ten thirty and I was just one hour late. They'd be sitting there grinding their teeth and planning new restrictions, which frankly would be taxing even their imaginations because there wasn't much left to restrict. They'd be wondering who I was sleeping with, what I was taking, etc. etc. It really cracked me up, thinking about them raging around at home and ringing round all my friends and promising themselves they'd be tougher tomorrow. And all the time I was a hundred miles away ...

They'd find out on Monday morning when my letter came through.

And then, Vonny turned to me cool as a cucumber and she said, 'Don't you think you ought to ring your folks up and tell them you're all right?'

I just gaped at her. The hypocrisy of it! There we'd been swapping stories about parental horror and now she wanted me to started being nice to them!

'What for?' I asked.

'But they must be feeling awful. At least you could let them know you're all right.'

'And tell them when to expect me back?' I asked. 'And to send on the woolly vests.'

'No, like I said – just let them know you're okay.'

'I think that would be a good idea,' said Richard to the ceiling.

Well, I was cornered, wasn't I? I went on about the letter coming on the Monday morning but it wasn't good enough. Mum and Dad were worried *now*. I tried to point out that at this stage in the proceedings, incandescent fury would be a more typical reaction, but no. Even Tar rounded on me. Then of course he wanted to ring up *his* mum and we had to argue him out of that. I hoped that'd put them off the scent but as soon as he backed down they started on me again.

They even had a whip round so I wouldn't get cut off in the middle of something important. And before I knew it I was standing there in front of the pay phone stuffing pound coins and thinking, Pig, pig, pig. How did this happen?

'Gemma ... where have you been? Where are you now?'

'I'm all right, I'm just –'

'We've been worried sick –'

'It's only half past ten –'

'It's eleven o'clock and you should have been in an hour and a half ago. I thought we were past this, I thought things were getting better. Your mother ...'

'Look, I'm ringing up to let you know I won't be back tonight ...'

'You ... you'd better be back. Picked up with some of those seafront friends again, have you? ... It isn't good enough, Gemma ... blah blah rant ...'

And he was off. That's all it took. I held the phone away from my ear and I whispered, 'Please, please don't do this to me ...' I was in the corner of the pub but I was aware of all of them looking over at me. I couldn't talk to him, he was shouting so much. I couldn't even look upset because they were all watching. I just had to pretend I was having a normal conversation with a normal person.

'Oh, we're having a great time, thanks. Yes, okay, I'll be careful. Yeah, thanks, Dad. I'll see you tomorrow ... Yeah, give Mum a big kiss ...'

And he was going, 'Why are you speaking to me like that, are you being sarcastic? Gemma, what's going on? Look, let's overlook this slip. You get back here WITHIN THE HOUR and we can discuss –'

'No, I've already eaten, we had baked potatoes. I'll give you a ring again, tomorrow probably. Okay, see you, Dad, thanks,'bye ...'

And I put the phone down.

I don't know why it upset me so much. I just wasn't ready for it. I was leaving home, I was running away, I just wasn't ready to start talking to them. I guess it took me by surprise.

I stood there for a bit staring at the wall trying not to cry. It wouldn't do for them to see me cry after speaking to my folks. Vonny came up to me after a minute and tried to peer into my face but I turned away.

'Are you okay? Gemma?' She came up close and touched my arm. 'Is everything okay at home?'

The stupid cow! What did she think things were like at home? I closed my eyes and nodded my head. It felt like she was drilling a hole in my skull. She just made everything so hard. I managed to whisper, 'Look, I've done it, is that enough?' She thought about it and nodded. I went out to the toilet to fix my face.

Afterwards they were going to a party, but I didn't fancy it by this time. I'd really been having a good time but now I felt shattered, totally shattered, as if I'd flown to the moon and back instead of catching the coach to Bristol.

Me and Tar went back and sat in his room. I was furious with him for siding with them. We almost had an argument and then I started to cry and ...

I couldn't really be angry with him for long. Once he saw me cry he got really upset about it. He started hugging me and saying, 'Sorry, sorry ...' and getting all wet-eyed. And I thought, I'm not coming all this way just to fall out with Tar about that pair of sergeant majors.

We got ourselves cosy. I wanted to light a fire but we weren't allowed to in case the neighbours thought the house was on fire and called the fire brigade. They weren't supposed to know the house was squatted. We weren't allowed to have the lights on either, for the same reason. I was beginning to get a bit irritated with the list of things we weren't allowed to do. But Tar stuck loads of candles in bottles and made coffee and we sat on the floor in a pile of cushions and had a bit of a cuddle, and we talked for ages about ... I dunno, everything.

Then bedtime came along. I had my bedroll with me that I used for camping. Tar had his mattress and he kept going on and on about me sleeping on that. I could feel myself losing my temper about it so I just said, 'Okay, okay.' I had his present to give him and I didn't want to spoil this.

I was feeling shy by this time. I put the bedroll down next to the mattress and got undressed and into my bag while he was out of the room.

And I thought, right. I've done my bit. He can do the rest.

Tar came in. He blew out the candles, got undressed in a corner and into his pyjamas. Then he slid into his bag and just lay there.

I was furious. Livid. I had the bag up around my nose so my hair and my eyes were peering out at him, three feet away with his eyes closed, all set to go to sleep. The worst of it was, I was getting cold and if this kept on I'd have to sneak out and get my pyjamas on.

I lay there for about ten minutes getting really chilly. And then he said, 'Can we have a cuddle?'

'All right, then.'

He pushed his mattress across so he lay next to me and hugged me. He didn't try to kiss me. Then he put his hand on my neck and I could feel his fingers slide down to my shoulder ...

I was watching him. I saw his eyes open and catch me looking at him and he closed them again, quickly. Then in a moment the fingers slid down a little further, down my waist, to my hips.

That was my present, see. Me. I wasn't wearing a stitch.

Tar opened his eyes and smiled at me and I smiled back and said, 'It's a double. The sleeping-bag.'

'Oh ...'

The big oaf.

'I've taken two bags and zipped them together.'

He got out of bed and was just about to slide in next to me when I said, 'Have you got anything?'

'Oh ... no ...'

It was such a pain. I was so cross. I sat up in bed and seized a cup of cold coffee I had by me. 'Do I have to do everything?' I snapped, and started slurping the coffee.

'I'm sorry, I'm so stupid ...'

Well ... I suppose I should have supplied them. How was he to know? Still, Tar was never a Boy Scout, that much was clear.

Then he said, 'Hang on ...' And he ups and outs the room with his jeans on and I thought ...

'Oh, no!' I knew what he was doing. He was going to borrow some off Vonny and Jerry ... I was half amused, half furious ... because, I mean, this was my first time. I didn't want to use boring old borrowed anarchist condoms!

And then he was away for *ages*. He must have been half an hour and then he came back quietly in case I was asleep, all sheepish.

'Sorry ...'

'What happened?'

'They were a bit reluctant to lend them.'

'Why?'

'Well, you're only fourteen, see, and ...'

I got the picture. There'd been a big discussion about whether Gemma was old enough. I was livid. I sat there and steamed. He was dithering around the room. He came and sat next to me and asked me if I didn't want to any more. It was dreadful. This was exactly the sort of thing I'd wanted to avoid. I thought he'd discover me wearing nothing at all under my sleeping-bag and it would just happen. Now he was sitting there in his blue jeans and I had my jumper back on, I'd got so cold waiting.

I said, 'Oh, never mind,' and I turned away and wrapped myself back up in my sleeping-bag as if I wanted to go to sleep. I could feel him standing there for a moment, then he got into his. He lay close and cuddled up to me.

Well. Sometimes you've got to work harder than you want to. I turned round and he kissed me and then he slid out and into my bag and he lay there very still for a bit, although I could tell he was really excited. He can be very tactful sometimes. We cuddled and it got very warm and then a bit steamy and pretty soon my jumper found its way up around my neck ...

Later on, Tar said in a little voice, 'I love you.'

And I said ...

Oh ... I felt so sorry for him, but I hadn't anything else to give him, you know? It was just a moment we had together. I mean, he was a really special person to me, but ... I just felt that someone could come along and blow hard and I'd fly away from him, go in the wind and end up ... next door or on another planet with someone else, anywhere. Just because the wind blew.

I didn't want to hurt him.

I put my finger on his lips and I said, 'Ssssh ...'

I could see him looking at me. He was hurt and I felt cross because I'd done my best. And what right had he got to love me?

I said, 'Don't say that.'

There was a long silence and then he said this funny thing ... 'Dandelion.'

I just looked at him, it was so out of context. I said,

'What's that supposed to mean?'

He sort of smiled and shrugged and I smiled back because I realised ...

He'd given me a picture he'd done of a dandelion. It was a lovely picture. I didn't know what the dandelion meant to him but I knew what he was saying. He was saying that he still loved me, even though ...

I wanted to say something to him ... to tell him that I felt so much for him, even though I didn't love him. I couldn't say dandelion so I said, 'Ladybird.' It just came into my head.

He laughed and said, 'Why ladybird?'

I said, 'Because they're nice, and everyone likes them, and they're pretty and red ...' He began to kiss my mouth.

'... and they like dandelions. A lot,' I said. I touched his nose with the tip of my finger, as if I was telling him off.

Tar smiled and nodded.

'Dandelion,' he said.

'Ladybird.'

'Dandelion.'

'Ladybird.'

And I really did love him in that moment, more than anyone, more than myself, even though tomorrow it might all be over.

He kissed my mouth and we snuggled up as close as we could get.

7
Richard

I AM AN ANTICHRIST
I AM AN ANAR–CHIST–A
DUNNO WOT I WANT BUT I KNOW HOW TO GET IT
IIIIIIIIIIIIIIIIIIIIIIIIIIIIIIIIIII
WANNA BEEEEEEEEEEEE
ANAR–CHEEEEEEE

The Sex Pistols

It was a stick-up. We were going to start with Barclays Bank on the High Street.

For the occasion I dressed up in my GLUE YOU tee-shirt and a pair of bright green Doc Martens with daisies painted on the toes. I got Tar to do the daisies for me after I saw his dandelions. He's brilliant. They looked great. I have such enormous feet. Oh, and my tight, calf-length leggings. I had to wear a parka over the tee-shirt though. It was a bit of a giveaway, really – GLUE YOU all over your chest and twenty tubes of Locktite in yer handbag.

Vonny dressed up as well in a sort of yellow and black stripy leotard and woolly tights that made her look rather like an enormous wasp, only of course far more attractive. I couldn't get Jerry to dress up at all, although he wore the blackest clothes he could find. But he always wears black. He dyes his hair, which is a start. I tried to get him to wear some black eye shadow or mascara, on one eye at least, but he wouldn't until Gemma joined in. He let her do it for him and I have to say he looked rather menacing. I expect he would have let me do it, only he thinks I might be gay. I'm not, in case you were wondering. I just play up to it. In fact, I'm celibate. I have been for five years now. It's not the sex I object to – it's the politics.

Gemma dressed up in her party dress and Vonny did her face for her like a forties film star – loads of powder and one of those Cupid's bow mouths in shiny red lipstick. She wanted to wear a pair of high heels too but I had to veto it. Sometimes you have to run. As for Tar, he was willing enough but you could tell he found it hard going. Gemma wanted to dress him in drag, but it doesn't do to attract too much attention. We let him off in the end. He obviously felt ludicrous enough as it was without having to look it.

This is the way it ought to be. Not Bonnie and Clyde. Not gangsters and the IRA and BANG BANG BANG you're dead ... really dead. More like Robin Hood. I mean the Disney version.

We got to Barclays and I went up to the door and wielded the superglue. That's the easy bit – you just sidle up and go squirt squirt into the lock. By morning they're LOCKED OUT and the money's LOCKED IN.

They hate that.

It was writing the GLUE YOU logo on the door and the anarchist sign and getting the calling card through the letter box that was tricky. It takes time. Have you ever noticed that bank doors are always exposed? Try hiding in the shadows outside a bank sometime. There's always a streetlight. They must have some deal with the Council.

Actually it wasn't that tricky. You just wait until no one's looking, but it always got Vonny a bit nervous. Banks do that to some people. If she had her way we'd just do the glue and then scarper.

You've no idea how much I enjoy doing this sort of thing. I could hear Gemma giggling as I did THIS IS A STICK-UP in green chalk. It was a lovely giggle. It sort of floated out of the shadows into the night air and I wished I could post that through the letterbox, too. I had to be content with my calling cards. They're not bad, though. I do them at home on my stencil set and colour them in by hand. There's a nice little picture on each one of a character from my *Golden Treasury of Nursery Rhymes*.

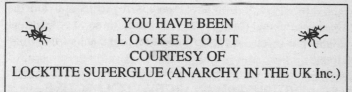

YOU HAVE BEEN
L O C K E D   O U T
COURTESY OF
LOCKTITE SUPERGLUE (ANARCHY IN THE UK Inc.)

I showed it to the crew before I pushed it in. Gemma giggled. Tar looked astonished. Vonny tutted and glanced up and down the road. Personally I'd quite like to be arrested but it hasn't happened yet. Can you *imagine* what the police would make of us?

Then I got a bit carried away finishing off the GLUE YOU logo, double colouring it with red chalk, and Vonny started pulling at me.

'Come on, we've another fifteen to do,' she hissed.

'We've got all night,' I said. But I put my chalks away and carried on up the road. No point in getting upset about it.

Anarchy loves theatre. That's the whole point. People forget that. You have to laugh at the devil, not fight him. They'll always have more guns, they'll always have bombs that go off with a bigger bang. No matter how revolting you become, they'll always be willing to be even more revolting to you. They've had so much more practice.

My tools are superglue and subversion. No one gets hurt,

everyone has a good time, including my victims. They get the day off work. I never heard anyone complain about that.

Vonny sidled up to me outside the NatWest on Chisem Street and hissed, 'Jerry's smoking ...'

I said, 'Oh.' I mean, what's new? 'When is Jerry not smoking?' I enquired.

'Yes, but he's giving some to Gemma ...'

I said, 'Oh, dear.'

Vonny said, 'What shall we do?'

I said, 'Play it by ear.' I posted my card and led the Outlaws up the road to the Midland, three shops further down. I ask you. What do you need four banks for on one street?

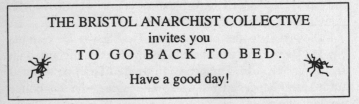

THE BRISTOL ANARCHIST COLLECTIVE
invites you
TO GO BACK TO BED.

Have a good day!

Although we're not really a collective, you understand. It's just me and whoever I can get to come along with me on the night.

To be quite honest, I didn't care one little bit if Gemma was smoking a bit of dope. Frankly, I'd rather Jerry didn't smoke on a stick-up. If we get caught it just confuses the issue. It's the sort of thing that gives them an excuse, something to latch on to. You know – drug-crazed punk anarchists glue banks ...

But still, this is scarcely a military operation. And why shouldn't he share it with Gemma? The reason why I said, 'Oh dear,' was that Vonny was having problems with it. The usual sort of thing. Gemma wanted to do one thing and Vonny wanted her to do another. It's called politics.

I hate politics.

Vonny walked alongside me.

'She's only fourteen, you can imagine the mess the police or the press would make of it.'

'Corrupting the youth of the nation, you mean?'

'Exactly.'

I beamed. 'But we are!'

The trouble is that Vonny comes out on a stick-up because she really does think we are affecting the financial running of the area. She thinks people will lose their money, the economy will get into trouble, that sort of thing.

Render unto Caesar, I say. I'm fishing for hearts and souls. The bank manager's heart, the bank clerk's, for Gemma's and Tar's, for Vonny's ... yes, and for yours, too. Go on – be a devil. Do your bit. Stay in bed today.

> Anarchy plc
> SUGGESTS YOU THINK AGAIN!!!

We had a bit of an argument outside the Co-operative Bank. Jerry reckoned we ought to let them off because they were co-operative.

'They're still a bank,' I pointed out.

They got glued.

Gemma and Jerry were having a good time by the sound of it. I was actually getting a little nervous myself. Her giggles were getting slightly hysterical and she was beginning to trip over things rather a lot. Vonny was getting extremely annoyed. She was walking in front of them glancing angrily over her shoulder. I gathered that Jerry had ignored her wishes not to get Gemma stoned. Tar was with Vonny and they were engaged in an intense-looking conversation, which I was willing to bet was political, and about Gemma.

Oh, dear.

It gets in everywhere.

When you walk down a high street in Bristol, you have so much going on around you. Butcher's shops, for example. We were standing outside a butcher's shop. I'm a vegan myself. It's an issue. All around us the streetlights were blazing away, burning up the fossil fuels. Banks and insurance companies investing in death and disease. Chemists selling cosmetics that have been tested by being dripped in monkeys' eyes. Plenty of opportunity for Vonny to spread a bit of political awareness.

And overhead the stars. It was a lovely night. When you stepped out and lifted up your head and looked up above the roofs and the traffic and the people you could hear the wind blowing in among the roofs and the stars overhead.

So what was Vonny doing?

Bending Tar's ear about Gemma.

Just what he needed.

Just the thing to endear him to us. Just what he needed after spending fourteen years being brought up by two monsters.

Vonny is a lovely person. She's ever so motherly, always bringing home stray cats and making biscuits and giving money to beggars. Always trying to make sure Jerry eats his veggies and washes his socks regularly and trying to make sure that things don't go to your head and that you don't giggle too loud.

I love her but sometimes I suspect her of being a closet Communist.

> No work today ...
> DON'T TELL ME YOU'RE
> **DISAPPOINTED?**

You may think I'm being a bit of a prat. I am. But I do actually think that it's just possible that one day enough people will start to think, Why am I having such a bad time so often, and why is it so important for me to give other people a bad time in order to make sure that I can carry on having a bad time myself?

If I can get just a couple of bank clerks to start thinking they might as well stay in bed a bit more often, then I've done something to change the world. And if I can do it wearing enormous green boots with daisies painted on the toes, all the better.

I have to say it wasn't the most successful stick-up I've ever done. There were too many distractions. Vonny was livid by the time we got home and Tar looked as though he'd been gimleted with a blunt skewer. I must have a word with him.

Gemma could barely stand up. Lovely life, isn't it, sometimes?

'How do you think her parents feel?' asked Vonny. 'They were just keeping her in. It's not like Tar, is it?'

Well. The thing was, Vonny had a point.

8
Gemma

We were having a WILD TIME. Gluing the banks. Sharing the washing-up. Eating baked potatoes and beans for dinner every day. Wow.

Nah ... it was all right, really. I was thinking too much. You know – where's the wild parties, where's the street life, where's the CITY?

But then, Tar was having such a great time, that's what made it all right. Honestly, I think he was in heaven. He liked everyone. He adored Richard. He even liked Vonny though she was obviously an enemy.

And, of course, he had me.

We could stay up as late as we liked and get up when we wanted. We could be together all day and all night. And I have to admit, it was pretty good. If Tar hadn't been there I wouldn't have lasted the day. But he was. So.

Since he had no money and they were feeding him, Tar had been doing the house up. Richard got his hands on several gallons of cream paint and Tar was getting up at nine every morning and slapping it on, room after room in a disgusting pale glub colour. Of course I was a dependant too. I hadn't let on about my hundred pounds, no way – so I had to help him. I soon put a stop to the nine o'clock in the morning bit, though. We got up about midday. We spent the morning splashing about in bed and the afternoon splashing around in paint.

Since we'd started sleeping together I fancied him like mad and we kept having to stop to have a cuddle and a grope. Whenever I undressed I had painty fingermarks ALL OVER!

Tar's great company. He must have thought about everything at some point or other, because he's always got something to say. But he always listens. He stands there frowning with the effort of trying to work out what he's missed, as if it's all his fault and not just me saying something stupid, which it usually is. And he's funny. I mean, he likes my jokes. We were falling around laughing half the time. We just got on together so well.

On the other hand he always had some annoying habits. I thought he was overdoing the being helpful bit. As far as I was concerned, all right, they were feeding us but we were working for our keep. It wasn't just our own room we were doing. But Tar was so pathetically grateful and guilty, he spent half his time rushing about doing jobs for them, cooking, cleaning up, you name it. But the other thing – the thing that really got up my nose – were the endless discussions about Gemma.

It was Vonny who was behind it, of course. She was so bothered about deciding what was the right thing and then making sure someone else did it. She was the same with everyone, actually. She was always on at Jerry to do something – open more squats with Richard or clean the kitchen or make their bed or do the laundry. She didn't have much luck there; all he wanted to do was sit around and get stoned. She had better luck with Tar. That got up my nose worse than her getting at me. He loved it, of course. She only had to ponder aloud what to do for dinner tonight and he'd be on his feet begging to be allowed to rush round the shops with the shopping bag. Gratitude wasn't the word. It was humiliating. As if he wanted another mother ... he'd only just got rid of the last one.

She didn't like me one little bit. You could see it in her face what she thought of me: spoilt brat. She didn't like the way I spoke or the way I acted or the way I looked. She thought I ought to be at school, at home and out of her life. She figured I ought to be tucked up back in bed.

I figured that was her problem.

Basically, she was running a campaign to get me out and back home. She didn't know me or she'd have realised – the best way of making me do something is tell me not to do it. But she was on at Richard as well and I could see he agreed with her. He was a lot more sympathetic but basically it was the same. If you were fourteen you *belonged* to someone – in this case, my mum and dad.

She was on at Tar about it ALL THE TIME. You could see him roasting. She poured the hot fat on and let him crackle, telling him how selfish he was being for dragging a young innocent like me away from the loving bosom of my family.

'How must your parents feel?' he wailed.

'About as good as Von is making you feel,' I told him. He had just the same expression he did when his real mother was wrapping him around her little finger, back in Minely.

Actually, Richard and Vonny made a perfectly reasonable set of parents. If I'd had them instead of the inadequate pair of bozos God gifted me with, I'd never have run away. It was perfect. I could spend the night with my boyfriend. They passed joints to me. I could decorate my room whatever colour I liked, stay out how long I liked. As parents they were perfect.

The only trouble was, I hadn't run away from home in order to find a new set.

I didn't say anything to Tar, but I was thinking, well, this was okay for now. I was going to keep my eyes open for proper friends. People more our own age or a bit older, maybe, who weren't going to worry about how legal we were, because they'd probably be fairly illegal themselves.

We were already meeting people. Richard and Jerry and Vonny had friends round. There was the night we were allowed, WOW, to have the LIGHTS ON IN THE HOUSE! And walk around in the brilliance of Real Electric Lighting.

Well, actually it was quite exciting after creeping round in candlelight for a week. They had a few people round then for the first time. Just people sitting round talking and drinking and getting stoned, no dancing or anything. Richard brought his sound system down. Me and Tar sat in the corner and watched like a pair of tame parrots. Occasionally people came up and were nice to us. They were all ancient.

One interesting thing that did come out was that we were going to have a housewarming party the next weekend to open the squat officially. A proper party, with dancing and loud sounds. Richard said he'd invite some people more our age there. Richard knows everyone, he's opened up so many squats. He mentioned some people living a few streets away who sounded interesting, said he knew some more not so far off who might come ... and I began to think maybe it would be worthwhile after all.

It was about right. Two weeks of living in candlelight and house painting were about my limit.

I still had that hundred quid I thieved from Dad's cash card. I hadn't had to spend a thing. They'd paid for all the food. Vonny and Jerry had even been keeping me in ciggies. I thought to myself ... right. So the next day I told Tar we were going out.

Would you believe it took me ages to drag him away? He was still mad keen on painting the wretched house. You practically had to make an appointment with him before you could do anything except paint, and one or two other things. I almost pulled him out of the house in the end.

We headed off into town to do a bit of spending.

The whole day unravelled in my mind as we walked down the road. By the time we got to Woolworth's I knew exactly what I was going to do with my money. The first thing was a huge, greasy, disgusting burger. It was almost the only thing I missed about home – meat. I'd been living off beanshoots and soya milk. Tar had been making vegetarian noises but I dragged him into a McDonald's and ordered two huge ones.

'Dead cow.'

'Dead cow,' he replied solemnly. We banged burgers and bit. It was unbelievably delicious. Then we got a couple of thick shakes and sat down to go through a copy of *City Limits*. There was a bop at the Albert Chapel. Punk. I gave Tar a few quid and told him, 'Be there.' Then I dumped him. I didn't want him around getting bored while I was togging myself out and getting presents. Besides, Tar would only want to be sensible. I was petrified of spending my hundred pounds on sleeping-bags and decent footwear.

I wanted to clear the lot.

I caught the bus to the market at the stadium to get togged out. We'd been there before, Sunday afternoon, the day of the stick-up. I hadn't spent anything then but I was keeping my eyes open. What I'd seen was confirmed at the little do they had at the squat.

I was about a thousand years out of date.

That bushy-tailed well-scrubbed nice sunny day look was definitely out. I looked older than Vonny for Christ's sake! She was done out in a Mohican and a ring in her nose while I was still in fluffy jumpers.

Black leather jacket – that was the first thing. I got a good deal – fifty quid for a nice tatty secondhand one. It was gorgeous. It smelt of sweat and leather and had a zip up the front that you might use to keep a gorilla locked out. Or in. I was going to get a pair of leather jeans as well, but it was too expensive and anyway, leather pants look naff, as I discovered later.

But it had to be BLACK BLACK BLACK. I got black tights and a short black skirt and a pair of filthy great boots. I got the whole thing for twenty quid at an army shop, although what the sergeant major was doing in a little black skirt is anyone's guess. Oh, and a little granddad tee-shirt done up down the front with scruffy laces.

I got my ears pierced. I got my nose pierced. Twice. It hurt, and I was only going to have it done once, but Vonny only had one, and I mean ...

Then I got my hair done. I only had about twenty quid left or I'd have got it dyed, but it was okay.

And I was ... well, I say it myself. Bleeding brilliant.

Now, I know what you're saying. 'Hundred-pound punk.' Well, okay. If you want to do that sort of thing properly you spend about two pound fifty. But be fair. It was my first get-up. The girl did good. I got some make-up and I had to go into the bog to get it on. Black lipstick and eyeliner, that sort of thing. And then ...

I looked at myself in the mirror and I thought, Gemma .... mmmm!

That punk look suited me. I was never a pretty pretty even when I was little but I reckon I got the best of both worlds, really. I mean, if you look all pretty and cute right from the start you don't even have to try. All you have to do is blink your eyes and everyone's falling over you. But if you start off like I did, looking like a half starved frog with dental problems, you have to get by in other ways. I used to look at myself in the mirror when I was small and I'd think, God, I have to go through my whole life looking like this! Then when I was about twelve I noticed people watching me, and I took another look and I thought, Mmm, there's something going on here after all.

Some people look at me and they see nothing special, just a girl whose mouth is too big and her eyes are too far apart. But others look at me and they see there's a lot more to me – the way I am. That's how I can tell right away if someone's going to be my kind of person.

The girl did good.

I dived into a craft shop and bought Tar's present. Then I went to meet him at the café we'd agreed on.

I was skint by that time. It was a shame. I'd been thinking we could have a really wild night and get drunk or even see if we could score something interesting. No chance now. Still, who needs money when you're looking good?

The really great thing was ... he didn't recognise me. Honestly. He was sitting at a window table and I sat at the table next to him and he stared straight through me like I was a stranger. I thought, Right, we'll see how faithful Mr Man really is. I started staring at him hard, as if I fancied him. I could see him getting all nervous. He didn't know what was going on. I stared and then I gave him a little wink and raised my eyebrows and he blushed bright red. Then, after a bit, he looked cautiously at me and gave me a sickly little smile. So the next time he caught my eye I winked and got up to come and sit next to him.

I thought he was going to die! But you could see the light dawning as I came closer to him and he squeaked, 'GEMMA?!?'

'Who do you think?'

Tar's face. You can see everything on Tar's face. He was gobsmacked.

'I can't ever go home now,' I told him. It was right. I didn't look like *anyone's* daughter any more, let alone Mr and Mrs Brogan's. We got up together and went to walk to the bop. Tar was a bit self conscious. People were looking at me, and he was proud to be with me, but he's shy about being proud, you know what I mean. Then after a bit he got used to the idea and then he started wanting to touch me. He grabbed me and started kissing me and trying to get his hands under my clothes but I smacked him off.

'This is practically being unfaithful,' I scolded him, and he giggled. But I didn't want him to smudge the lipstick and stuff, see.

By the time we got to the bop I was flying. There was a reggae band on when we arrived. A few people were dancing about but most of them were still sitting, waiting for the main band. We got drinks, lager. I went to the bar and bought them. Looking like that I could have walked in and bought the building, let alone a drink. I sat next to Tar and held his hand between my thighs under the table.

I felt so good.

It was loud in there. I loved the noise. I loved the crowd. I loved being me. We got up and danced around a bit until the band left the stage. We went and leaned against a wall and had another drink and waited while the next band got ready.

It was a punk band. I don't know who they were. They came on and started fiddling with their gear. There was a sort of buzz from all those people. They didn't do any of that testing, testing, 1 2 3 and faffing about making sure the sound was right. They did a couple of chords, and then ... it looked as though there was some sort of argument going on. The singer started shouting at someone in the audience through the mike.

It was ... it just started getting out of hand. The band joined in and the crowd gathered up right under the stage and shouted back and I thought there was some real trouble on the way. The band looked about ready to trash the place. They weren't playing. This bloke at the front was really winding up the audience. He was really going for it. The floor was full of people and this guy was SCREAMING abuse at them. He was sticking his fingers up at them and mouthing FUCK OFF and they started screaming back at him. The whole place was enraged. Then he leaned forward and spat – a big gobful – you could see it spraying over the people at the front ...

Then the band started up.

I couldn't work it out. It was so violent but they were playing this song that was just like screaming abuse but put to music. Suddenly the audience was pogoing up and down and the lights were flashing and the whole place was throbbing and the people up at the front were spitting at the singer so he was slipping and skidding, the stage was so wet with gob ...

That was it. It was the act! I just screamed with pleasure. I never saw anything like that. I ran out into the mess and started with them, jumping bang abang bang abang up and down and howling ...

That band. I wish I knew who they were. They must have been famous or become famous soon after because they were just so *obscene* and rude and wonderful. The music was like being beaten up, only it didn't hurt, you know what I mean. It was a lynch mob out there except, funny thing, there were never any fights.

Tar was there too right next to me, jumping about. He goes ape sometimes. He was leaping up and down, up and down, his black hair was flopping about in his eyes and he was grinning like a maniac. It went on and on. The band just finished one number then went straight into the next. The sound system was howling and screeching but no one cared. Then there was a smoochy number and honestly,.. there were couples I *swear* were actually ... you know. Me and Tar slammed into each other and started trying to stick our tongues down one another's throats. He licked me all over my face. Then the band played fast again and we went on and on and on ...

We'd stumbled on this real punk den more or less by accident. You could tell the girls who were the real punks. They looked like absolute *slags*. They didn't care about *anything*. I felt completely over-dressed. When I had to go to the loo I found a hole in my new tights so I ripped it open and made another hole and ripped that open so my white skin showed in big holes in my black tights. I ripped my new little skirt at the front and tried to tear a hole in the tee-shirt but I couldn't do it, the material was too strong. So I just undid the laces halfway down and rushed back out and started jumping about.

I couldn't see Tar any more but that didn't matter. I pushed my way right up into the crush in front of the stage and pogoed up and down and started spitting at the singer with all the others. It was great but it was so hot and hard up there you couldn't stay for long. By this time there were people climbing up on the stage next to the singer and the crowd was so packed there they could run off the stage and right across the crowd, walking on their heads. Some of them got maybe ten, twelve steps before the crowd got too thin, or they'd trip up and fall back into the people. Someone trod on my ear.

When I needed a bit more space I went back and started dancing there. I was dancing and dancing and dancing. I caught sight of Tar bouncing away like an idiot. We banged into each other and danced next to one another for a bit. Then he had to go and get a drink and cool off but I carried on. And on and on and on and on.

People kept coming up and asking me to dance. I danced with them, then I lost them. There was one guy asked me if I wanted a drink. I said yes, and he went off to get the drinks. I stood and waited a bit but that music – the band started up this number that was so good so I just ran off into the crowd and started dancing again and I forgot all about him and his drink and everything ...

I didn't see him for about half an hour. I danced with a few other people. At one point Tar came up and said he'd had enough, he was going home.

'See you later, then,' I told him. I just grinned. He sort of hovered about.

'I can't go without you,' he said, looking peeved.

'Wait for me then,' I told him and I bounced off.

I wasn't going to leave, why should I? He could see that. But about ten minutes later he came up and wanted to go again and I thought, What a pain. I didn't say anything though. I saw him leaning against the bar looking miserable and I thought, Oh, yeah? I mean, I'd done it all for him – dressed up, gone to the bop. I still had my present in my bag and there he was mooing about looking like his dad had just whacked him one. But I wasn't his dad. I thought, Sod you, and carried on dancing. I wasn't going to stop, not for him, not for you, not for anyone.

Then after a bit this guy I'd been dancing with turned up with my drink. He stood there in this horrible pair of thin black jeans and a safety pin in his nose. He looked like he'd been awake for about ten years. He looked like he'd been bleached and then left under the wardrobe.

'Have you been carrying that around all this time?' I laughed.

He laughed at himself and nodded. 'I've spilt half of it,' he said. I thought, Well, you're keen. But he wasn't pushy, he didn't mind me doing my own thing. I drank the beer straight down and we set off on the dance floor again. He was a brilliant dancer, we were spinning around all over the place. I was drunk on dancing by this time. I didn't care about *anything*. I caught sight of Tar out of the corner of my eye a few times and I thought, Stuff you, you can suffer for a change. I mean, I'd put up with his limp friends and their baked potatoes for over two weeks. How come he couldn't go with me for just one evening?

You could see this other fella thought I was a catch. He was right! I danced up his leg. We were thrashing and skittering, we were both drowned in sweat. There was another slow one and he was all over me. I didn't care. I thought, It's just a dance, it's just fun. I didn't mind at all. I was wearing this tee-shirt and I was so wet with sweat it was sticking to me, and he just couldn't keep his hands off me. Well, why should he?

I don't know how long I was dancing for. I could have kept at it forever. But finally he put his hand on my hip and leaned over and said, 'I've got to go now. Why don't you come home with me?'

Just for a second I almost jumped back. It was stupid but I honestly hadn't been expecting that. He wasn't asking me back just for a cup of coffee. The kind of life I'd been living up till then, no one asked you back to their place to sleep with them. It was all parents at home, gropes on the beach.

I looked around, and I thought, You can have a one-night stand every now and then without being a complete slut, right? And I fancied this guy. He had the right look. I mean, I wouldn't say I wanted to spend my life with him but I was ready for whatever was coming my way.

I looked around. I couldn't see Tar anywhere.

'Yeah, okay,' I said. 'You wanna go now?'

He nodded and tipped back his drink. I went to get my bag. And there was Tar.

I might have known he wouldn't go without me. He wasn't at the table but he'd seen the whole thing and being Tar he wasn't going to come up and say, 'You're mine,' or, 'What do you think you're up to?' But there he was, showing me he was still here and that he'd waited for me. He was the colour of green cheese.

I looked at him and he looked at me.

'Someone's asked me back to their place,' I told him. He just looked. I made a dash for my bag. I almost made a run for it, then, 'Here,' I said, 'have you got any bus fare?' I dug about and found some money. I couldn't get it out quick enough. I just wanted to get away from him. I shoved the money in his hand. He looked at me. Then I got annoyed. I don't know why. I turned round and shouted at him, 'You're not my bloody mother, either!'

Then I went. This bloke – I didn't even know his name – he was waiting for me with a little crowd. They were the real thing. What they were dressed in probably didn't cost a tenner all added together and there were about ten of them, girls and boys. I could see them all watching me and watching Tar. They were real nasty punk, you'd think they'd slit your throat but I knew already they weren't like that. It was just a show, right? Just a style ...

One of the girls winked at me.

I got in among them and they closed around me. I walked out of the door into the night air. They all started talking at once, laughing. Someone said something to me and I answered back. I was feeling happy again. I hitched up my bag and stuffed it under my arm. Tar's present was still in it.

'Hang on a minute,' I said.

I ran back into the hall. Tar was still standing at the bar. I ran up to him and grabbed him.

'Over here,' I said. I shoved the present into his hands and then I dragged him to the back of the hall and pushed him out of the door at the back and followed. I don't know why I did it. I was really made up to go with that crowd. They were my crowd, I knew they were my crowd. It was almost like they'd been waiting for me.

We ran off down the road. When I was sure we couldn't be followed, I stopped him running and we stood there looking at each other.

'You should have seen your face,' I told him. Then we started laughing and laughing. As if the whole thing was funny. As if the whole thing was set up as a joke. But if I hadn't found the present, I would have done it to him.

I regretted it afterwards. Not going, I mean. I wanted to. But I couldn't do that to Tar. Not to Tar, could I?

* * *

We never talked about it but we both knew I'd nearly gone, and we both knew I could do it again, any time. He was very tender and loving. I suppose he thought he could make me want him like that but of course I hadn't nearly gone off because he wasn't nice enough.

I put my torn tights and skirt and stuff away. It was party gear, you know? Maybe I'd wear it at the housewarming, maybe it just wouldn't be that sort of do. But I was going to wear it again, some time. Some time soon.

9
Vonny

My feeling was it was important to get her back home before she really took off. You could see that she was going to go over the top. Just walking down the street, you could see her peering over heads at anyone she thought might be interesting, fighting her way to a shop that looked her sort of place. Poor old Tar didn't stand a chance in hell to find out what sort of person he was, of course, and *he* was the one who really needed to.

That's what really annoyed me. She had all the time in the world. She didn't have problems, not real ones. Tar had lived in that horrible family for so long, he was so open, he was trying *so* hard. Now that he was out of it he needed a bit of space. But you didn't get any space when Gemma was around. She filled it all up.

But I did like her. I just wished I'd known her ten years further on, that's all.

I was furious with her when she came back from that bop dressed in leather and all the rest. We'd been feeding her, paying her bills, we'd even been supplying her with fags.

She said, 'It's my party clothes,' and went into this model-girl pose. I was obviously supposed to be charmed but I wasn't. I was on the dole. I was paying out of my miserable thirty quid a week so she could eat, drink and smoke and all the time ...

'This isn't a party,' I told her. 'And I'm not your mother.'

She pulled a face.

The trouble is, she obviously needed one. A mother, I mean.

Jerry of course was totally useless. He liked having a young girl around to get stoned, that was about as far as it went. Actually, she really brought things to a head between me and Jerry. All he wanted was to enjoy himself, nothing else meant anything. Not even me when it came down to it. Well, I like to have a good time but I just think there's more to life than that.

Richard knew she wasn't doing anyone any good, certainly not poor Tar. The trouble with Richard is, he doesn't like to get his hands dirty. He was responsible, you know, but he thought somehow it all ought to be fun. As soon as the hard decisions had to be made he'd pull a face and go, 'Politics.'

Tar was important. He was in trouble. People had one of two reactions when they met Tar: you either wanted to mother him or fleece him, usually both – just like his real mother had. Gemma did it too. She wasn't exactly manipulating him, she wasn't that sort of person. But she was just so full of herself, she might as well have been.

After she got herself punkified she thought she'd found The Only Way To Be. Of course, being Gemma, she got right in it up to her eyeballs. She came home that night with a ring in each ear and two in her nose. She had three more two days later. She'd got Tar to do it with a sterilised needle. She borrowed the needle off me.

'I can never go home now, I can never go home now,' she kept crowing. She was going to get her tongue pierced as soon as she could afford it. Yuk. Although, come to think about it, she might have just been shocking me.

Then it was Tar's turn. She shaved his head except for a

really long Mohican stripe in the middle. Then she dyed it green and red, and used loads and loads of gel to make it stick up. It was hilarious! We were all laughing, but it was cruel, because it didn't suit him at all. He was prepared to try anything once, or even twice. Come to think about it, Tar was willing to try anything as long as it kept coming, but this really didn't suit him. He's this long gawky-looking kid, and there was this long skinny neck and then this creased, worried looking, spotty head poking out of the top, and the mouth full of ivories and that blinding red and green crest on his head. He looked like some sort of parrot.

'You're not going to leave him like that, are you?' I begged, wiping my eyes.

'I think he looks great,' said Gemma. I could see Tar tensing up and clenching his teeth and trying to convince himself he wanted to look like that. He was like one of the things you see on a postcard for tourists. Of course Gemma was just teasing. She clipped him down and toned down the dye. He still looked ridiculous though.

I was dreading the party. So far Gemma had been in the house most of the time, but once Gemma found the Chapel she was raring for it. Fortunately she didn't have any money but she spent the next week trying to find some casual job as a waitress or something. She didn't have any luck, thank God.

Meanwhile I was working on Richard. He was reluctant to do anything but – it was just so obvious. I mean, Tar was one thing. Even he should have been at home with his family, except that his family was so awful it was impossible. But Gemma ... I didn't want the responsibility and I didn't want to have to watch what she was doing to Tar. And let's face it – I didn't particularly want to have her around in the first place.

We had it out with her the night before the party. I more or less had to do it all on my own. I was barely speaking to Jerry by this point. And Richard pissed me off. He's quick enough to take the lead if it's anti-authority, but when it comes down to being responsible, he just sits in the corner looking miserable.

She knew exactly what was coming.

It was fair. A week's notice, if you like – give her time to get used to the idea. She'd had her fun, she could stay for the party. But after that ...

It wasn't fair on us. She was only fourteen and it wasn't as though she was being knocked around like Tar was. All right, her parents were obviously making life unnecessarily hard for her.

'Unnecessarily hard? I can't do anything ...' she whined.

But running away from her problems wasn't going to solve them. Basically, it was time for her to start arranging to go home after the housewarming party.

I expected a scene, of course. And we got one. Tar sat there looking miserable. Gemma was *furious*. It really made me sympathise with her parents. If it wasn't what she wanted, here, now, then and tomorrow, it was unbearable. We were doing it as nicely as we could. She'd stayed two weeks already. I even offered to speak to her parents myself but she refused to give me their telephone number.

'I wouldn't trust you with a roll of toilet paper,' she sneered. Which was really unfair. We'd done everything we could for her, but for Christ's sake! It was highly illegal. We'd fed her, hidden her, everything. But that didn't give us any right to suggest anything. Not to Gemma.

I tried approaching Tar afterwards, to try and get him to talk some sense into her. He could see the point. He was uncomfortable with the fact that he'd encouraged her to come but he really didn't want her to go. I tried to get her number out of him, but he was too loyal.

'Don't ask me that,' he said. I didn't press it.

Well. What more could we do?

I think Richard was feeling guilty about giving her her marching orders. He went around afterwards arranging for her to have a good time at the party but he made a big mistake in my opinion. He came in one teatime beaming all over his face and announced that he'd invited a few people their own age round.

'Who?' I asked.

'Oh, you know,' he said, grinning like a cat at the air. 'That bunch on City Road ...'

A vivid picture of a girl in a net and a boy with no front teeth came flashing into my mind.

'The ones you introduced me to ...?'

'That's right.'

'Richard!'

'What?'

I just glared. I couldn't believe it. That bloke had no alarm bells.

'Have you ever looked into their eyes?'

'Why?'

Of course, Richard never looked anyone in the face.

I didn't know what those kids were on, but they were on something. I certainly didn't think it was a good idea to put them and Gemma in the same room together.

10
Gemma

It was so typical of Vonny to give me the news just before the party. I was really looking forward to it. I got out my party stuff and dyed my hair, I was really looking the part. And in comes the posse. It was horrible. She'd got Richard on to her side, that was bad enough. But even Tar started agreeing with her.

'I don't want you to go, you know I don't want you to go,' he kept saying.

'Then what are you on about?' I hissed.

And he just ducked his head and muttered, 'But they're right ...'

I went right off Tar after that. I mean, what was the point of all that I love you stuff, if he just teamed up with them and sent me back home?

Thanks, Tar.

And I'd done everything for him, I'd done it *all* for him. I'd never have gone away if it wasn't for him. I might have thought about it but I wouldn't have done it. Now I had and there he was telling me I belonged back at home. Great.

I gave him a bit of the old cold shoulder after that. You've got to have a bit of stand-by-me. I was getting fed up with him anyway. Now he was trying to be Mr Responsible, he could find someone else to hold on to at night.

* * *

That was Friday. On Saturday we got ready for the party. I was really determined to have a good time; it might be my last day of freedom. We spent all day making food and clearing out the rooms and getting the sounds wired up. Jerry locked himself in upstairs with Richard's sound system, making a party tape. Vonny and Tar and me were making salads and stuff, and Richard was running about baking bread – olive-bread, olive oil bread, cheese bread, all different sorts. I stuffed myself. But I got fed up when he left to do an hour or so in the bicycle shop so I went upstairs to help Jerry while Tar and Vonny stayed downstairs and played House.

I got too stoned with Jerry, I suppose. I was all excited about this party but when it came ... I dunno, I just wasn't in the mood. Basically Auntie Von had put the spokes in as far as I was concerned. I just couldn't help thinking how they all thought I was a kid and no one liked me.

The other three went to the pub, but me and Tar of course had no money so we just hung around at home glaring at each other. Or rather, I glared at him while he slunk about trying to be nice. But not nice enough to back me up about staying on at the squat.

We sampled the wine they'd bought in, ate some of the food. Before he went out Richard gave us some cookies he'd made – hash cookies. I was waiting for the lights to start twinkling or something, but nothing happened so I had some more but still nothing happened. I thought he hadn't put enough in. I was still waiting when they came back.

Richard said he had some people our age coming round but as far as I could see it was just the squat crowd and a few friends of theirs. They were all standing round in groups, talking about, I dunno, how to run your car on rice salad or something. I mean, you spend all those years being Little Sammy or whatever, you leave school, get out there on your own and what do you do? You turn into Big Sammy ...

96

If that lot grew their hair a bit and put on suits it could have been a party at my parents' place. Here it was animal rights and anarchism; back home it would have been the Church jumble-sale and the local Conservative Club, but that was about the only difference. They wore the clothes and they had the haircuts but ... well, put it like this, *their* parents really did a good job on *them*, that's all.

Things began to liven up as more people came. I had a few smokes. Tar kept coming and going. At one point he turned up – I was by the salad bowl stuffing myself – and he turned up all excited and said that they'd hatched this plan to go and open another squat.

I said, 'What for, we've got one?'

'No, you don't understand, it's just to free up as many properties as we can find ...'

It turned out one of Richard's friends had spotted this place and it was a big old house, just perfect. Of course Richard got really excited about it, like he does, and Tar had volunteered, like he does. They were actually planning to go and open it up that very night.

I said, 'We're having a party!' I mean, why spend all day making salad and hash cookies, and then go out? What for all that beer and wine? My last party on earth and they go and wreck it by opening a squat!

Tar was lost. He was beaming and smiling and I suddenly thought, Something was happening to him. His face seemed to be stretching out and it looked as if his teeth were escaping out of his mouth and his eyes were rolling around.

'You look really weird, are you all right, are you all right?' I said, but he dashed off to organise a squat committee or something.

I started stuffing more salad and thinking to myself, This is unreal, this is a squat, and they're running away from their own party!

Then Tar started to follow me about going, 'Is anything wrong? What's the problem, Gemma?'

And I was going, 'Oh just shut up, why can't you leave me alone?'

I was going much too fast, smoking joints and pouring booze down my neck just because I couldn't think of anything else to do. I couldn't seem to stop myself. Later on more people turned up and it livened up more and I began to feel a bit better. Someone made up a punch. God knows what they put in it ... and whoa! Everything got very fast very quick then and ... well, I could tell I was going to be really ill if I carried on like that.

The place filled up suddenly. Suddenly you couldn't move. Everyone was screaming and shouting and dancing. I was feeling so strange. I had a dance but my head was still spinning faster and faster. Then I had a couple more joints and ... and ... So I went upstairs and sat in the loo for a bit. Then someone wanted to come in so I went into a bedroom and lay down for a few minutes on the bed until my head settled down.

It was horrible – like someone was stirring my stomach with an electric spoon faster and faster and faster and faster ...

I lay there for ages waiting for it to stop. When I felt able to sit up again the music was still thumping away downstairs but I had no idea how late it was. I still felt extremely ... well, extremely extremely. I didn't feel drunk or hung over, but there was still this horrible tight bubble in my stomach and it felt like at any minute it was going to swell up and go ... Pop!

I got up and looked out of the window. All I remember is, everything was orange and it looked like cats and weasels and things were creeping round out of sight behind the dustbins and lampposts. I don't mean I could see them but they were there out of the corner of my eye. I looked around

It was a motorbike engine and he reckoned he could get it going and sell it. He'd learned about engines when he was really young. He'd had this strange childhood. His mum lived in caravans and they parked up in the winter and travelled around to the festivals all over the country in the summer. That sort of thing. So of course he'd known how to fix engines since he was about eight, because everyone was always taking the vehicles to bits and doing their own mechanics.

'Yeah,' said Lily. 'Big Honda 1000cc, brm, brm, Big Chief Go Places.' She was teasing him, but he just laughed, he didn't mind at all.

The room was filling up with candlelight. I was getting worried about something catching fire. There were candles on the table in between the pans and the dishes of their last meal, maybe twenty or thirty of them, blazing away. There were candles on the mantelpiece, candles on the floor, stuck on books, shelves, tables – even on top of the doors. It was getting hot in there!

'She collects candles,' said Rob.

'Candles are magic, I collect magic,' said Lily.

Then when they were all lit ... I don't know how to tell you this. She came up and pulled me to my feet. Gemma was there, grinning at me.

'You did it,' Lily said.

'Did I? What?'

'They were trying to turn you into an animal but you broke out. You got away!'

'Yeah?' I said. I felt like an idiot. I was standing there staring at the candles wondering what was going on.

'You're the bloody Titanium Man! Yeah ... Tar, the Titanium Man!' yelled Lily suddenly. She grabbed hold of my arm and stuck it up in the air. I tried to pull it down but she just pushed it back up and started to dance around me.

110

private! But Gemma said, 'Go on, tell her, it's all right, tell her, tell her ...'

So I tried.

It was hard. I didn't know them. Gemma kept jumping in. She wanted to share everything with Lily, whether it was hers to share or not. She was talking about my parents like they were a pair of monsters and I didn't like that. My mum – she just can't help it, it's not like she does it because she wants to. Even my dad. They just can't cope. They got stuck and they can't cope. Probably they should never have had children, that's all.

Lily kept shushing Gemma. She didn't say much, she just listened. I didn't know what she made of it.

Their place was a big old house on City Road, on a corner. Richard had opened it up for them; he must have opened up half the squats in Bristol. They had a flat on the ground floor and this big garden. Inside it was messy, packed with stuff, all sorts, books, clothes, tools. There was an engine half taken to pieces on the floor. That was Rob. He was always building engines or taking them to bits.

Lily put the kettle on and some music. I started talking to Rob. That was okay. That was nice. He had two teeth out in the front so he looked like a real bruiser, but he was very gentle and polite really. Only that gap in his mouth made you think he could be nasty if he wanted to.

Gemma and Lily started lighting candles. It looked like a nice thing to do at first, but then I got confused because they kept bringing out more and more. There were these endless candles. Lily kept producing them out of the cupboard. It got funnier and funnier. Even Rob was amazed; he had no idea where she got them all from and he lived with her. We were laughing our heads off every time they got out another box.

'Big special occasion,' said Rob. He started telling me about the engine on the floor which he'd fished out of a skip.

11
Tar

It was all going so fast. I was scrabbling and snatching but I wasn't catching a thing.

Gemma was so excited. Her and Lily, grabbing hold of each other and talking and hugging. None of the things I had mattered to her – the squat, my new friends. She was leaving me behind. They were all on a different wavelength from me. Gemma looked so happy, happier than she ever was with me. But she was a bit hysterical at the same time and that made me think that maybe in the morning she'd want to come back.

It was weird, walking like that through the streets of Bristol. Lily was wearing nothing but this string vest dyed black. I was having kittens, I was sure we were bound to get into a scene or an argument or something. In fact a couple of blokes who'd been drinking started shouting at us but we just walked past them and it was all okay. I began to feel I was being paranoid. I was the only one worried about it.

Gemma hardly noticed me at all, she was so excited, but Lily kept looking back at me and I thought she was wondering, What's wrong with him? Then they started talking about me. I knew that because they kept shooting little glances at me. That went on for a bit. Then Lily came back and took my arm.

'Tell me about your mum,' she said.

I just looked at Gemma. I was appalled. That's all so

I watched Lily look at him. Then she winked at me and said, 'I'm gonna get him ...'

She jumped up and grabbed him round the neck and pressed herself into him. 'Well done, man, you broke the door down ... brilliant, brilliant, yeah!'

Tar stood there, his hands fluttering nervously around her bare bum. He glanced anxiously at Rob, who stood up and started to pat him on the neck and back.

'Brilliant. I love you, man, I love you,' he said.

I said, 'It's all right,Tar, it's all right ...' because he looked so worried about it.

Lily let go and looked around the room. Everyone was staring at us. She scowled. 'Sod this. Let's go. Come on ... This place is dead!' She said that in a loud voice so they'd all know what she thought about them.

'But ... all our things are here,' said Tar.

'They'll be here tomorrow. Or we can get you some new things ...'

'That's right, you put your order in,' laughed Rob. We all headed for the door. Somewhere out of the corner of my eye I saw Vonny glaring at me. I thought, YEAH! Because I fucking done it! I'd got away ... She stood staring like a waxwork while we all trooped off out of the door in a line like a circus.

guess poor old Tar was dying to get a good look at Lily's boobs but he didn't want to upset Rob. Actually, Rob would have lifted the string vest up for him if he'd asked.

Rob gave him a big smile and stood up to shake his hand and that made poor Tar more nervous than ever.

'Yeah, really nice to meet you,' said Tar.

'Those are a really nice pair of boots,' said Lily, nodding down at his feet.

Tar looked doubtfully down at his boots. They were nothing special. He had a good shine on them. He spent ages polishing his boots, I'd noticed it before. 'Are they?' he said, trying to work out if she was teasing him or not.

'Yeah, I love 'em,' said Lily.

'Thanks.'

He stood there looking awkward and unhappy while Lily closed her eyes and danced with her head. Poor old Tar, I felt sorry for him. They were only winding him up. I stood up and took his arm.

'He's the one I ran away with,' I told them.

'Oh, right ...' Lily beamed. 'Yeah, that's really great, everyone should run away, you did the right thing. You did the right thing for Gemma too.'

Tar smiled uncertainly. He'd been told so often that I ought to be at home with Mumsy. Now this amazing naked girl was telling him he was doing everything right.

I said, 'Yeah, if it wasn't for Tar, I'd still be at home going mad.'

Lily was sitting there watching Tar and I was worried because I thought she might decide to go against him. I hadn't got any idea at all which side he was on, but I wanted him to be on the right side, too.

'Tar had a really bad time at home, he got knocked about by his dad.'

'Yeah, right ... leave the bastard,' said Rob.

Then the music stopped and she scowled. 'Are they crazy or what?' And she got up and went across to put on some more.

We talked and talked ... I don't know how long we talked. I felt better and better. Her bloke Rob came to sit with us and he was just like she said – really soft and slow but right there. I mean, he looked like he'd slit your throat for a penny but he was so warm. He was great but ... it was her, Lily ... she was the one. She'd done what I'd done – run away from home. She'd done it when she was twelve! Can you imagine? I thought, Wow, imagine being so sure about what you want, you can run away at twelve! And I thought I was something for doing it at fourteen. She was more real than anyone I'd ever met.

I'd started to think I was wrong about myself ... you know, that I was just a stupid kid with big ideas after all, just like my mum and dad and Vonny and Richard and Tar made out. But here was this amazing person talking to me and I felt, wow, this is me, Gemma Brogan, and I'm getting somewhere ...

Some time later, Tar turned up. I should have known he wouldn't just dump me.

'Oh, right, here you are,' he said. He was smiling that big smile, but I was on another planet by then. 'We went out to have a look at the new squat but you were asleep. Are you all right?' he added, his face going all serious for a second. Then I saw his eyes catch Lily sitting by me, string vest half off her shoulder, nipples sticking through. His face went sort of still and he had to concentrate on looking at me.

'This is Lily,' I said.

Tar did his nod. 'Yeah, hi, hello,' he croaked. I could see him looking nervously at Rob. Rob is always so polite, more polite than anyone else, all smiles and please and thank you. But you could tell he'd been in a few really nasty fights. I me or where I came from. She talked about music and bands and she talked about herself and her boyfriend, what he was like, how amazing he was.

'Yeah, he's on the right side, you know,' she said, nodding her head and puffing down the smoke.

'I don't even know what the right side is,' I told her, beginning to giggle again.

'The right side. Your side. My side. You know.' I didn't know if she was talking about the world or this room or just us. I asked her if she knew the people in the squat well.

'Nah.' It seemed Richard had helped them open up their squat about six months ago. 'He's okay, he's out of his head. But the rest of them ... they're playing the wrong game,' she said. 'They're playing the same game as the banks and big business ...'

I said, no ... they were all out the next day squirting superglue into the locks. I was proud because I thought she couldn't know that but she just laughed.

'Big deal, so what? The banks don't care, why should they? Nah ...' She laughed and shook her head. 'They'll get in the back, send for a locksmith and put the charges on to their customers. No trouble. Listen ... I'm a businessman myself.' She laughed at the thought. 'Listen, they live in a squat and they like to think they've got it all worked out, but they don't even know what they're thinking about. They'll be out with their mighty tubes of superglue on Monday, and on Tuesday they'll be back in college to make sure they get nice fat exams so the bank'll give them nice fat jobs in a couple years' time. Five years from now they'll be working for the same bank and moaning their faces off because their salaries aren't fat enough. Maybe they'll break out the superglue again. Yeah ... superglue for bigger bucks!' She laughed and jived about on the sofa. 'That's the big business game. I do my own business, thanks.'

Suddenly she put her arms around me and hugged me. She held me close. I just hugged her straight back and I felt the tears coming. I'd been thinking I was having a good time but she only had to touch me and I was crying.

A couple of people came into the kitchen and saw us like that and then went out again. She didn't say anything. After a bit she began to move to the music again still hugging me tight and I realised she'd stopped moving to hold me. I was the only thing that made her stand still. I began to move and we stood there a little longer, just swaying to the music.

'Yeah,' she said. 'Isn't that great? Isn't that great? The music's the only drug ... yeah ...' I put my head on her shoulder and tried not to think.

I don't know what it was she had. She was sharing her magic with me and I could feel that tight bubble in my stomach get softer and softer and softer.

'Come on, let's see what's going on ...' She broke away and moved to the door, still dancing in that way she had.

I followed her through.

I sat on the sofa. The girl, the magic girl, was still dancing around the room, dancing as she went and kissed her boyfriend on the ear, dancing as she put someone's drink on top of her long sausage of cups, dancing as she pushed another on top of that so that ... whoops! The drink spurted all over the floor and all over her. Everyone laughed – even the girl whose drink it was laughed. The magic girl licked the wet off her arms and looked over to me as if to say, See? You don't have to behave like them, you don't have to behave like anyone. Then she reached over and plucked a joint out of someone's fingers and came over to sit next to me.

We talked – I don't know, all sorts of stuff. I took a couple of puffs but then she had a look at me and took it off me.

'You don't need that either,' she laughed. Even sitting down, she was still dancing. She didn't ask anything about

about her pinching their drinks and their smokes. If it had been anyone else they'd have been offended, but with her it was like it was a privilege. Or maybe they just didn't dare complain.

Did you ever see someone and think straight away, I want to be that person? I want to look like her and think like her and have the same effect as she does ... you know? This girl – nothing mattered to her. All the rules, all the things you do do and don't do, the manners, everything – she had none of that. If she didn't like it she just didn't do it. If she did it, it was good. She didn't have to say please or thank you. She didn't have to be offered anything; it was already hers. She was more herself than anyone else ever was and as soon as I clapped eyes on her I knew I wanted to be myself just as much as she was herself.

I didn't have the courage to talk to her but it made me feel so good just watching her, just knowing you could get like that, that someone else had done that.

I stood at the door for a while. I was so excited. After a bit I wanted someone to talk to so I went to look for Tar, but he wasn't there. I went and sat down in a hard chair near to this bloke; he was one of the people from the squat.

I asked him, 'Where's Tar?'

'Dunno.'

I took a swig of my drink and I thought, Shit, he's left me here, he's left me here to go and do anarchy. I felt like giggling. I got up and had another drink and sat there glugging away at it, just because there was nothing else to do, no one else to be with, nowhere else to go.

Then the girl was there, dancing about, moving her head to the music in front of me.

'Hi, what's your party like?' she said, as if she couldn't imagine not having a good time.

'Great,' I said, and I started to take another swig but I

started giggling just as it got to my mouth and spluttered it all over me. I held my head and giggled and tried to calm down before I made a real idiot of myself.

She said, 'Yeah, great.' I smiled at her, trying to look as if I was having a really great time. She held out her hand.

'Can I have some of that?'

'Sure.' I was, you know ... wow, she thinks my drink's worth drinking. She took it and went jiving off. I felt a bit naked, sitting there without my drink. I thought, How pathetic, I mean, she didn't feel naked even with no clothes on. I watched her nervously as she boogied about with my glass. She sniffed it but she didn't drink any of it. She just put it down on the mantelpiece and started to pick cups off the floor and stick them together to make a long tube.

'Power,' she said. She was swinging it round at a group of people sitting on the floor like it was zap ray or something, 'Pow, pow ... power ...' She laughed, chucked the stick of cups into the bin and went dancing off, waving her body to the beat. The people on the floor smiled self-consciously. You couldn't tell if she was teasing them because she thought they wanted power, or because she already had all of it.

I got up and made for the kitchen for another drink. I was pouring it out when there she was again, behind me.

'You don't need that stuff, what do you think you need that stuff for?' she said crossly. She wasn't smiling. I looked at her in surprise.

She reached out and took my drink off me. 'Why do you think I took the last one off you?'

I clutched my head. 'I know, I know, I don't know what I'm doing,' I wailed.

'You're doing okay, you know that?' she said.

She seemed to know everything about me already. I just stood there like an idiot clutching my head and going, 'I know, I know, I know ...' And of course I didn't know anything.

the room and all the things – the wardrobe and the chest of drawers, even the window frame – they all seemed to be looking back at me, like they were alive. I was thinking, What's going on? And I suddenly realised – I'm stoned! That's what it was, I was stoned out of my tree ...

I thought, Hash cakes! The cookies, of course. Richard had told me not to eat too many and I thought he was being wet because he looks wet, but he wasn't. I'd eaten ten times too much and now I was absolutely flying.

I thought, Wow, this is something, although I wasn't enjoying it all that much.

I went down to see what was going on.

Downstairs was half empty. Little groups sitting on the floor talking, odd people sitting in chairs, crashed out. I looked about but Tar was nowhere to be seen. I went into the kitchen to get a drink of water. I had a mouthful of rice; it tasted so good I started eating and eating and eating and eating. When I'd finished it all up I had another glass of punch and went back into the sitting room.

A couple of new people had turned up. There was a guy standing talking to a couple of people from the squat. He looked different from the rest. And there was this girl.

She was dancing. I mean she was doing things and dancing at the same time. She'd go and put on a new cassette, or find a better track on the old one or just look through what was there, then she'd go over and pinch a fag or a joint off someone, or tidy up fag ends or paper cups or something ... and all the time she was moving to the music, dancing, swaying her head, just really going with the music. She just couldn't stand still. She was smiling all the time, not at anyone, just to herself and the good time she was having. Her mouth was even wider than mine and her eyes turned into two black, happy little gaps in her face when she smiled. She was beautiful.

She kept dancing over to her bloke and kissing him or rubbing up to him. You could tell he was as proud of her as if he'd poured out a glass of moonjuice. I just couldn't take my eyes off her. It was as if she was in a completely different room, at a completely different party from anyone else in the room. She was different from everyone.

After a bit I noticed what she was wearing and ... POW! I couldn't believe my eyes at first. I looked around and saw all the guys eyeing her up and I almost burst out laughing because it was so daring and at the same time ...

She had this black net string vest on. That was it. It took a while to sink in. At first glance you saw this vest, it was just clothes. And then suddenly your eyes went POP, right through it and there she was, bare as a baby. But some baby. I mean, you could see everything. It was quite long for a vest but even so when she bent over to put on a new cassette you could see her bare bum.

Everyone was watching her but it wasn't just because she was more or less naked. She had the power. People were talking about this and that but they were all just pretending. She was everything that was going on in that room. Some of 'em couldn't bear to watch her like I was. They carried on talking and watched her in little sneaky glances out of the corners of their eyes. Some of them were staring at her gobsmacked, mouths hanging open like fridge doors. But they were all looking. And she was lapping it up, jiving around doing little jobs, making little remarks to people, laughing at jokes.

Her bloke, all scruffy and stubbly with a tatty Mohican and at least two teeth missing, he was loving it as much as she was. She'd get a joint off someone and she'd take it over to him and give him a toke and then jive back. He behaved as if she was dressed in jeans or a tee-shirt, except that he touched her bum a couple of times. No one seemed to mind

'Someone must have thrown it out by accident,' he said. 'It might be worth something. We better knock on the door ...'

I just laughed. He didn't know about skips. He didn't know about the kind of things people throw out. You can find anything in a skip. Carpets, clothes, books, radios, all sorts of stuff. You know – Granny dies and out it all goes because it's old, or because Granny was an old bag and so everyone thinks anything she had is as useless as she was.

You can get anything in a skip. He was all goggle-eyed. He couldn't believe that anyone thought of those piccies as rubbish.

I told him, maybe the rest of the book was in there. He looked at that skip like it was a treasure chest, which it was, really. And I thought, Ah, a convert. So we really got stuck in. He was keen. He ended up making a tunnel under an old door so he could mine his way right into it. He had his feet sticking out over the edge while I kept watch. It was great. We didn't find the rest of that book but we found some other quite nice books, including one with plates in – just a few – drawings of hillsides and stuff. He was so made up about it.

'This is crazy, fancy chucking this out,' he kept saying. I just grinned. Those things didn't mean anything to me, I'd have chucked them out myself. I'd rather have found a decent spanner or some cable. But he was thrilled.

When we'd found all the books, we cleared out a load of wood and carried it back to the house and dumped it in the garden. See? Free fuel. We heated the whole house over the winter out of skips and it never cost a penny.

Tar was beginning to get the idea. He was talking about how his dad used to go on and on about the cost of heating, when all the time he could have gone out and helped himself.

Of course his dad never would. People are ashamed to get things for free. If roast pigs were running about the street they'd let 'em go because of the social stigma.

That's how bad they had his old man. 'But not you, eh?' I said. And he smiled.

Tar went in for a bit to show the books to Gemma. I started chopping up some of the wood for later on.

Wood isn't the only thing you can get from skips, but do you know, the amazing thing is, it's still stealing? Someone even owns the rubbish! I was in a skip digging about – not for wood, someone had dumped a load of nuts and bolts and sheet metal in this one. I've got a whole workshop out of skips. Anyway, I turn round and there's this policeman walking over, looking all important like he's caught me kicking old ladies.

He nods at the stuff. 'That's someone's property,' he tells me, going for his notepad.

'It's been chucked out.'

'That's the owner's business.' He waves the notebook at me. 'Name, please, sonny.'

I couldn't believe it. 'They don't want it, that's why they're throwing it away,' I pointed out.

'In that case it belongs to the Council who will be disposing of it,' he goes. 'Now I'd like your name and address.'

'The Council have to pay to get rid of it,' I said.

'Don't argue with me, son.' And he holds his pencil in the air and waits.

I mean, what can you do with people like that? I was telling Lily about it afterwards and she was furious; she started kicking things all around the room. She just couldn't bear the thought of people like that wandering about causing trouble.

'Bastard thought police!' she growled, and kicked a hole in the door.

There was no point arguing with him. He would have had those books as landfill.

I gave him my name all right.

'Mouse ... that's M O U S E ...' I pronounced it Mowse.

'I can spell, I can spell,' grumbled the copper.

'Michael,' I said, climbing out of the skip. That copper was so thick he never clicked till I was halfway through my address, 'Six, Mousehole Road, Disneyland.'

The last thing this copper wanted was to turn up at the station with a kid on a charge of nicking from skips. He was just throwing his weight around, having a bit of fun, see.

'Now listen here, sonny ...' he goes.

I says, 'Right, let's go round the station and you can arrest me in front of all your mates, okay? What's the charge – unlawful possession of rubbish?'

There was this pause while the policeman looked at me, a real nasty look, like I was a piece of dog shit. They don't like being sussed. The thing to remember is, not to mind being arrested. What have they got then?

'Clever little git, aren't you?' he said.

'Cleverer than you,' I said, which was true, but no compliment to me. Then I legged it. He went after me but he stopped pretty quick.

'Pity your brain isn't as big as your gob,' I yelled. He just turned away and pretended nothing was happening. He was scared he'd look a prat chasing me. He did already.

After we dumped the wood we went round to my mate Dev's place. We sat and had a few joints. I slid out the back with Dev to do business and have a chase. When we came back out, Tar was sitting there going on to Sals about skips and how 'mazing it was what people threw out and all that. He was so full of himself, so I thought, Right, lesson number two.

Actually we should have gone back to see Lils. She'd be feeling a bit ragged by now. But I was having a good time, I liked the guy and ... well, Lils is pretty tough 'n all. So I took him down town and we had a look in the shops.

I was going to go straight round to Marks and Spencer's and show him how to liberate the food, but on the way we passed by an Allen's bookshop.

Inside they had this absurd book on display. It was enormous, about half a metre tall – one of those art photograph books – black and white piccies. Naked women but not rude. Well, some of them were pretty rude, actually, but art rude, you know? The sort of stuff you're allowed to look at.

Old Tar loved all that. He kept going through it and discovering pictures even more wonderful than the last one. Look at this, wow, look at that one. He really went for it. That sort of thing doesn't do anything for me. I mean, I liked the rude ones, but he actually liked them for other reasons. My favourite thing about that book was the price. Sixty quid! For a book! Christ. That was a work of art, whoever thought that up ought to get a grant. I don't think anyone was meant to buy it, it was there as a kind of advertisement. You know, see what an amazing bookshop we are, we have books so expensive that no one can even afford them!

He said, 'Someone'll really buy it and it'll be theirs then.'

'I should coco,' I said.

'It'd be like owning the sky or something,' said Tar.

I was getting to really like him.

I was half thinking of lifting a few books but the shop assistants were taking an interest so I figured we'd better move on.

Marks and Spencer's. I was having a good time and I thought, It's time for a celebration ... us meeting them and them meeting us ... and because Gemma was coming to live with us, although he didn't know that yet.

We were standing by the meat section. I said, 'Are you two veggies?'

'No.'

I stuffed a couple of fat packets of steak in the basket.

'Look, I don't have any money,' said Tar, looking all nervous.

'Neither have I.'

We walked down the aisle. I didn't let him see when I tucked it under my coat. He just suddenly noticed that the basket was empty. I saw him out of the corner of my eye looking at the floor behind him to see if I'd dropped the stuff.

Then it clicked.

Poor old Tar! His face nearly fell off. I got a couple of cans of beans to buy and we stood in the queue. I was getting nervous myself by this time, despite the chase I'd done earlier. Tar was so scared and twitchy, he was looking round all over the place to see if anyone was watching us. I thought someone would be bound to notice but those women at the checkout are so bored you could wheel out an elephant and they'd never notice.

He was full of it once we were clear. He was dancing around me, beaming away. He gets really carried away, Tar. One minute you think he's really quiet and then suddenly he starts bouncing like that.

'Let's go back in and have another go,' he says.

I just shook my head. 'Next time,' I told him. He didn't know how to look. You have to look like someone boringly buying something for a boring tea. Tar was putting on this desperado face. But on the way home we had to call in at the offie for some beer, and when we came out he showed me what he had under his coat. A bottle of wine and I'd never even noticed.

I banged him on the back and grinned, and he beamed at me like I'd just given him a hundred thousand pounds. Well, I had. He could have anything he wanted after that. See?

* * *

He was as high as a kite on the way back. Gemma took one look at him and said, 'What's got into you?' Lils was all ready to be pissed off because I'd been so long, but when she saw how I'd spent the time with Tar she was okay about it. Me and her went into the back and did a chase. We were doing too much, really, but we'd been bingeing that weekend and it's important to come down slowly.

Tar was sitting on the floor showing Gems that book he'd got from the skip, and telling her about the book in Allen's and all the rest of it. Gems was treating him like a bit of a divvy and that annoyed me. I mean, just because she was leaving him behind. I'd like to see her cope with all the stuff he had.

I looked at Lily. She was craning over Gemma to have a look at that book and Tar started telling her about how he wanted to paint. She was interested, Lily. And I thought, It doesn't have to be messy. It doesn't have to hurt. Maybe we could find a way of bringing him in with the rest of us instead of just elbowing him out like that.

We had a big meal. Steak, wine, the lot. Lily really got into eating meat, we hadn't had any for weeks. Then we got a big fire going in the garden.

We've got a brilliant garden. You'd love it. There's a big tall tree at the end of it that hangs right over the road. There's a little bed with flowers and a few veggies in it that we'd planted earlier in the spring but we'd never done anything more with them and the weeds were coming back. I got inspired that night and started digging but the spade broke.

There were dandelions in the grass. Tar was going on about the dandelion he'd painted and how he wanted to do a really big, bright one some time with the pastels Gems'd bought him.

It was a beautiful evening. Gems was lying there with Tar in her arms. They looked so happy together. I wanted her to change her mind. We were going to get our bags and sleep out, but later on the rain started so we all went to bed.

In the morning I looked out of the window. The bonfire was wet but part of it was still smouldering away. It was a damp day. I've got this picture very clear in my mind, because it wasn't something you see every day. Tar was sitting there on a milk crate by the bonfire staring up at the tree. He was crying. I thought at first it was the rain on his face, but it was tears all right. I just thought, Shit.

I gave Lily a rub to wake her up so she could have a look.

We both leaned against the window, quietly, half behind the curtains so he couldn't see us. It was early.

'Ahhhh ... ' Lils leaned her arms on the window-sill and watched him weeping there by the fire.

'Isn't he lovely?' she said. I put my arm around her. 'Isn't he lovely?' she said again.

13
Tar

I went back to my room and I got out the pastels that Gemma had given me and had a go at the dandelion. I had a big piece of cartridge paper that Vonny gave me on a board over my knees. The pastel sticks were bright, just what I'd wanted. But it was no good.

Vonny came in and asked how I was. I said, 'Okay.' She asked where Gemma was and I had to tell her that she wasn't coming back. Then Jerry came in and asked what was going on. Then Richard. I just sat there and wished they'd go away.

Sometimes I feel like I'm some kind of organ plucked out of a living beast. Every little twitch shows up; it's like having to confess all the time. I can make my face go ever so still if I want to but then I forget and it starts twitching away and everyone knows exactly what I'm feeling every second.

I just wanted to bury myself about a hundred million miles under the ground.

They dashed in and out and talked about it, watching me and nodding to each other. They started on about Lily and Rob.

'Scum,' said Jerry. That shocked me. They looked scummy but they weren't really like that.

'I wouldn't like to find one of them in my shoe in the morning,' said Vonny, which made me laugh.

I looked at Richard, because he's the one I trust the most. He looked terribly upset but he didn't say anything. They grouped around me and hugged me and tried to cheer me up but none of them made me feel as good as Lily had when she was calling me the Titanium Man.

'I liked them,' I said.

'Oh dear,' said Richard.

Vonny was furious with Gemma. She thought she was being really irresponsible. Jerry kept going on about me getting over her and maybe it was all for the best. Funny thing, all the time at the back of mind I could see this tiny picture of my mum raging at me and my dad was standing behind her as big as a mountain with his face getting darker and darker and darker.

'She just wants to fly,' I said.

'She has to walk before she can run, let alone fly,' said Vonny

But I want to fly, too.

Rob came round the next day or the day after. I was in a state. I'd more or less decided to stay away from Gemma. I was hoping that if I gave her a break, she might miss me and want me back, although let's be honest, there wasn't much chance of that with Lily and Rob about.

'She wants to be friends still, it isn't that she doesn't want to see you,' he said.

'I just want to leave it for a bit,' I told him.

'What about me and Lils?' he said. 'We want to see you –'

We went out for a walk. I didn't tell him what the others had said about him. We did a couple of skips, wandered around the art shops and the bookshops, but ... I was too messed up. I was glad when it was over. I told him to say to Gemma, you know, that I'd not be seeing her for a bit.

Rob said, 'She'll be disappointed.'

'I don't think so,' I said. He didn't reply. It was the truth. She was leaving me behind.

It was about a week before I saw them again.

'Someone here to see you,' called Vonny. I knew who it was at once, because of the way she said it, like the toilet had just overflowed or something. I looked down the stairs and there was Lily, weaving about at the bottom of the stairs, dancing with her head and grinning up the stairs like a cat or snake or ... like Lily.

It was odd, seeing her there. It was always like that with Lily. Whenever you saw her out of her house she looked out of place. Like you looked out of your window and you saw a python sliding away under the privet bushes. Like she was having an incredible, dangerous adventure just walking down the road. I suppose she was.

'Come with me,' she said. I'd been planning on staying away a few days longer but ...

I got my coat on and followed her out of the house.

It was a damp day. I'd only seen her at night or in the house, half naked. Now she was dressed in this long skirt that dragged in the puddles.

She walked along by me smiling all the time like she does, like she has a secret.

'How's Gemma?' I asked.

'Oh, she's great, she's fantastic, you know our Gems,' said Lily, and then she laughed at me. I must have looked disappointed because she wasn't sad like me. 'Don't get all hung up on that romantic love stuff,' she told me. And she started clutching at her heart and her throat and moaning, 'My life is at an end, I cannot go on without her, oh, woe, oh woe ...' and she ended up leaning backwards over a wall with her hand at her throat and her tongue hanging out.

I guess it was bit like that, wasn't it? I was hung up on Gemma. I suppose I wanted something to cling on to after getting away from home – another prop, another crutch. Maybe that's all it was.

Lily got off the wall and put her arm through mine.

'She's been missing you,' she said. 'We all have. And me.' And she stood on tiptoe and kissed me on the lips. A real long kiss. Then we went off down the road, with her arm in mine and her warm body right against me and I thought, Crikey.

We got to the house and she made me wait in the hall.

'We're home!' she yelled.

'Hang on a mo ...' That was Rob.

Then the door opened. Gemma came running out at a hundred miles an hour and wrapped her arms round me and kissed me all over my face, just like she did that time I met her off the coach.

'I missed you, I really missed you, I was so AMAZED at how much I missed you,' she said. And then before I had time to think about it they pushed me into the room and there was Rob with a can of lager in his hand nodding and grinning and next to him ...

It was the book! I couldn't believe it. That book, that sixty quid's worth that you had to be God to own. They had it up on this old wooden easel and there were ribbons and flowers they'd picked – loads and loads of dandelions, a great big yellow heap of dandelions. And a big card with, 'For Tar, love from'... and their names written on it for me.

'For who? For who?' I said, because it didn't make sense. And they said, all together, 'For you! For you!'

I couldn't believe it! They'd opened it up at one of the pictures I thought was really amazing, and it was covered in flowers and paper leaves Lily had made. And the whole thing was draped in red silk; it was a kind of monument to me.

'But ... how did you get it?' I mean, that book was kept right next to the pay desk all on its own, right where all the assistants always were.

'You're the only person who could afford it,' said Rob.

'Yeah, and now you've got three people to love instead of just one,' said Lily, and she gave me a big kiss – a proper one, about two minutes' long, it felt like. I could hear Gemma clapping her hands and whooping and Rob yelling, 'Yeah ... yeah!' They started counting, to see how long we could go on.

I started crying then, right in the middle of kissing her. Sort of leaking tears, not sobbing, but they were on my cheeks. They thought I was pleased and I was but it wasn't just that. I was still so sad then about losing Gemma, and Lily saying that and kissing me reminded me. Then Lily stood up on tiptoe – I'm quite a lot taller than her – and she licked all the tears off my face.

'I'm gonna live forever now,' she said.

They'd spent the whole week liberating that book. They'd gone to the bookshop every day to stake the place out, looking for a time when no one was there. They even dressed up in different clothes so no one would recognise them. That made me laugh, actually, because Gemma and Lily might get away with it, but Rob with his big tatty Mohican and two front teeth out – there's no way you could disguise that.

Anyway, so after about six days they still hadn't worked out how to do it, when Rob heard an assistant talking about how someone should have come in and they hadn't and he was late for his tea break. So the under manager or something like that comes in and lets this guy go for his break. Then the phone rings and the under manager has to go to the phone.

Rob had been planning on going in as a student with one of those art portfolio cases to hide the book in. He didn't have it with him because he was still staking the place out. But then suddenly there he was standing next to the book and there's not an assistant to be seen and he's totally unprepared ...

He just put it under his arm and walked out, right past everyone, past the assistants in the fiction department between him and the door, past the girl at the sales desk and the other shoppers walking to and fro, past the staff stacking books and pricing them. He just walked past them all with this amazing showpiece book tucked under his arm, right under all their noses. He got to the pavement and Gemma saw him and they both just walked fast round the corner and then they legged it.

For me. They did it for me.

Gemma came over and started going through the book with me. We were showing each other our favourite pictures and smiling at each other. All the time at the back of my mind I was thinking, What now? What now?

Lily and Rob were sitting at the table. Rob was shaking something on to a strip of foil.

'Oh, yeah,' said Gemma.

Rob handed the foil to Lily. She lit a match and held it under the foil. There was this thick, sweet smell and a curl of white smoke. Lily held the foil to her mouth and 'Glop!' she said. She sucked down that curl of white smoke and clamped her lips down. And held her breath for ages. Then she breathed slowly out. She smiled like a snake.

'Now I feel good,' she said.

'What is it?' I asked.

Lily waved her fingers in the air like it was spooky and magic and she said, 'Heroin, yeah!'

'Is it? Is it really heroin? Is it?' I said. I was horrified. Rob was doing another lot. I was thinking, She's a junkie, she's a junkie, she's a junkie ...

You know those stories. You take one little sniff and that's it, you're hooked for life; you end up on the streets robbing old ladies and putting your hands down old men's trousers for a few quid for the next fix. Rob held out the foil for

Gemma and she grinned at me and struck a match and 'Glop,' she said. I watched her letting the smoke ooze out of her nostrils. But she must have been doing it wrong because Rob and Lily jumped up and shouted at her,

'Don't let it go, don't let it go ...!' And Gemma chased the smoke she'd let out with her mouth.

'That's pretty important smoke,' said Rob.

I was thinking, Oh my God, oh my God ...

Then he did one for me but I shook my head. Rob laughed and sucked it down himself.

'Hey!' Lily was angry. 'Hey, that's Tar's, what're you doing?' He just smiled and opened his mouth to let the smoke out. He looked like a ghost. Lily was getting seriously annoyed, but then he got out the little packet and shook it at her.

'Plenty more where that came from,' he said, and Lily grinned.

'Go on, try it, it won't hurt,' Gemma told me. 'It doesn't do you any harm, it just feels good.'

'I don't want to,' I said.

Lily was amused. 'Aren't you gonna be a junkie with us?' she teased. 'Are you a junkie, Tar?'

'No.'

'A little heroin isn't going to change you into one. You have to think like a junkie if you want to be a junkie.'

'Yeah, you don't need smack to help you ...'

Gemma sighed and leaned back in her chair. I looked into her face to see if I could see anything different. She looked ... happy.

'It's all right, Tar, try it. You don't have to do it ever again if you don't want to. But try it once. Try everything once. All that stuff you hear about one little hit and you're a junkie for life is just stories, you know.'

'Stories to scare the kids, stories to keep you in your

place,' said Lily.

Rob had done another one. He held it out for me. 'Junk's the best. That's why the doctors keep it for themselves.' He gave me a slow wink.

'I know what's better for me than any doctor,' said Lily. I looked at the foil and I thought, God, I don't know what to do ...

'Look, he's actually going to miss the chance to feel better than anyone else in the whole world,' said Lily.

'More for us,' said Rob. Then I thought – what did I have to lose? Rob held the lighter to me, I lit it up and held it under the foil and I watched the white powder turn to a little blob of brown running up and down the crease in the foil. Then I went 'Glop' and ...

Sometimes maybe you need an experience. The experience can be a person or it can be a drug. The experience opens a door that was there all the time but you never saw it. Or maybe it blasts you into outer space. This time it was Lily and Rob and Gemma spending all that time to make me feel one of them, but it was the drug too. All that crap – about Gemma leaving me, about Mum and Dad, about leaving home. All that negative stuff. All the pain ...

It just floated away from me, I just floated away from it ... up and away ...

I leaned back and I looked at the book and I looked at them and Gemma smiled at me, a big soft smile, and her eyes were like marbles.

'Better?' she said.

I just nodded. I didn't feel incredibly wonderful or anything, but it was gone. All the hurt. She came over and sat next to me and sort of wriggled under my arm.

'Tar,' she said. 'Will you go out with me?'

'Yeah,' I said. 'Yeah, I will.'

'I nearly blew that, didn't I?' she said.

'You're gonna live here now, with us,' said Lily. 'Yeah, both of you. Aren't you?'

What could I say? I felt I was just beginning to learn how to live.

'Yeah!'

14
Lily

YOU GET UNDER MY SKIN BUT I DON'T FIND IT
   IRR-I-TATING
YOU ALWAYS PLAY TO WIN BUT I WON'T NEED
   REHA-BIL-I-TATING
OH NO
I THINK I'M ON A-NOTHER WORLD WITH YOU ...
   WITH YOU
I'M ON ANOTHER PLANET WITH YOU ... WITH
   YOU-OO
ANOTHER GIRL
ANOTHER PLANET
ANOTHER GIRL ANOTHER PLANET

The Only Ones

Everything is free. That's a secret.

The only thing that isn't free is you. You do as you're told: you sit in your seat until they say, 'Stand.' You stay put till they say, 'Go.'

Maybe that's the way you like it. It's easy. It's all there. You don't have to think about it. You don't even have to feel it.

I sometimes wonder how this planet keeps on sticking to my feet. They did everything they could to pin me down ... my mum, my dad, school. They put me in homes with kind guys and they put me in homes with bastards. They did things to me you can't even talk about. I'm okay.

What about you?

It's mind control, see. You have to go to school, get those exams, get to university or college, get a job, get married, don't miss the boat, do it now or you'll shoot your life down the drain. Yeah. They got you as soon as you were born. They never risked a second of your life. When you have kids they'll be telling them they have to wear a plastic mask and put a penny in the slot above their nose before they can breathe in.

Listen: Auntie Lily knows the way it *really* is.

Air is free. What, you know that? Good for you. Okay. Food is free. Ah, you didn't know that one! Listen. This is how you do it.

First you gotta find the FreeFood shop. You go out of your front door and you walk down the road. Sooner or later you come to the FreeFood shop. You can't miss it. It might be called Sainsbury's or Tesco or Morrison's if it's a big FreeFood shop. It might be called Smith's or Scholl's or Singh's if it's a little one. It doesn't matter what it's called. The food's piled up everywhere – on shelves, in great heaps and stacks on the floor, in boxes and bags and bins. You want it, you name it – it's yours.

You go inside. You have a look around and see what food you want. You put the food you want under your coat or in your shopping bag and then you take it home and eat it.

Yeah. I expect you thought that you had to go to school, get educated, learn a job, do the job, get paid, take the money down the shop, give people the money before you could take the food home, huh?

You listen to other people too much.

Once you know how to do it, you look about and you'll see FreeFood shops all over the place. The only thing you've got to worry about is that there's usually someone about who thinks the food belongs to them, so you have to make sure you're invisible.

That's easy, too. Because you can be anything you want to be. It's a big secret. You're magic! You're terrific. You're anything you wanna be. Believe it!

Liberate the food! Yeah!

If one of those people who think the food is theirs catches you, it's no use arguing; they're too far gone. You better leg it instead. And once in a while – maybe your aura has got a few holes in it today – you may get caught. Then you get the police and you go to court. If you have money, they'll fine you. If you have no money, you'll get Community Service. That's okay. It needn't happen often. I know people who've never been caught in years. All that stuff about going in and out of prison, that's just another form of mind control. But even if you do get caught, I'll tell you ... Community Service is maybe forty or a hundred hours. What's the alternative? Going out to work every day for the rest of your life? I mean, what kind of sentence is that?

Sometimes I look out of the window and I see all the straights crawling past, going to work, coming back from work, going to learn how to go to work, whatever. And I want to shout out, 'Hey! Listen to me! It isn't like that, it really isn't like that ...'

Only I never do it. It's useless. They must weigh about sixty thousand tons. I'm so far away from people like that, they can't even see me.

Do you want to know more? Listen, I'll tell you everything.

You can *do* anything you want.

You don't believe me. You think, she's out of her head. Yeah, I'm out of my head – on being me. What are you on? On being them. You don't even know. I bet you were never even given a chance to know.

Remember when you were little and they used to say,

'Naughty girl, naughty boy,' because you broke something or said the wrong thing? They told you, 'You are a *bad* person.'

But it wasn't like that, it was just you were doing a bad thing. It wasn't you who was bad. You're beautiful. You're wonderful and everything that you do is wonderful because it's you doing it. You're that strong. You can do it bad and know it bad or you can do it good and know it good but it doesn't *do* anything to you. You're still you.

Listen. You can *be* anything you want to be. Be careful. It's a spell. It's magic. Listen to the words. You can be anything, you can do anything, you can be anything, you can do anything. Listen to the magic.

You *are* anything ... everyone, anyone. Whatever you want. I'm showing you. So long as you stay yourself inside, you can eat dirt and it'll taste good because it's you that's eating it. You can even lick their arses if you have to. You listen to them, teachers, parents, politicians. They're always saying, if you steal you're a thief, if you sleep around you're a slut, if you take drugs you're a junkie. They want to get inside your head and control you with their fear.

Maybe you think your mum and dad love you but if you do the wrong things they'll try and turn you into dirt, just like mine tried to turn me into dirt. It's your punishment for being you. Don't play their game. Nothing can touch you; you stay beautiful.

I've done everything. All of it. You think it, I've done it. All the things you never dared, all the things you dream about, all the things you were curious about and then forgot because you knew you never would. I did 'em, I did 'em yesterday while you were still in bed.

What about you? When's it gonna be *your* turn?

15
Gemma

JUST LURKYING ABOUT, LURKYING ABOUT
LURKYING ABOUT, LURKYING ABOUT
WE'RE JUST
LUUUURRK-LURKYING ABOUT

Lurky

I'm flying, but a lot of people end up dead inside. You can't tell to look at them but as soon as they open their mouths you know they've lost it. They got murdered by life.

I look back at where I came from and I think, What a mess most people make of their lives. My dad. Too scared to live, too scared to die. He works all day for that firm, managing this, managing that. Apart from the fact that it's other people who do the work – I mean the *real* work, the making things; he just burns himself out making himself look important, he doesn't actually do anything. And he hates it. And what for? He makes this money and spends it on a new TV when the old one still works, or a new car because the one he's got is old, or he spends it on a holiday to get away and relax from that ghastly job he's got to have because he needs the money ...

I don't need money. It's the people who want things gotta work.

You should come round to our place sometime. You'd love it, everyone does. You'd come in and there'd be people about but we wouldn't expect anything. You could sit in a corner and watch or you could talk or do what you wanted. There'll be music, there'll be something to drink, maybe there'll be food later on if some turns up. We usually open up the French windows and people sit in the garden. It just turns into a party. We don't have to plan it. Like, Col brings round some booze and Sal turns up with something to smoke, and then someone else turns up with more booze and we all get a bit drunk and then we think we want some more ... so everyone pools in what money they've got and I turn the music up.

And it's a party.

Then at night we'll light the fire. People'll go round and find wood in the skips and the fire'll burn all night long. There's always something going on – dealing, music, people. There's Dev, the dealer. He doesn't go out much but sometimes he comes to sit by the fire and he rolls joint after joint. There's Col and Sal. She used to be with Dev but they split up. I get on really well with Sal, she's right on my wavelength, we're almost as close as me and Lily. Almost. Col's okay, he's a bit boring; he does too much stuff, I reckon.

Col ... he could be a casualty. Well, you get casualties. Life's a dangerous business. I reckon Col and Sal'll split up before long. And there's Wendy and there's Jackson and there's Doll and Pete-Pete. We're never at a loss for people.

But at the centre of everything it's me and Tar and Lily and Rob.

Tar's just *so* much better now. You wouldn't recognise him. He always used to be so anxious and worried. He takes it easy now, you can tell just looking at him. He's sorted out that business with his mum and dad. He had to leave them behind. I mean, he'd left them physically but he was still carrying them round inside his head. Lily said to him over and over, 'What are you carrying their shit for?' It's their problem. They made a mess of their lives; he doesn't have to make a mess of his for their sakes.

I really love him. When I think how close I was to chucking him! It was a close thing. I must have been crazy. I guess I was so excited, I felt that everything had to be different after I met Lily and Rob. It was them who talked me out of it. I was going on about how claustrophobic he made me feel, and how he was always staring at me like I was a fish in a tank. They said, 'No, no, he's really nice, he's special, why don't you be nice to him? You gotta be nice to your friends ...'

I said, 'But I don't love him.'

Lily laughed at me and she said, 'You gotta look after him, he's yours, can't you see that?'

Yeah. He's mine. We got each other. I'm his.

I ring up my parents from time to time, just to let them know I'm okay. I'd like it to be all right between us. I'd like to ring up and just chat or invite them round for a visit, but I don't dare. They're still into this owning me trip. They'd tip off the police and get me back home – a bloody mental home or a remand home if it wasn't their home.

I said to my mum, 'When I'm sixteen, I'll come and visit you and we'll be friends.' She said nothing. I know what she was thinking. She tries to keep her mouth shut but it slips out from time to time.

She still can't forgive me, see? She thinks I've done something bad to *her*. See what I mean? I'm just getting on with my own life and she thinks I'm doing her down. No wonder I couldn't even breathe in that house.

The first time I rang up home after moving in with Lily and Rob I was scared stiff. I kept putting it off and putting it off. I mean, what could I say to them? I'd turned into something they could never understand. But the others kept going on at me.

Tar always rang his mum up even though his parents were even worse than mine. He's such a good little boy it makes me sick sometimes. He and Rob and Lily were on and on at me.

Rob's really soft about mums. It was all right for him, his mum's really great. She's an amazing woman. She came round to visit us once and when she saw the sort of thing we were up to, she just laughed.

'Don't get caught,' she said. That's all. Can you imagine it? It was so wonderful to see there were people like that. I mean, it's like, once you break away and get out of the brainwashing, you can liberate your children and your grandchildren and all the generations to come. Rob had his first joint when he was about eight. He didn't smoke tobacco and she reckoned it was the way she'd brought him up. She was really pleased with the way he'd turned out. Most people who smoke hash smoke tobacco, too, you see, but Rob grew up with it so he had more sense. Mind you, he rolls his first joint as soon as he gets up.

Even he doesn't tell his mum everything. He made us all swear not to tell her about the heroin. She'd have blown her lid. A lot of people can't handle junk. You have to be special to be able to use it.

Anyway, he was always on and on at me to get in touch with my mum, and so were Lily and Tar. I said, 'I just know it'll be horrible, they'll make me hate them, I know it.' But they kept on and on. So in the end I did. They went round with me to a telephone booth to back me up.

I got Dad.

'Gemma, is that you?'

I was full of it to start with. 'Aren't you going to ask me how I am, then?' I said. I was grinning at Rob and he was nodding. This was about two, three weeks after I met them.

My dad said, 'Is that you?' again. He sounded like a little grey man.

I said, 'Yeah, it's me, all right. How are you, Dad?'

'Gemma, Gemma,' he said. He was weird. He sounded ...

Lily pushed her face into mine. 'He's scared of you,' she hissed.

I thought, Wow! And I knew it was true. He sounded like a little boy stuck outside the headmaster's office. I could have whooped because I knew that whatever spell he had over me was broken for sure. But I didn't want to be mean to him. I stared at the phone and licked my lips, then I said, 'Yeah, it's all right, Dad. It's nice to talk to you.' Pause. 'How's Mum?'

'Gemma. She's worried sick. We both are. Why didn't you ring? You could have rung us any time.'

'Don't get at me, Dad, I'm doing my best,' I said. 'Is Mum there?' I didn't want to start talking about what he thought I should have done.

'We love you, Gemma.'

'Dad ...'

'I know we made mistakes but we both love you, you know that, don't you?'

That shocked me. I was embarrassed because ... I love you. I don't ever remember him saying that to me and now that he was saying it he sounded so broken and beat up. But it made me angry, too, because it was like, you know, a trap? I mean, they'd covered me in shit and now I was out of their control it was, I love you ...

He could have said that any time before.

'Look, Dad, just don't, just don't start on me. I'm not coming back. I'm having a good time.'

'Gemma, you're fourteen years old ...' Then I heard sounds over the phone and I thought I heard Mum's voice.

'Is that Mum? Can I have a talk to her?'

I could hear her in the background. She was saying, 'Grel? Grel? Is that her, Grel?' She always called him Grel, God knows why. His name's Andrew.

He said, 'Just a minute.' Then to me, 'Gemma, why are you doing this? Are you punishing us? Don't you think you've done enough?'

I could have laughed. He didn't have a clue. Punishing him! That was his scene. I wasn't doing anything to him. I didn't have to.

'I'm just having a good time, it's nothing to do with you any more,' I told him.

'I think it is something to do with us, Gemma,' he said. 'And I think it's time you stopped this. Do you realise the upset you've caused your poor mother?'

I was getting upset. First it was loving me. Then it was what I was doing to him, now it was what I was doing to Mum. I put my hand over the mouthpiece. 'I don't think I can take this,' I said.

'Stay cool, stay cool,' Rob was saying.

Lily said, 'You're doing great, Gemma, you're doing beautiful.'

I could hear my mum on the phone saying, 'What's she saying, Grel? What's she saying?'

'Look, just let me talk to her, will you?' I said.

He said, 'What's going on, have you got someone with you?'

'Never mind that, can I have Mum now?'

'She's been worried sick, ringing up the police, ringing up the papers and not a word from you, Gemma. Not a word in four weeks ...'

He was really getting going. I could hear Mum behind him trying to get to the phone but he wasn't having it.

'She's done everything for you, you might at least think of

her ...' And I was really beginning to get mad because he wouldn't let me speak to my mum. He was only going on like that just because she was in the room. He always felt he had to act up for her.

Then Rob grabbed the phone.

'Hello? Mr Brogan?' he said.

'Who's that? Who's that?' yelped my dad.

'I'm a friend of Gemma's, Mr Brogan. I just want to tell you, you've got a beautiful daughter. You ought to be proud of her, Mr Brogan,' he said.

My dad said, 'Oh, so she's found a bloke, has she? I suppose you know she's under age, whoever you are ... '

I began trying to pull the phone away from Rob. I was so angry, I was so embarrassed for him.

Dad was going, 'Gemma? Gemma? I'd like to speak to my daughter now, please.'

Then Lily grabbed the phone. 'I think she's beautiful too,' she said. 'And if you want to know, I'm under age as well. And don't start telling *my* bloke he's messing around with my best friend, okay, Mister Man?'

Then it turned into a bit of a fight with everyone yelling and snatching for the phone to tell my dad what for. Tar started really screeching.

'My turn, my turn!' he was screaming. He was so loud he got hold of it and then he held it to his ear and he just stood there. I could hear my dad's voice going, a little tinny crackle. But Tar just stood there listening. I guess he just wanted to hear, he didn't have anything to say. We were all quiet, watching him. Then the tinny crackle changed and I could just make out my mum.

'Hello, Mrs Brogan,' Tar said.

'Hello, David? Is my daughter there? I'd like to talk to her, please,' my mum said, and Tar handed me the phone with a funny little look. Everyone gathered around me with their heads close to the phone and listened in.

My mum said, 'Gemma ... Gemma, is it you? Is it really you?' I was so pleased to hear her voice. I forgot all about the things she did to me.

'Mum, hello, Mum, I love you, Mum, I love you,' I was saying, and Rob was nodding and Lily was going, 'Yeah, yeah.'

'Are you all right? Have you got enough to eat? Do you need anything?' she was saying.

'Yeah, Mum. I'm fine, I'm great, everything's fine. How are you?'

'Gemma, come home, please come home ... please ...' she said. And she started crying.

I wanted to hug her and hold her. I had to hug the phone, it was the nearest I could get to her. Dad made me angry, but Mum just made me love her.

'I can't come back, not yet, Mum, not yet. But I'm okay, I really am and I miss you, Mum, and I'll come back as soon as I can,' I blabbed. I was just about crying already.

'Oh, Gemma,' she said. 'Oh, Gemma ...' And she couldn't even talk, she was crying so much.

I wished she wouldn't cry.

I could hear Dad trying to get the phone back but she pulled herself together. He was going on in the background, raising his voice to her. It made me cross.

'What's he going on about now?' I said.

She said, 'Don't be angry with your father, Gemma. It's been a terrible strain. He hasn't been sleeping, the doctor's put him on pills.'

I felt rotten then, but Tar reached over and put his hand over the receiver so she couldn't hear and he said, 'Bloody junkie.'

It was *so* funny. It was awful. There was a second's pause and then everyone started spluttering and laughing silently.

Lily clapped her hand over her mouth and slid down to the floor of the booth and hid her face in her hands. I had to bite my cheeks to stop myself laughing.

I gritted my teeth and said, 'What sort of pills?'

'Sleeping pills, you know. Quite strong ones.'

Rob and Tar were holding on to each other.

'He's in the most awful state,' finished my mum.

I was howling and laughing and laughing and I had to do it all without making a noise. It was so funny! All that stuff about him worrying about me and there he was, packed up to the eyeballs with downers and smoking fags. Lily got up off the floor and hissed, 'Ask her if he'll send some down. We'll give him a good price ...'

I was killing myself. Mum was saying, 'Are you all right, Gemma? Are you all right?' And then I heard Dad saying 'She must be on drugs or something ...' And of course that made me howl even more. I could barely stand up. We were all getting really hysterical.

Then Mum started crying again and I felt rotten so I just said, 'Look Mum, there's a spot of bother here, I'll ring you back later ...' and I slapped the phone down and we all just roared with laughter. It was hysterical. It was rotten, I felt awful, but it was so funny ... none of us could help it. Rob was staring at Tar and saying, 'You bastard!' but he was still laughing. And Tar was saying, 'Sorry, sorry ...' But none of us could stop.

I rang her back later on my own, and it was okay. She sort of understood, I think. She made it sound as though she did. But I kept thinking about it the whole time and I kept bursting out laughing for the rest of the day.

Once she accepted that I wasn't coming back we got to have some intelligent conversations. She still cracks up and starts crying sometimes, which is a pity because I'd ring up more often if it wasn't for that. I hate that. It doesn't do any good.

My dad's okay, too. I try to have a normal conversation but it never gets much past the 'How are you, what's the weather like over there?' kind of thing. Sometimes he tells me he loves me but it never sounds all that convincing. I guess I get on better with my mum, all in all.

Vonny and Richard come round from time to time. I don't know whether it's because they like us or whether they're just keeping an eye on us. It's nice. I like them. Even Vonny. Now she can't be some sort of Auntie Thing, it's okay. Mind you, they don't know the half of it. I don't tell her everything. Junk, for example. I don't tell them about that. They wouldn't understand. They have their drugs – hash, a bit of speed, booze. But junk. I dunno. One day, maybe I'll tell them just to watch their faces.

Yeah. There's a lot of drugs around here. Drugs are just part of life – pleasure, business, they bring you up and take you down, they make you feel good. They take you to another planet, sometimes. Sometimes you have to find your own way back.

I know what you're thinking. You're thinking, O-oh, she's a junkie, she's only been away from home six months and she's a junkie already.

You poor brat, you've been brainwashed. Look, drugs are fun. They make you feel good, that's all. Sure, they're powerful, that's why they're dangerous. So's life. If you're in control, then it's okay.

They never dare tell you that, of course. It's not because they want to keep you off drugs. Oh no, they like it, they want you to. They just want to make sure you take the ones they want you to take. It's all part of the big mind control. Tobacco, booze, medicine – good; hash, acid, junk– bad.

You think about it. What's that row of little bottles in your mum's medicine cabinet? How many is she on a day? How often do you reckon she's clean – once every three months when the prescription runs out and she toddles off down to the doctor and gets some more? Medication, they call it. Thanks, I can prescribe for myself, I don't need no experts telling me what's good for me.

What about Cousin John puffing his way through twenty fags a day, filling the air with his poison, breathing all over his baby and watching it cough and having a good laugh about it. What about your dad, going to the pub every night for three or four or five pints? It'd be an education to take a scan of what his insides look like after thirty years of that. You don't know what goes on after you're safely tucked up in bed. Ever hear the clink and ring of a bottle on glass after lights out? Take a look at the drinks cabinet and see.

Then one day they catch you with a joint in your hand and it's, 'Oh my God, she's on drugs'... and then it's police, social workers, tell the school, teachers checking your eyes in the morning, into care, and before you know it you're going crazy and all their worst dreams come true.

It's all mind control. The tobacco companies, the drug companies, the booze companies – they've got it sewn up. It's all right to take the stuff they churn out. Tobacco – makes you look cool. You're going to look pretty cool in an oxygen tent with your legs cut off. Go to the doctor. Here, take this, take that, this'll make you feel better. Meanwhile they're dumping all the stuff that doesn't work on the third world and you wake up one morning and your baby's got no arms and one eye in the middle of its neck.

No thanks.

Yeah, I like to smoke a little hash. I like to breathe in a little smack. It makes me feel good.

I got to admit, heroin's the best. I mean, THE BEST. The others, well ... Acid, your thoughts come alive and they start to live a life of their own. Hash, your senses sort of wake up.

But with heroin, ahhh. You can just sit in a sewer all day and be soooo happy and feel soooo good.

Chasing the dragon ... yeah. It's like Chinese magic. That smoke, that's your Chinese dragon, and when you breathe that dragon in and he coils about in your veins, like Lily said, you feel better than anyone else ever did. You feel better than Churchill after he won the war, you feel better than the caveman when he discovered fire, you feel like Romeo did when he finally got to bed with Juliet.

That's why it's dangerous. You have to be strong to feel that good, because after a while you have to open the door again and step out and ... go to work or ring up your mum or whatever. You almost don't dare to do it because it's one hundred million dollars of feeling good. You don't dare take it just to escape because when you get back, you might not like it much. Yeah ... to do heroin, you've got to have a life.

No, really, it *is* dangerous. Even I know that. Rob and Lily used to have a thing. That was before they came to Bristol, when they were still living in Manchester. They got into a bit of a mess up there, especially Rob. He had a hard time for a bit but he managed to kick it on the head. He'd been clean for a month when we moved in.

Lily – well, she's something else. Rob says she used to take loads and loads in Manchester. Then when she saw how he was in a mess, they both packed up and went to Bristol and she went right off it, no problem at all. Then once he was clean again, she started up just like that. Now she takes loads and loads again. She frightens me, she takes so much. She says that's because she's stronger than anyone else. Well, she is.

Actually, Rob was never addicted to the heroin. It was the needles – jacking up. He had a thing about sticking the needle into his arm and pushing down the plunger. He used to do it with gin and vodka; he even used to do it with water when he hadn't got anything else. But that was before we all got together. Things are different now. Sure, heroin's strong. But we're stronger. You have to be able to stop and start when you want to. Like, we do a bit, or we have a little binge and then we lay off for a few days, or a week. We all gave up for a week once, me and Lily and Tar and Rob. We just said right, that's it, no more for a few weeks. And we did it. I could do it again tomorrow.

We dug the garden, Tar got on with his dandelion. He's doing a really huge one on the wall of our bedroom. When we first moved in he started on it straight away. When it's finished it's going to take up a whole wall. You should see it – dense black in the back and these amazing arrows of yellow and orange.

'That's you,' he says, colouring in a petal. He still says that to me sometimes – you know, dandelion. He whispers it to me at night when we're cuddled up. Only I don't say ladybird back any more. I say, dandelion. Dandelion, dandelion. I love you.

He'd stopped doing it for a while, but when we gave up junk for that week he almost finished it. And Rob got on with his motorbike. It had been lying in bits on the floor ever since we moved in; he hadn't touched it. Then he got stuck in and he got the wheels on and the engine in place. Pretty soon, we'll pack it in again and then he'll finish it, I expect.

It wasn't difficult, coming off. I could do it again any time. So long as I feel like that I know it's all right.

16
Tar

It's a beautiful winter's day.

Here in Bristol you don't get much frost. The sea gets channelled up the Bristol Channel and keeps us all moist and cool. But these past couple of days it's been really cold. Yesterday there were tiny little frost crystals on all the walls and the twigs and branches. There's a lot of trees in this town. Today there was another frost and all yesterday's crystals had more crystals growing up them, like fairy land. Ice flowers everywhere you look. I went out as soon as I realised. I stood looking for hours.

Me and Rob and Sal went out and made a slide down Richmond Road. It was already so slippery we had trouble walking up it. Once we got to the top, you could sit on a piece of cardboard and slide for miles down into the square at the bottom. We were at it all morning. We got Gemma out, and Col. Even Lily came out in the end. We forgot everything. Then this old black guy went past and started on at us for making the pathway dangerous and Lily lost her temper as usual.

'Son of the morgue! Sod off and die!' she yelled at the poor old bloke. Lily really knows how to turn a good insult.

Lily doesn't go out so much any more. 'Too many straights,' she says. She used to do the shops with us in the summer but we don't have to do that so much now. Me and Rob do quite a bit of dealing these days. Not to make money, we never have much money, but just enough so we can buy some smokes and some hash and a little junk from time to time. You can shoplift most things but it isn't clever to try and pinch drugs. Apart from anything else, they usually belong to your friends.

Dealing's okay, it's a business. You go round and visit your friends, buy a little, sell a little, take a little. We usually have enough money left over to get food and stuff, so we don't have to do so much shoplifting. That's nice, because although it's fun, it wears you down if you have to do it every day. Rob's sixteen, he can sign on. Lily'll be sixteen in a few months but meanwhile we only get what we make ourselves.

I really got into the shoplifting for a while. I got Gemma to sew these big pockets into my coat so I could really stuff myself with things.

I used to walk into the supermarket thin and walk out again fat. I even used to try and keep up with Rob, which was dangerous, really, because he's in another class.

Rob's been at it since he was a kid. He used to train for it. He grew up in tepees and trailers and lorries. He'd get up in the night and go into someone's tepee, and then he'd crawl round inside, hiding behind the chairs and the table and dashing out across the open spaces while they weren't looking. Can you imagine?

'Practising,' he says. For shoplifting, see? And he never got caught either.

Yeah, the summer was beautiful. Now it's winter, it's cold. I suppose you wouldn't expect it to be so good.

I remember those nights out in the garden by the fire. They really were the summer for me. Big bonfires – we kept them going all night. Whenever it got low someone'd toddle out and find some wood in a skip. There was the swing. Did you hear about that swing? Rob and I built it up in the big sycamore tree at the end of the garden. Huge great tree, its roots were breaking up the wall on the other side, tearing out stones and rubble ...

Anyway, we climbed up and cut off the branches to fit this swing in. We had to fight Lily about it, she went mad, she said we were mutilating her tree. She went on and on about it, but when we'd finished it, she loved it. It was one great long piece of rope, must have been five yards long, with a cross-piece of wood at the bottom. You had to go right back to the other end of the garden pulling the rope after you, right up on top of the little shed ... then you let go ...

It was amazing! Not just how long it was, but because you went right out beyond the garden and over the road. People'd be walking along or driving or on their bikes and they'd hear this whoosh of air overhead like some giant eagle or something was coming down. And there'd be someone flying out above their heads! We used to do it with no clothes on. Stark naked. People used to almost crash their cars. It was such a gas. You can imagine – you're driving along and then suddenly this naked girl appears howling and flying through the air.

We were all in love with one another. We were in love with ourselves. We still are. And me and Gemma of course.

When she took me back in I was so happy. I was just so happy. I really felt like I'd arrived, I belonged. We were just all over each other. I was nervous at first that she'd want a bit more freedom in the next few days, but it wasn't like that at all. She'd really missed me. She didn't realise until I'd gone. She wanted me so much. And then when I came back, she was in love with me as much as I was in love with her. It was a miracle. In the summer we'd sit next to one another for hours and hours, by the fire holding hands, and I was so grateful and happy that it had worked out.

I still love her, but it's different now. I don't *need* her any more, you know. If she chucked me now, I'd still be really upset, but I know that I'd get on with my life. Back then, it felt like the end of the world.

Maybe that's the difference with me these days. I used to get this feeling that life was rushing past me and I had to grab hold of it or I'd lose everything. But when I moved here, I remember thinking, I'm in control now. It was the first time I felt I had my life in my own hands. There I was scrabbling and struggling to keep things together. These days, I just let go of them. And it isn't me who falls. It's the rest of the world that goes away – up or down, I don't know. Just away.

The trouble with the dealing is, there's always drugs about so you tend always to take them. But I'm glad we don't have to do so much thieving. We had a couple of close calls, actually. There was this one time we ran out of booze, so Rob and Col decided to go and do an off licence. I went along, I don't know why. They'd done it before but this sort of thing was brand new to me.

We got to the place. Rob whips out this brick – and crash, straight through the window. Then the alarm; it crashed about, it was terrible. I thought the whole world would be on top of us. We all dived in. I was a bit slow, I'm always a bit slow. I was too busy watching up and down the street but the other two dived in and grabbed bottles as fast as they could. But it was a good job I was a bit slow, because then I saw a cop coming. This cop was haring up the road, he must have been just round the corner. I yelled, 'Pigs!' and everyone charged out and up the road, dropping cans of beer and smashing bottles of wine.

We made it to a railway cutting, up the side and into the trees. The policeman waited at the top of the ridge. We heard the police cars wailing up the road, screeching to a halt. Then it was a manhunt!

They roadblocked the two sides of the cutting. They had men up and down the side. I mean, fifty quid's worth of booze and they had this operation that must have cost thousands. If they'd given me half that money, I'd never commit another crime for months. They even had a loudspeaker.

'We know you're in there ... come on out, lads, and we'll see what we can do for you.'

Yeah, sure.

We were hiding in the shrubbery, giggling. Actually, I got a bit panicky at one point and I thought we'd better give ourselves up. You know how they go on: It'll be better for you, the magistrate will think better of you if you do this, we're going to get the dogs now ...

But Col and Rob knew better. They'd been up to this sort of thing all their lives. We just sat tight. After a bit the pigs got bored, or they decided we'd legged it. So they went. And after they went, we went too.

I was scared shitless, actually, but it was fun looking back on it. We don't do that sort of thing these days. It's too risky. If they came to our homes, it'd be serious. Apart from the fact that I do a little dealing, it would really do Lily in. She's in a bit of a mess, if you ask me, although no one says anything about it.

I dunno, perhaps she knows what she's doing. Sometimes I do really honestly think she has special powers. She thinks she does. You know that book they got me? We've still got it. I keep it in a drawer. In the drawer there's a cutlery box we found in a skip, an old one made of wood with a silk lining. Inside there's this piece of silk, a scarf or something. It's really old. We found that in a skip too. It's wonderful. It might be seventy or even a hundred years old or more. Someone wore it when they were young and beautiful in the nineteen twenties or further back. Then they'd got old and kept it tucked away because it was full of memories. Then they'd died and the people who came after threw it out.

But we found it, so it isn't wasted. And wrapped in the silk is the book. Lily calls it the Sky Bible because of that remark I made when I first saw it. Rob kept repeating it. 'It must be like owning the sky.'

Lily lights incense sticks and candles, and fills the room with smoke and candlelight. Then she takes the book out very slowly, very carefully.

'Sky Bible, what we gonna do today?'

And she lets the book fall open. Last time it was a piccy of a naked woman. Not young, quite old and baggy. She was sitting on an armchair smoking a cigarette and looking out of the window. All the smoke was coiling around the place. She wasn't pretty or anything but the photograph was really beautiful. I thought so anyway.

'What's it mean, Lily?' asked Gemma.

Rob said, 'Have sex in an armchair?' He's a bit irreverent about it, it annoys Lily.

Lily screws up her eyes and thinks carefully. Then she says, 'Nah. It says, we gotta do some heroin today ...'

Everyone fell about laughing. But she really meant it, she got quite annoyed.

'Strange, that's what it said last time,' I said.

Lily patted it. 'The Sky Bible knows how to have a good time,' she intoned.

I could never work out if it's a game or not. But I think if anyone's magic, Lily is. It's funny – sometimes she's dead against any sort of hocus pocus, other times she acts like she's the Queen Witch. You never know what's going on with Lily. She worries me sometimes. She thinks that whatever she happens to be thinking is fantastic. And the problem with Gemma is, *she* thinks whatever Lily is thinking is fantastic.

I tried to talk about it to Gemma the other day, but she just got annoyed. She thought I was getting scared, told me I ought to lay off the junk. I'm not worried about it for myself, I never take smack two days on the trot, just to show myself. But I do worry about Gemma. I can take it or leave it, but she never says no.

It's one of the problems that we all do the same kind of thing. There's always one of us wants a chase. Of course we never use needles, we've got more sense than that ... but I might want to have a break but Gemma'll feel like she wants some. Or if both me and her decide to have a break, Lily'll turn up or Rob will or Sally ...

You sort of infect one another like that.

It'll be all right. I just have to remember I got away from my mum and dad. If I can escape from that, I can escape from anything.

17
Gemma

One day I'm going to have babies. One day I'm gonna move to the country and grow flowers and vegetables. Maybe I'll have a little flowershop. Maybe I'll sell the things I grow. And in the summer when I need to get off my head I'll go round the festivals and meet all my friends.

One day. But right now, I'm a city girl. It's all here, in this half a square mile. You can stuff your face on it. You can just bend down and pick it up, anything you like.

In the city, you gotta have money. For the first six months we lived off nothing but after that ... well, you need money to do everything. You need money for the bus, to go to bops, to buy yourself things. The only thing is, you gotta find an easy way of making it. Work in the factory for forty hours a week? No thanks, I'd rather be skint at home.

Money's easy, that's another thing Lily taught me. It was – I dunno – last spring? We were all really skint. We'd been having a bit of a binge that week, too much really, but it's nice to do too much once in a while.

We'd had a couple of grams at the beginning of the week. Then Sal came round. It was about the time she'd given Col the elbow and she was missing him but she didn't want to take him back. She'd been away visiting her brother in Manchester so she'd been clean for a week and she was gasping. She bought a couple of grams. We always share everything, so we got through that lot together.

That wasn't too bad, but then Dev turned up back from Amsterdam.

It was just one thing after another that week. He had, I don't know how much; he always has a bagful when he comes round. I don't even know how long that lasted ...

After you've done a junk binge, you feel it. Cold turkey. You feel horrible. If it was measles or the 'flu or something you might think, Well, so I'm ill, it won't last long. Coming down isn't any worse but the difference is, you know that all you have to do is take one little snort and instead of feeling like dirt you'll feel better than anyone ever did before.

That's what makes it so hard. All you can think about is, junk, junk, junk.

If Dev'd still been about he'd have looked after us, but he'd cleared off that morning. We should have asked him to leave a bit behind so we could come down slowly, but he left really early and we forgot to ask the night before. Our usual dealer was away for the weekend, otherwise we could have got some on credit. It was awful. That was the first time. Up to then coming down hadn't been so bad but this time – I don't know – this just seemed to get worse and worse. I was taking Anadin and all sorts but it wasn't doing any good at all. There's only one thing can make you feel better when you've got cold turkey. More junk.

Lily was worse than any of us. 'I'm really gutted, my head can't cope with this,' she kept complaining. Lily hates feeling bad. Feeling bad is against her religion.

She was sitting down, jumping up, going to bed, coming back. In the afternoon me and Tar got into watching this movie but Lily just couldn't get into it. She got into this whispering session with Sal. I got irritated about it, they wouldn't tell me what was going on and I hate being left out. Finally Lily dragged Rob off to the bedroom. I thought they'd gone for you-know-what, but five minutes later they came out and got their coats. Lily was back in her string vest, it was the first time I'd seen her dressed like that for weeks.

'Where're you going?' I asked.

'When I come back,' said Lily, 'I'm gonna make you all feel soooo GOOD!' She stuck her bum out sideways and winked at me. Rob grinned, a bit shakily. Then they went out.

They were away about two hours. Me and Tar gave Sal a grilling but she kept her mouth shut. I got really ratty about it in the end and she started snapping, so I shut up, but I was burning up with curiosity. Then we heard their voices in the hall and I knew whatever it was they'd done, it'd worked, because they were both happy.

Lily came banging in and shrieked and just flung this money at the ceiling.

'Yeah, free money, free money!' she yelled. There was a big handful of tenners coming down from the ceiling. She started jiving round the room. Sal grabbed hold of her and kissed her. Rob grabbed the notes and went bombing off to get some.

I was going, 'How did you get it, how did you get it?' I thought they must have robbed someone. But she wouldn't say, she kept just jiving about and putting music on and lighting incense and getting the place ready until Rob came back. He was quick too, he's not usually that quick. He usually stays round there a bit, specially if it's one of the dealers we don't know so well. Lily had her fix first. Then she gave me that big Lily smile and she said, 'Sixty quid, not bad for ten minutes' work, eh, Gemma?'

'Go on then, tell me, I've been going mad.'

'I turned over a punter,' she said.

'What's that mean? Did she rob someone? Has she mugged someone?' I asked Sal. Sal giggled and shook her head. She was watching Rob stick the needle in his arm like she'd never seen anything so interesting in her life before. I couldn't wait either but I was so curious.

Lily said, 'I've been a little prossie for half an hour.'

I was just amazed. I kept asking her questions – how she did it, what she had to do, where she did it, how many she did it with, how often she'd done it before, what she charged. She got annoyed when I asked her if she enjoyed it.

'It's a job, Gems, nobody likes working,' she said, glancing at Rob.

Later when she calmed down, she said she got a hit off it, but she didn't enjoy it the way I meant. She got hyped up from it, like she used to when she was a kid and she walked across the river on the edge of the rail bridge. It was a dare.

This is how you do it.

She stands on the street corner. He waits a little bit down the road. Then the punter in a car comes along and pulls up, has a chat. He makes himself seen, so the punter knows she's not on her own. They decide to do business. They decide what the service is, what the price is.

'We all knew what the goods were,' said Lily, and she grinned.

She gets in the car, the car pulls away. He walks up and down chewing his nails and fretting. Fifteen minutes later the car drops her off, she gets out and she finds him and hands over the money. Then she goes back to her place, does another punter.

Two punters. Hey presto. Sixty quid.

Yeah, money's easy. You can earn it standing in a doorway or flat on your back or in the back of someone's car. You use your body same as other people do – carpenters, mechanics, gardeners. You can go to work and earn it in a shop or you can work for yourself on the street corner or at home. Money's easy, same as everything's easy – once you know how.

I know what you're thinking. You're thinking, how terrible,

how demeaning, how awful, oh, dear me, oh oh oh ...

Yeah, about as demeaning as going out to work five days a week. About as demeaning as going down a mine. About as demeaning as sitting in an office all your life while the sun shines on someone else. About as demeaning as getting married and having kids and then finding out he's a bastard who knocks you about and wants to give you one five times a week and you can't say no even though you hate him, and all for less in a week than Lily can earn in a couple of hours.

Who's the sucker?

I was amazed. Even after I was full of heroin I was still amazed and I kept saying, 'You didn't, you're pulling my leg, aren't you?'

'I was a little prossie for half an hour, now I'm Lily again. And I'm having a really good time ...'

I had Vonny and Richard round here the other day and ... Oh, I couldn't resist it. I'd already told them about turning over a few punters. I love it. You can see their faces trying to work it out. They just *hate* being disapproving. They think they're Mr and Mrs Alternative, really subversive. Gluing up the banks, smoking a few joints. I'm only fifteen and I've done things neither of them would dare do.

When I told them I was on the game, Vonny sat for a bit trying to decide what her position was, then she said, 'That's *awful*, Gemma.'

'Well, I'll try anything once,' said Richard. 'But I wouldn't advise it as a career move.' Which actually was just about right. He surprises me sometimes. Anyway, I was going to tell you ... I couldn't resist. They were sitting there and they wanted to know what I'd been up to. So I thought, I'll show you what. And I rolled up my sleeves and showed them my track marks. Where I'd used the needle.

I won't bore you with the details. I was almost sorry I

bothered, they went on so much. Actually, I say that, but I didn't mind. I like talking smack. I could talk about smack all day, it fascinates me – what it does to you and the way people react to it. But they were just appalled, far more than when I told them I did punters. It went on for hours.

'There'll be tears over this,' said Richard.

I laughed. He doesn't know me!

'Everyone thinks they're stronger than heroin,' said Vonny. 'That's how it makes you feel. But there'll be deaths.' She got really wound up.

She got up and started pointing round the room like the Angel of Doom. 'Some of you are going to die.' There were a couple of younger ones there, little beggar girls who made a bit selling to the even more down-and-out beggars. They just sank back into the carpet and stared at her as if she'd Come To Get Them. It was so funny.

'You know all about it, you've been through it, have you?' said Tar. And of course Vonny had to admit she'd never even tried it. Everyone started laughing at her after that, even the little ones. Vonny just stood there looking sulky.

'There'll be deaths,' she repeated.

'Yeah! You're all gonna die! Yeah!' Lily was funny. She was dancing round the room like a ghost. She was on form that day, like she was at the party where I met her. She danced up to Vonny. 'Live fast, die young, babe, before you get any older,' she sang. Vonny looked at her like she was going to be sick, like she'd no right to be thinking like that.

I enjoyed it at the time. But they come round too often, both of them together, or one at a time. And it's all they ever want to talk about. I reckon they're more addicted than I am.

We get really young kids round here buying smack sometimes. I mean, I was fourteen when I started and now I'm fifteen and a half but some of these are thirteen and I've even seen twelve-year-olds turn up. I feel guilty about selling to them, but then I think, what else have they got? These kids didn't leave home to get a slice of life like me. They left home because they needed to escape.

They couldn't handle home. Trouble is, they can't handle the street, either. They don't take smack to have a good time; they take it to escape. They don't go on the game to make money; they do it just to survive. They ought to be working in a café or at school or being milk monitor for the nursery round the corner.

It's different with them.

They really ought not to be on the game, though. Apart from anything else I wouldn't trust men who want girls that young. But there you go – there's no other way they can earn money. That's true for us, too.

What else do you have to sell?

That's about as far as it goes if you're under age. You can get some lousy job where you work 2,000 hours a week for some fat git sweatshop. Or you can spend a couple of days a week on your back ...

There's this one little kid I pass on the way to work. She hangs around the corner of Brook Road flogging her lamb chop. She has this long wimpy bloke with her, he can't be more than fourteen, but I wouldn't put her down as a teenager. She dresses up in make-up and high heels. I suppose she thinks she looks sophisticated, but actually she does good trade because she looks like what she is – a little girl all dressed up.

She does a trick and they go together and spend the money on sweets and heroin.

When she comes round here I try and talk to her. I say to her, 'Look, you can be anything you want, you don't have to hang around here ...' And she just looks at me and sighs. She likes to linger here. I suppose it's the company. If I go on at her too much, she sighs and says, 'Can I go now?' as if she needs my permission to leave the house.

I sometimes wonder if I shouldn't turn her in for her own good, but Lily reckons she ran away for a reason, and she's probably better off where she is.

Maybe. At least she's in control of her own life. But I feel bad about those kids. They deserve some sort of life. Me, I've made my own choices and I'm happy with it. Yeah. Yes, I am. I'm in control of my life and I love it, and I love myself and I love Tar and I love my friends.

The thing is, I know my limits. I'm sensible about it. Lily says I do everything sensibly even when I go over the top. Too right. I take care of myself. I eat well. Always make the punters use a condom. I don't work on the streets; I do it through the massage parlour. I don't share needles, except with Tar. I'm not a junkie. I can stop it whenever I want. I do sometimes, for a week or so, just to show myself I'm still on top. I don't have Aids. I don't even have non-specific urethritis.

Lily goes out and works on the street, even though she could get a job at the parlour with her looks. She says she doesn't want to work for anyone except herself. Basically she believes in magic. Believing in magic the Lily way means that you never get harmed no matter what you do ... and if you do, it's because you were meant to.

It's a funny thing with Lily but it seems to work for her; nothing seems to harm her. I don't mean she never gets hurt. Things happen to her. She got turned over by one of the punters the other day. This guy beat her up and took her money. She came back with a black eye looking for Rob because he was supposed to be keeping an eye on things. It wasn't his fault, though. The guy drove her off before he did it.

But the thing was, she was all right again in half an hour. She was back on the street that evening. I'd have been terrified to go out there again, but there she was, chirpy as ever. She was even proud of it. That's her secret, I suppose. Everything that happens to her she's proud of. She makes it special by it happening to her.

Me and Sal, we've got this amazing job at the parlour – Dido's Health Parlour. It's nice and clean. It's safe because you're on the premises and there's the other girls around and the management don't want anything bad to happen or they lose their business. You get a better class of punter. Lily has to take them as they come, straight off the street. Some of those lorry drivers have been sitting in the cab twelve hours, sweating. At the parlour, if you think the customer's a bit ripe you just fling him a towel and say, 'I'll come and give you your massage when you've had your shower.'

Of course the management don't want people to get turned away so you can't pick and choose. You can't say, 'I don't fancy him, I'll have him instead.' That's not fair on the other girls. But if someone asks you to do something kinky they send in Joe and he shows them the door. And the boss, Gordon, is really good. If it's someone really gross or someone you really can't stand he'll try and overcharge him or get rid of him somehow. If the customer still wants it, he offers him to one of the other girls for extra money. Usually Elaine, because she really doesn't care. Yuk! As it is, I like to do a little junk – not enough to be out of it, just enough, you know, so I'm not totally all there.

It's a public service, really. After the bank holiday you get this queue of men in the waiting room. I mean they don't get it at home with their wives or they're too shy to find a girl of their own. So they come to us. If it wasn't for us they'd probably be out on the street hunting down young girls. Sal and I have a joke about it.

'You on PPD today?'

'Yeah, Pervert Prevention Duty.'

I get three hundred quid a week some weeks, if I go for it. Pretty demeaning, eh? Fifteen years old, three hundred quid a week. I keep thinking I'd like to go back and show my parents. Not what I'm doing; not what I'm earning, either, 'cause they might guess. Just me. Just show them me, so they can see I'm doing all right.

Only, not yet. I'd like to wait until I'm clean before that. I do too much, I know that. I'm planning on getting myself straight for a few weeks. I'll go and see them then. I keep meaning to ring them but ... it does my head in. I just can't bear to talk to them these days. Even my mum. I miss her, but I can't talk to her. It'll come. I can wait. I mean, she's not gonna die tomorrow, right?

18
Tar

SINCE I GOT BETTER
I BIN HAAPPY THIS WAY
AND BETTERBETTERBETTERBETTER'S THE WAY
I'M GONNAGONNAGONNAGONNA STAAAAY-YA

Lurky

If I lean out of the window and look down the City Road I see all the houses and the windows and doors in them, with rooms and rooms behind the windows and doors. I feel like I'm looking behind a forest or into a deep ocean. Behind the streets there's office blocks and shop buildings. On a hill there's a group of tower blocks. They look like frilly bricks from this distance.

I'm part of a tribe. We live behind the windows and doors. Sometimes we go out in the streets, quick enough to shop or to visit each other. In this part of town, in the houses and the flats, one above the other, side by side, there are many tribes. Shop assistants, clerks, office workers, that sort of thing. The Asians, running their shops or keeping their homes; the West Indians, the Irish, the Poles, the people who like this and do that – all tribes, mixed together and jumbled up. Going about their lives, rubbing shoulders, doing deals.

I don't have much to do with the rest of them. I only see them. I have my own life to live.

I had Richard round here the other day to say goodbye.

He's going on a trip to South-East Asia. Thailand, Bali, then on to Australia. He wanted me to go with him. I laughed. What with? I don't have any money.

'I'll lend you some,' he said.

I just shook my head.

I impress myself sometimes. He thinks I'm worth offering a thousand quid to and I don't do anything. I get on with my life, I do my business. I don't try. And he still thinks I'm worth giving a thousand to. I know he said lend, but we both know I'd never get round to giving it back, no matter how good my intentions were.

I knew what was behind it, of course. He thought if I went with him I might leave the smack alone. He used to come round regularly to nag me.

'It'll kill you. It is killing you. You're really boring these days,' he told me.

I said, 'So are you.'

He just shook his head.

'I don't have to go running off to Asia to keep myself interesting, Richard,' I told him.

'I hope you find it just as interesting being dead as you have being alive,' he told me.

That's the trouble with most people. They want to live forever. When you turn round to them and tell them that you're just living your life and if that means you'll be dead in three years, that's okay by you, they hate that. There's no answer to that. If you don't mind not reaching twenty there's no argument against heroin, is there?

You have to face facts. There was this thing with Alan and Helen, this really spooky thing. I was just getting to know them quite well. I can't remember where I met them, but they used to turn up at our place to score. Then they got into a bit of dealing. He was the handsomest bloke I ever met. He was dark and all hairy. Hairy chest, black hair on his arms. He had to shave twice a day. Well, he never did, of course, but if he wanted to keep clean shaven he had to. He had beautiful eyes, like liquid gold, and those even, good-looking sort of features. He could have been a model, except maybe he was even a bit too pretty. People used to sit staring at him. I used to myself. Then if he caught you looking, he'd fling back his head and put out his arms into this model-man pose.

He was a laugh. He always played up to it, posing like a model in the magazines. He had this really silly shirt, with a picture of a dragon on the front of it, all picked out in tiny little fairy lights. Sometimes if it was getting dark he'd turn the shirt on and sit there with his head flung back, like Erik the Viking, and this stupid shirt flashing on and off.

Helen was a frizzy blonde, quite pretty, with a turned-up little nose. She was from Birmingham, I think. She was quite lively, I didn't really know why she was with Alan, because he was a bit thick. I think she just thought she had it made because he was so good looking, and he made quite a lot of money dealing.

Anyway, Rob had some sort of a deal with them, for some stuff. There was a shortage on. Me and Gems had a little bit but we didn't want to share it because it was all we had, it was just a tiny little bit. It happened like this. They were out of town organising this stuff, and they rang Rob in the evening to tell him it was sorted and he could come and get his. He went round straight away to their place and the light was on, but he couldn't get an answer. He banged on the door and shouted up ... nothing. They were in Brook Road, just round the corner. He didn't want to make too much fuss. It's bad manners, you know, to make a fuss outside a dealer's house, so he came back to wait at home.

'They only rang me up half an hour ago and they never said they were going anywhere. I told them I was coming round,' he said. He looked awful, sitting there chewing away at the skin round his nails.

'Maybe they got busted,' said Lily. She was sitting on the floor with her arms round her legs all wrapped up in a cardigan. They were both really going through it. I really felt for them. Yuk. It's like, every little thing that happens is too much. It almost hurts sometimes, even when someone's just saying hello.

He hung around for half an hour and then went back; same thing, no answer. We were getting a bit worried by this time. Alan and Helen never went anywhere. If they said they'd be in, they were in. Everyone was thinking the same thing. You see, it wasn't all that likely they'd been busted because the police'd still have been round there half an hour after they rang up. On the other hand ... well, we all knew people OD. You heard about it. But ...

Rob was getting paranoid because he was scared to go round in case they had been busted and the place was being watched. I went and walked past to have a look for him but I didn't dare knock. When I got back Lily was getting really pissy, blaming Rob and getting on at me and Gems just because we had some and they didn't. She wanted someone to go round and bust in. There was a window open at the back, but it was up on the first floor; it would have meant shinning up the drainpipe.

'You do it, Tar, you're all right,' said Rob.

'No way, it's your stuff.'

'You're all right, how'd you like to go breaking into someone's place when you're coming down?'

We started squabbling until Lily suddenly lost her temper.

'Just bloody someone go round and sort it out, okay?' she screamed, and she started walking round the place kicking things. She was getting really wound up. She started punching the doors and making a mess of her hands. So Rob and I looked at each other, and we decided to go together.

We didn't have to climb in the window in the end. Gemma remembered that this other friend of ours who lived a few doors down from Alan and Helen had a key in case they got locked out. He didn't want to give it to us at first, but once we'd explained to him, he handed it over.

'You can come in with us if you'd like to make sure it's all straight,' said Rob. But funnily enough, the guy didn't want to.

We just opened the door and walked in. It was like normal at first. They were just sitting next to each other on the sofa. Helen had slumped a little sideways on to him and he was just sitting there staring straight ahead as if he was thinking about something. It smelt a bit funny. She looked like she was asleep. His eyes were wide open.

Rob said, 'Are you okay?' and I thought at first he was talking to me but he wasn't. We both knew at once. They were blue. Then I saw the needles in their arms.

Rob looked at me. Then he went into the room and started creeping about opening drawers and looking on the shelves.

I went up close to have a look. I touched him on the arm and he was quite cold. Behind me Rob was rushing about, faster and faster. I think he was freaked out but I didn't mind so much as him. They looked just like themselves but they weren't moving. Alan was still gorgeous. She'd gone a bit thin lately, it didn't suit her. So had he but it made him look even nicer if anything. I wanted to kiss her on the cheek because I knew she couldn't wake up. It was like the Sleeping Beauty.

It was all so realistic. I kept waiting for him to move, and then for her to move and then for him to move, but they never did. I touched his cheek again. I thought of cold meat.

'Bloody get away from them and help me!' hissed Rob. We started pulling stuff out of the drawers and running about.

He found it in the end – two bagsful, it must have been not far off an ounce.

That was a lot of junk. It was more than I'd ever seen.

'It's probably dead pure as well,' said Rob, nodding at Alan and Helen. We giggled ... you know, dead pure.

'What shall we do with it?'

'Well they're not going to need it.'

I felt like we were stealing it even though they were both dead. I had this feeling they were waiting, that they were trying to trick us into stealing their stuff. I looked at them and shook the little bag at them as if to say, Is it all right? Then I noticed little details I'd missed the first time, like the sticky under their noses and in their eyes. Then I saw a fly walking across his face and I just flipped. I yelled and ran. Rob ran after me. We were down those stairs and out of the house in seconds.

Once we got the stuff back home we were all scared stiff of using it. Then someone heard the police give a warning on the radio to all the junkies that there was some extra-strong stuff about that was killing people. You get used to taking your usual hit, see, and so people were ODing. Wow! We had a party for Alan and Helen. That bag lasted for ages. It took the police a week to get round there and knock the door down.

I ring up my mum sometimes.

I do it when I'm alone. It's private. I don't know why I do it, they've got nothing to do with me any more. Just to see if she's all right, or what they're up to, or just checking that they're still there. Or maybe I do it because I want to show myself that I can take it. I can deal with her these days. Sometimes I have to remind myself that I can.

I'm usually walking down the road and I decide to do it just like that. I just walk into the phone box and pick up the phone and dial and there she is. Suddenly. Like she was at my elbow the whole time but I never saw her, all these months.

She has this way of answering the phone. She drawls Maybe it's the booze, but I think she's watching herself in the mirror above the sofa in the lounge where the phone is, and she's thinking how cool she looks with her fag in her hand and her lipstick smeared off her lips and her dress hanging off her shoulder. Really – she thinks she looks cool. She's lost her whole personality to that poison and she thinks it makes her look cool.

'Heeeeeeeelllllooo,' she says, like she's on a film. My heart starts going like a fire engine.

'Hi, Mum.'

And straight away, she changes. I can feel her moving quickly, I can hear her put her drink down and sit up. Then there's this pause. She's waiting for me, letting me dangle. She used to scare the shit out of me like that. These days, I let her dangle, too. I wait for her to speak.

Off she goes. Am I all right, how dare I not get in touch before, do I need help, how much she's missing me, do I have somewhere to stay? How she keeps hearing about kids sleeping out on the streets and she prays every night it isn't me.

What god would possibly want to listen to her?

'No, Mum, I've got it sorted out, thanks.'

'But, darling, is there anything you need?'

'I was just ringing up to see how you were. You haven't left him, then?'

'He's your father, David.' Pause. 'Darling, tell me about it.'

Pause.

'Tell you about what?'

'Everything.'

For a minute I start getting confused. Then I hear her drink clinking on her teeth, and I think, Oh, yeah. I know what's she's up to.

It's pathetic, really. She only has this one trick and she plays it over and over again. And yet she nearly gets me with it still. It's the same thing – dangling, you see. Asks you some twisted question, or makes these remarks which aren't quite right. And you get nervous and then more nervous and then more and more nervous with the long silences, so you end up babbling away and all you can hear is her sucking her fag or sipping her drink, so you end up saying anything, promising her anything on earth, just to get her to acknowledge you.

And then when you're just about begging her to say something, to say anything, she launches a rocket at you. Like, 'He beats me up, darling ...' Or, 'I think I might have cancer.' Or, 'I want to leave him but I have to have someone to help me ...'

So when I hear her teeth clinking on the glass and her sucking her fag and waiting for me to start falling at her feet, I just keep quiet and then I say, 'I haven't got anything to tell you.'

She says, 'David,' in an injured voice. Then she gives me the rocket anyway. 'He's been beating me again.'

Maybe. Maybe not. I just keep my mouth shut and let her have a taste of what she tried on me. And it works, too, that's the amazing thing. She starts blabbing and blabbing and blabbing and then the blabbing turns to blubbing

'I can't help you, Mum. You have to help yourself. You have to leave Dad and pack in the booze. No one can help you until you do that. Can't you see that, Mum? I tell you what,' I say, 'I'll come back if you do that.'

Of course I know she never will.

Sometimes my dad's there. He takes the phone.

'David? David? Are you all right, David?'

I haven't got anything to say to him. I just breathe down the phone, 'Hurrrrrrrrrrrrrrrrrr,' very softly but loud enough for him to hear. Just like I used to hear her breathe when she was letting me dangle and breathing out her fag smoke.

'David, is this some sort of joke?'

I listen a bit more, but I really have got nothing to say to my dad. So I put the phone down, carry on my way. I don't know if I'll bother doing it again.

I always think that, but I always do.

19
Gemma

WHEN SOMEONE TEMPTS YOU YOU CAN'T REFUSE
IT'S GETTING COLDER AND YOU KNOW YOU'VE
GOT NOTHING TO LOSE
YOU NEED IT
NO YOU GOT NOTHING TO LOSE
YOU NEED IT

The Only Ones

Lily was in her pyjamas. She almost never goes out these days, so she doesn't need to get dressed. She was looking at herself in the mirror. Then she turned round to watch Sally push down the needle and smiled that big Lily smile.

'Yeah! Sal?'

'Better,' sighed Sally. She took the needle out of her arm. She wiped it carefully on the tissue and put it down. Sally is always so neat and delicate.

We always use separate needles ever since we started work. You've got to be sensible. We used to share because it was only with each other. These days I only ever share with Tar. If I got something like Aids, he'd get it anyway.

Then Lily said this thing right out of the blue. She said, 'I'm going to have a baby.'

Christ!

'Oh, my God! What are you going to do, what are you going to do?'

174

'Oh, Lils,' said Sally sadly.

It was *so* awful. Sally was pregnant a while ago and she had an abortion and she felt dreadful for ages after.

I said, 'Have you told the doctor yet? Has he given you a date?'

Lily glared at me. I could feel myself shuffle back on the bed a bit, because she really has a temper and she doesn't often glare at me because we're soul sisters.

She leaned across to me. 'Listen, Mrs Sister. You know what dead babies do. They come back and *haunt* you. They're all over the place, I see 'em. Yeah – dead babies floating on the ceiling looking for their mums 'cause their mums had 'em scraped out and they never had a life ...' She kept glancing across at Sal as she said all that stuff. I started remembering how when Sal had her abortion Lils was all quiet about it, just smiled and never said a thing. Now Sal was looking upset, and I thought, O-oh ...

'I'm not gonna kill my baby. That's my baby. No one's gonna kill my baby.'

'I didn't say kill it.'

'I said, I'm going to have a baby. I'm going to *have* it. There's gonna be a baby. A baby, Gems ...'

I glanced at Sally. Even though she looks so prim Sally's got a terrible temper. She said, 'You're on the game and you're a junkie, Lily. You ought to have an abortion.'

'Are you telling me to kill my baby? Are you telling me ...?'

'You ought to have an abortion for the sake of your baby.'

'You want to kill my baby? You wanna? You wanna kill it? Come on, come on, you kill it then, you do it now.'

'Your baby is a junkie. Your baby is inside you and it's full of junk, same as you. You want to give birth to a junkie? Is that what you want? Is that how much you love your bloody baby?'

Lily's eyes were absolutely bulging out of her head. 'I'm

a fucking junkie, are you telling *me* I'd be better off dead because I'm a junkie? Are you telling me that?'

'I'm telling you it's not fair to your baby to be pregnant with it while you're full of junk. What sort of a mother ...?'

She didn't need to say any more. Lils was up off the bed walking up and down the room, poking herself on the chest and trying to find the words. I just held my breath. When those two start, you take cover. I was getting ready to disappear under the table.

Finally Lily got it out. 'I can give it up any time I want ...'

Sally just laughed. I mean, it wasn't funny but under other circumstances it would've been. The number of times we'd tried to give up – I'd lost count. I dunno why. It used to be easy. Maybe the comedown's worse when you've been using for a while. First you get the shivers. Then you get the aches, then the cramps start in your guts, then it's the squits and you're diving into the bog every five minutes. Then your teeth start aching, and your bones begin to hurt, and then you feel sick in the pit of your stomach and then you're throwing up.

And all it takes is one little needle and Lady Heroin makes you feel ... mmmmm. The days when you could say what Lily said – they were long gone.

I was gobsmacked. It never occurred to me she might want a baby. I mean, apart from the junk, well, it could be anyone's.

Lily gave Sal this look. She looked ... And Sal was sitting on the bed still and she started to get up because it looked as though Lils was going to land one on her ...

Then Lily just turned round and walked out of the room.

It was *awful*.

Sal sat back down and lit up a fag. I just stood there. I said, 'Let's have one.' She gave me a fag and I paced up and down the room smoking, trying to get calm. Sal took a few more drags then she said, 'I think I better go.'

I said, 'Don't go, don't go, it'll be all right, it'll be all right.' She'd gone white; she had a temper almost as bad as Lil's. She didn't run around screaming but she was just as bad. Next door, Lils put some music on – 'Lurking About' – feel-good music, our theme tune. The music was filling up the house; the feel-good wasn't coming in through the bedroom door yet, but I could just imagine Lily jiving around the front room, getting herself back.

I said, 'See? She'll be okay.'

The track was about halfway through when the door opens and Lily comes back in. She was jiving about, glancing up at me and Sal, but jiving about like she was in her own space. She was singing along. 'Lurkying, lurkying, lurkying about ...'

She fiddled with some stuff on her dressing table. She started to smile her big Lily smile .. then she came over and sat on the bed and put her arms around Sal.

'Okay, Sal? Okay?'

'Yeah, I'm okay.'

'All right, Sal, mates again. Soul sisters ...'

'Yeah, soul sisters, eh?' Although Sal didn't exactly sound convinced.

Lily got up and started walking up and down in the space between the bed and wall. 'There's gonna be a baby, right? It's a fact. That's just all there is to it. Right ... a baby. Right? Think about it. I'm gonna be a mother. Everything's gotta change. Right? Like Sal says, I can't do junk if I'm a mother. See? I can't. You can't come round here smacked up when I'm gonna be a mother. See ...?'

I said, 'Yeah, yeah,' just to keep things cool, really, at that point.

'There's gonna be a baby, Sal, I'm gonna have a baby. I'm gonna be a mother and you're gonna be its mother and so's Gemma and we're all gonna get clean and live the real life ...'

She looked at us, just willing us to think like her. She said, 'You're not gonna come round here junked up, you're not gonna give me smack when I'm pregnant ...'

'No, right, no,' I said. Even Sally was nodding now.

'See?' Lils was grinning from ear to ear. And I began to feel it.

'*Everything's* gotta change. You don't do smack when there's babies. It was good but now it's on to something else ...'

I began to see what she was on about. We started talking. It turned out she's over a month gone already. We'll have a baby in the house for Christmas.

A baby.

It means you have to live another life ...

You can see it, can't you? Lily can't be on smack while she's got a little baby growing inside her. That wouldn't be fair. And it's not fair on her to do it all on her own. So, we're all going to pack it in together, just like we've done everything together ever since we met. Out of solidarity to Lily. Out of solidarity to the baby.

That's how it happened. The change. Because it all started making sense. After about a couple of days no one could talk about anything else.

Lily and Rob had already started making plans. He was gonna get a job and we were all going to move off the City Road, where, let's face it, it's pretty squalid. And Lil was coming off the game and she was gonna grow veg in the garden and keep chickens and everything.

Lily'll be its mother, of course, no one can be its mother and father except her and Rob, but the baby will belong to all of us. Rob and Tar are going to build a swing in the garden, a little one just for the baby. All right, it'll be a while before it's big enough, but still. And they've been out round the skips looking for a cot and all that sort of baby stuff. And

Sally and me are going to knit – imagine! Me knitting!

And the first thing – the big thing – we're all going to give up smack. That's it. It was good for a while. No, I don't regret it, why should I? Okay, there's been casualties, there always are. You walk across the road, there's casualties. But now it's gone on for too long. It's time ... we've all known that for a long time, it was just a question of the right thing, the right time. And now it's come, courtesy of Lils, as usual.

The way I look at it, I had a love affair – but now it's over. Me and Junk, we've fallen out. It's just so right that we all get led out of it by a little baby. You know? Like baby Jesus.

A baby is different, isn't it?

I'm really looking forward to being clean again. It's this weird thing with smack. First off it makes you feel so good. But after a bit, after your body gets used to it, it stops working like that. You start needing it just to stay normal. You know? So you wake up feeling disgusting because you're coming down. So you do some and you feel okay, but that's all you feel. It's like medicine. You get like some old woman who has to take her pills in the morning in order to get through the day.

So what you do then is take more and more and more, chasing that dragon, chasing that hit, chasing that feel-good feeling. You take more and more and more, and more often. Then you get sick of it and give up for a few days. And that's the really nasty thing because then, when you're clean, that's when it works so well. That's when you can take a hit and mmmmmmmmmmmmm!

We've all been talking about it and we've realised – we all feel the same way. I was getting scared. Rob and Lily do so much. Every day. Tar and me have days off, at least.

Actually, though, Tar scares me, too. He's got so cynical. You know Tar, he was always so delighted by things. He used to get so emotional about, I dunno – me, a flower, the stars out at night, it was all wonderful for him. These days he doesn't care any more. I don't understand him these days.

I don't feel that I've changed, except I feel so rotten a lot of the time. But he has.

Sometimes I think I preferred him the way he used to be, almost. Not really, he used to get so upset, but ...

And the other thing is, he lies. About smack. You know? Like, we've run out, it happens from time to time. He tells me he has none left, and I think, Shit, that means coming down. But then he sneaks off and when he comes back he's got eyes like glass, and I say, 'You've just had some.'

And he admits it. That actually happened the other day. He just sat there smiling and nodding, 'Yeah, yeah, I had a bit ...' And he starts explaining to me that he didn't have enough for two and how if we'd shared it we'd both feel awful so he thought it would save a lot of trouble for both of us if he took it on his own. And he's serious. He's actually convinced himself that this is sensible behaviour and he gets really put out when I don't agree.

'You could have given it to me,' I said.

And he said, 'I could have done. But I didn't.' And he smiles like a snake at me. Then he's going on about how he's got to go out and score some so he *needs* it more than me. I have to go and rub up old men at the parlour. Does he think that's fun? Does he think I like that? Doesn't he know I'd rather be out of it when I do that?

But it doesn't make any difference. He believes anything he tells himself. 'I *need* it, Gems,' he says. Yeah.

Imagine! A baby ... Actually it's made me go all broody. What if I got pregnant? We could bring them up together and they'd be really good friends just like me and Lily. I know you can't tell how your kids are going to turn out but I really think we all live so close together they'd be bound to be friends. I'm sixteen now. I could go on the dole. I could pack my job in ...

That'd be nice. It's started to get me down doing that job. I keep telling myself that it's just a job, it's easy money. It's no worse than any other job. People have a prejudice about sex, but it's just something you do with your body. I jolly myself into it. Sometimes I think, I'm here to make these people happy, and I do. On a good day I see these guys walk into the parlour looking like dogs and they walk out like princes. Let's face it, they'd never get a girl like me if they couldn't pay for it. But ... well, it's still a job, you know? I can think of better ways to be spending my time. It's easy money, that's all.

I'm thinking I'll stop doing tricks at work – I mean, full sex. It'd be up to me, you don't earn as much but you can still do all right. Maybe when we're all clean I'll pack up altogether and have a baby, too.

Did I tell you, Lily turned blue the other day?

It was really frightening. We were all out in the back bedroom with the works. We were taking turns. There were some friends of ours in the front room, so after we'd done we went through to see them. Lily was last so she was on her own. I thought it was funny at the time because Lily is never last usually, when it comes to getting her smack.

I only went back because I'd left my fags in there. She was lying on the bed and I thought she was asleep but she was this strange colour. Blue. I just stared; I didn't realise what I was looking at until I saw the needle in her arm. Then I thought about what Tar said about Alan and Helen. The needle was still in, you see. There was a little blood had found its way into the works and ...

'Tar, Rob, Tar, Rob!' I screamed. I thought she was already dead. I jumped over and I hauled her upright on the bed. Then I remembered the blood in the works and that's supposed to be really dangerous, you can get air in your bloodstream and if that little bubble gets round to your brain ... So I tore the needle out quick and I ripped her arm doing it and this black blood oozed out of the hole. Black blood. I was thinking about Alan and Helen, I never thought it could happen to any of us. Rob came in, then Tar. She was getting bluer and bluer. Tar pushed her back on the bed because he wanted to press her heart, but Rob was pulling her upright; he had this feeling she ought to be upright. I started slapping her face, whack, whack, whack. Then she twitched.

In the silence that followed she took two little sips of air. I could hear them. It was so shallow, her breath.

We all stopped breathing then, I think. And so did she. I slapped her again and again and again and she took another breath, a deep shuddering one this time, and a little pink came into her face.

Then we got her on her feet and started marching her round and round the room. She started to come round and she was muttering something. I was really terrified because – it was really strange this – I thought she had some message, you know, from the other side. Because she'd died, she'd stopped breathing, her heart had stopped. I had this awful feeling that she was coming back from the dead with some terrible message for us, like in a horror story. I really wanted them to put her down and just let her die ...

Then the words started getting clearer, and all it was was 'Leave me alone, leave me alone ...'

She was all right after that. She began to come round. It was so weird because she was just normal. I mean, if I hadn't gone back for another few minutes she'd have been dead. And here she was, just like Lily, normal.

Later, when she came out of the smack a bit, she tried to make a joke out of it. 'Live fast, die young,' Lily kept saying. But it just wasn't funny. But what was weird, *she* was laughing. She found it funny. I honestly think she wouldn't have minded dying. Like it was just another adventure.

It turned out she'd stayed behind and had another little one. But the stuff was stronger than usual. We'd all been remarking on that in the front room while she was dying in the back room.

The really awful thing was ... I mean, the other awful thing was ... You see, it was nearly two weeks ago, that. No one has said anything. I know, I know, it's just a blob of jelly at this point, it isn't a person or anything. But I still keep thinking of how whatever it is went blue inside her as well. It'd be dreadful if the baby wasn't all right.

I know I'm being stupid. She wasn't out for long. It's very early days. If anything is wrong she'll probably miscarry or something. But it would be so dreadful. If she has a miscarriage I'll think about that all the time.

A baby! Imagine ...

20
Rob

We were going to get Dev to drive us down, but that was too risky. He wasn't giving anything up. Why should he?

I haven't got a licence, but I've been driving since I was a kid. I'm seventeen, I should take the test but ... I've got better things to do, I suppose.

The cottage belongs to a friend of Wendy. Wendy's my mum. It's a sort of holiday let, but this was April and it was a bit early in the season so it was a stroke of luck it was free that week. A whole week. Wendy used to take me there in the winter when I was a kid. At the time I'd been bored but now, when I thought about it, it was perfect. Miles from anywhere, beautiful countryside, no people, no hassle, no problems. They'd all fall in love with it. I was really looking forward to it myself. We drove along and I felt like I was taking them to another world.

We'd finished off the last of our smack before we set out, and we had just a tiny little bit, a dab, just to get us to bed that night so in the morning we could start right from scratch. Bare-brain riding, Lily called it. Riding life with nothing on ...

Tar was next to me, map reading. Lily and Gemma and Sal were larking about in the back. It was a great feeling, watching Bristol slip past. Getting on to the M4 and seeing the countryside. I don't think any of us had seen the countryside for two or three years. Fields, space with no one in it. Trees.

We were leaving everything behind. All the shit. The baby was the real magic spell and Lily was the witch who was making it. What does that make me? A magician, I suppose. It's a bit like that. Me, a dad. With my magic wand.

Gemma and Sals were really into it. Sal had been a bit doubtful at first, but now she was as keen as anyone. It was a real chance. She and Gems were already talking about having babies themselves.

'It's gonna be like a farm at this rate ...' I said. And they all howled with laughter.

I dunno. I know Lils better than any of them, see. This baby. Well, it's part of life, isn't it? Whether it's a good thing or a bad thing, babies, they just happen. But I wasn't so sure how great it was going to be this time. I kept my mouth shut. Anyway, you never know. You never know with Lils, that much is true.

They had a few spliffs and they were sitting in the back there singing the No More Song.

> NO MORE NEEDLES
> NO MORE FOR ME
> NO MORE NEEDLES
> NOW I AM FREE ...

And then giggling and nudging one another and beginning another one.

> NO MORE PUNTERS
> NO MORE FOR ME
> NO MORE PUNTERS
> 'CAUSE NOW I'M FREE-EE ...

The stuff they were giving up. I said, 'You lot are going to give up your whole lives.'

'Nah,' said Lils. 'That's the one thing I'm gonna keep, 'cause I'm too precious, I am ...'

Tar was, I dunno, not so up as the others. I was annoyed, because it wasn't his baby and he could've been a bit more supportive. Lily was eyeing him up and I thought, She's going to have a go at him later on unless he comes round a bit. He was going on about a lot of the stuff they give to babies in hospital – you know, when women go in to give birth they give them this to stop the pain, then they give them that to start the labour, something else to keep the baby breathing – I mean, half the world is drugged up at birth.

I said, 'I don't think now's the time to go on about that,' because it couldn't make it any easier for Lily to pack smack in, if he was telling her about all the crap they were going to fill her and her baby with in hospital. He glanced at me a bit resentfully but he kept his gob shut after that. He had a few joints but ... he looked a bit anxious to me. We spent most of the time talking about the route.

NO MORE HAND JOBS
NO MORE FOR ME-EE
NO MORE HAND JOBS
'CAUSE NOW I'M FREE-EE ...

We were all talking about how great it was to give up smack. I was watching, thinking, Who's going to make it? Who's going to make it?

NO MORE JUNKIES
NO MORE FOR ME-EE
NO MORE JUNKIES
NOW I'M FREE

***

It was dark when we got there. Griffin Cottage. When we got out of the car we stood for a bit on the grass.

The dark and the quiet were so intense. It was like standing on a hill in outer space. You couldn't see anything but you could feel how it went on forever and ever all around you ...

'It must be as dark as this all the way to the next star,' said Tar. Yeah. It was so dark the dark was like, filling it all up, as if it had been poured in. And there was nothing going on. No noise. If you held your breath there was nothing. That was so amazing after being in Bristol for all those years, because in Bristol you can always hear the cars buzzing away or the noise of people doing things. There was no one doing anything within twenty miles of here.

I thought, Tomorrow I'm going to be able to do anything. I think we all felt like that.

Inside was smaller than I remembered. This tiny sitting room and two bedrooms and the kitchen sort of tacked on the back. The toilet was an outside one. That part of Wales is like that – timeless. It was cold, it was colder inside than it was outside. There were a few logs left in the basket by the fire and me and Tar went out and got some more. We took it in turns chopping logs while the girls made some tea and got the stuff out of the car and tidied up a bit.

Every time we swung the axe – thup, into the wood – you could hear the echo come back a few seconds later.

I said, 'It's the mountains.' We peered into the darkness. We shone the light out down the hill but we couldn't see a thing. It was too far off.

I said, 'They're out there somewhere.'

He said, 'Standing around watching us.'

I said, 'Nah, they don't take any notice of us.'

He said, 'Do you think they're friendly?'

I said, 'Yeah, definitely friendly.'

Whole mountains without a light on them. There were stars out, it was quite a clear night but there was no moon. We turned off the lamp and stood on the wet grass waiting for our eyes to acclimatise. But it was so dark they never did. We used the gaps in the sky where there were no stars to try and work out where the mountains were, but we couldn't really do it. Those mountains had really hidden themselves well.

'What do you think of it?' I said.

'I could live here,' he said.

I laughed. 'You'd get bored. It used to drive me mad when I was a kid.'

'No, no. I really love it here.'

I said, 'Be honest, you didn't think much of this idea, did you?'

We were standing next to each other. I could just make him out. This ghostly voice.

He said, 'I didn't think anyone really wanted to.'

I waited.

'But I think now ... maybe we can do it.' I could feel him looking at me. It was funny – I couldn't see a thing but I could feel him. 'What about you?' he asked.

I laughed. 'Oh, yeah. Well, we gotta, haven't we? For Lils.'

Personally I was determined to have a real go at it. I had a little package in my pocket no one knew about, and I almost thought about throwing it away, but I didn't want to muck things up. I'm lousy at that coming down bit. I'm all right after that but I do need something to let me come down slowly. You have to find the best way of going about it. That little packet was right for me.

We stood for a while breathing big long breaths of air. It was cold and pure, you could feel it falling down into your chest. You could feel it inside you, doing you good. Then we went in to light the fire.

We all had our little dab and a bit to drink that night – not much, a couple of cans of Special Brew, because the last thing you want when you're coming down is to wake up with a hangover.

I got up early. I said to Lils, 'Do you want a cuppa tea?' and she smiled yes. She looked so beautiful lying there in bed. I kissed her and went out into the kitchen.

Tar and Gemma were already up, outside, drinking coffee. They called me to come and see and I went out.

It was tremendous. This soft, cool, clear air and now you could see it all, miles and miles of it, mountains and hills and forest. There was a buzzard circling about. Little birds hopped about in the firs nearby. No one said anything. We just stared and sipped our drinks. Then I went to get Lily up and she sat on a pile of logs and we all just looked and looked. It was like soaking something up. I felt I could soak it up forever and never be full.

Lils patted her stomach. 'This is all for you, yeah,' she said. We all laughed and I thought, Lucky little git.

We did the big breakfast, bacon and eggs and that, then we went for a walk. We were all still feeling a little run down, like you do at the beginning. Sals said in Bristol by this time, she'd be feeling shitty, but out here it was okay. It was this feeling that the air was so good we couldn't feel bad at all. Which was a bit of a mistake, really, looking back.

We walked down this track, downhill. It soon ran into woods, big tall trees, quite a lot of light coming through. We saw squirrels and birds. It was nice. Then there was this walk up the hill and that did us all in – none of us had walked more than down the road for years, I suppose. Then we went down another hill and this time we were in a plantation, little trees all packed in together.

That wasn't so good. It was man-made. It was dark, they pack those trees so close together. We carried on.

It was the woods, I suppose. It was all dead – dead little

trees all packed in neat little rows, like a tree factory. Nothing growing underneath and nothing in between as if these baby trees were poisoning the ground.

Actually, I was all right. I'd had a little dab out of my packet earlier – you know, just wetted the end of my finger and stuck it in, not enough to get a hit. Just enough to keep the heebie jeebies away. I didn't even notice the others, but I was thinking maybe I hadn't done enough and I ought to slip off and do a bit more when Lily suddenly said,

'Fuck this. Fuck this!'

We all jumped. Right out there in the middle of nowhere. She was standing there with her foot up to the ankle in this rut full of water. She was livid. She was only wearing these black felt shoes she wears all the time, not really what you go for a country walk in. I had a look round and I could see everyone was looking shifty and jaded and I thought, O-oh.

Lily turned round and stomped back up the hill towards the cottage. We'd been planning this really long walk over the hills and dales to get the toxins out of our systems. I could have carried on a bit, but you could see at a glance that the others had had it.

We didn't talk much on the way back, but I did have a chat with Sally. She didn't seem too bad either and I had an idea maybe she'd had a dab an' all. I was going to ask her, but it was a bit risky. About halfway home Gemma suddenly turned round and she said, 'God, I didn't expect to feel this bad, this is awful ...'

Me and Sals just laughed. It was funny – what did she expect? None of them was expecting it. Me, like I say, I'd taken precautions. But when Lils looked at me I stopped laughing because, shit, she really did look awful. Clammy. She'd been doing a lot lately. Well, let's be honest, we all have. I'd have given her a dab as well, but they'd all been making such a big thing about getting right off it once and for all and I didn't want to make it worse for her. You know, you build yourself up to do something and then you fail – it doesn't help, does it? Besides, there was the baby. That was why we were all there, right? Not just for Lily. For the baby. And it was my baby too.

'It'll be easier tomorrow,' I said. Lils gave me this dirty look, and I thought, I wonder if she knows?

We got back. We built a big fire to try and make it cosy and we started smoking joints to try and keep the heebie jeebies away.

Tar and Lily were having the worst time. Sal and Gemma were sitting together bolstering one another. Gems was saying, 'I don't care how bad I feel, I'm not going to crack.' She's strong. She meant it. She and Sal they're two tough ladies.

Lils wouldn't talk about it. 'Yeah, I'm all right, you worry about your own head,' she said. But she wouldn't look any of us in the eye.

As for Tar, he was looking very fishy. I think the joints were a mistake for him. Tar's one of those people who don't take to hash so well. He started to get that anxious look he used to have, and he was going for little walks on his own, which made Lily ask him if he had a little stash of his own, which he denied. I'm fairly sure he didn't actually, because he was a mess. He started talking about getting some booze.

'You'd only get a hangover, and then what about tomorrow?' asked Gemma.

'I need it, I need it, Gems, you don't understand,' he said.

'You can't make coming down feel good, you just have to go through it,' Sally told him. By this time, Sal and me were smirking a bit at one another when one of us said something like that. It was, like, I know you know and you know I know but neither of us is going to say anything. Lils had the cramps by now, so did Gemma. Tar didn't get the cramps so much, but pretty soon he started throwing up. Whereas me and Sal ... well, I was moaning about how foul I felt and so was she. But ... well ...

Finally, it must have been about four o'clock in the afternoon, Tar said, 'I've had enough of this, I'm going to hitch in and get some booze.'

I said, 'I'll give you a lift.' There was a village nearby but they didn't sell anything. The nearest offie was a good five miles away and anyway, Tar was only sixteen. They might refuse to serve him.

He didn't want a lift at first. He said he wanted to go on his own. But of course once it was established he was going, everyone wanted something to drink, so I ended up driving him in anyway.

Well. We got there all right, bought some cider and beer. Then he said, 'I'm going to walk back.'

I just looked at him.

'No, I want to.'

'Five miles, Tar.'

'I just want to clear my head.'

I thought, Oh yeah. I didn't say what I was thinking, but we were both thinking it. I watched him in the mirror as I drove off. He stood there watching my back but he didn't move until I was out of sight.

Things had gone downhill quite a lot while I was gone. They were all looking foul; there must have been an argument or something judging by the atmosphere. Gemma was getting violent stomach cramps. I thought, Wow, she must have been doing a lot to get those sort of symptoms. I handed over the cans and while they were opening them, I went into the bedroom for another dab. I figured, well, one of us better keep a clear head. But Lils followed me.

She just looked at me and said, 'Gimmee.'

I spread my hands. 'What do you mean, Lils?'

'Don't muck me around, I know what's going on. Now just give me mine, I want mine, all right ...?'

I fished around in my pocket. 'What about the baby?' I said.

'Don't give me that crap, you want me to get like Gemma? Yeah, that'll do the baby a whole lotta good. Right, yeah ...' She snatched the package off me and then pulled a piece of silver foil out of her pocket.

'I only had a dab,' I said.

'Yeah, how many? You haven't been coming down at all ...'

She wasn't that angry. I reckon she was pleased really, because if I hadn't brought any, where'd she be then?

Don't get it wrong. We weren't getting back on it but ... going away and just expecting to drop it was a bit unrealistic. You have to do these things bit by bit.

We didn't have any needles, we had to have a chase. Then we lay on the bed and listened to Gemma having a bad time. Sal was joining in but she wasn't so convincing. Lils had already guessed that she had some; they'd had an argument about it while I was away. They were really making a racket, moaning and groaning. After a bit we started to giggle. I mean, poor old Gemma was falling to pieces, Sal was making a fuss to keep her company, but in fact she was just like me and Lils, and all it took was a little dab I had in my pocket and Gems'd be as right as rain ... No, but I know it wasn't funny, it feels awful. But, you know ...?

Well. It went on till, I dunno, ten o'clock? Gemma was getting really agitated because Tar wasn't back. The village was only about five miles down the road and he'd been gone over five hours.

'Something's happened to him, he's done something silly,' said Gemma. She thought he'd topped himself or something!

I tried not to look at Lily but I couldn't help it. We both started snorting and laughing. It was no use, I couldn't keep a straight face with Lily looking at me like that. Gems didn't seem to notice that all the rest of us were okay. And as for Tar ...

It was just so obvious. Tar didn't have to kill himself. If he was that desperate there was a much easier way. Not that I'd fancy hitching all the way back to Bristol. He wasn't exactly wearing his woollies and overcoat. Come to that, I don't think he even owned one.

Poor old Gems, she was so worried about him. Her stomach cramps were really bad and ... it was getting silly. Then Sals started on at us because we were laughing about it.

We had to spill the beans. Lils got cross and she said, 'Look, Gemma, it's obvious ...' and she told her that Tar had certainly hitched back home for more smack.

That was the worst bit. Gemma was furious. She wouldn't have it at first. She more or less accused Lily of lying, and that's a bad thing to do. They started shouting and that's when Gems clicked that Lily and I had some.

And then there was a real major row.

'But what about your baby?' said Gemma. 'You just don't care, do you? You're doing that to your baby ...'

I thought, O-oh. I cleared off quick into the next room because you can tell Lily anything, but don't tell her she's doing her baby any harm ...

It was horrendous. They were screaming and yelling. Sal was quite pissed up by this time and she was having a go as well, which was a bit unfair because *she* was all right. I sat on the bed next door and listened. They were really digging up the dirt on one another. Finally Gemma came barging into our room in tears. Gemma's no good at that sort of thing, she starts crying. Sals and Lils'll carry on forever. We could hear them screaming at each other and Gemma said, 'Give me some, just ... give me, will you?'

I pulled the packet out. I was getting a bit worried because there wasn't much left but I couldn't say no, could I? She calmed down. Lils came in a bit later. She said, 'Are you all right now, Gems?'

'I'd have done it if just one of you bastards had hung out with me,' said Gems. And the whole thing started off again. I thought, This is no fun.

21
Gemma

We never even spent the second night.

On the way back no one said anything. A couple of times I tried to say how awful it was, but I just got 'Next time, next time, next time ...' We were all scared silly.

I'd tried to give up about half a dozen times, but I'd never been scared before. I mean, you've gotta take risks, we'd all been scared about ODing, or about getting stuck forever on junk, or about buggering up our veins, that sort of stuff. But that's just normal. This time was different, and I knew I really was a junkie this time because, what's a junkie scared of? Not Aids, not overdosing, like you might think. We were scared because there might be no more smack at the other end. It was the first time I'd felt like that. It was the first time I knew I couldn't get by without it.

Rob dashed round to Dev to score, but I was all right because Tar was at home when I got there and of course he'd already scored.

He was sitting on the settee. 'Home already, Gems?' he said, with this silly little I-told-you-so smile.

I walked across to the kitchen area and found the stuff in our usual stash place. I got my works together, put the kettle on. I sat down on the settee and did it.

You have no idea. You have no idea.

I could feel him watching me. 'You really hitchhiked all the way back?'

He pulled a face. 'I should have taken a bit with me.'

'Rob did.'

'I thought so.'

'Why didn't you ask him, instead of hitching all the way back?'

'I don't know.' Then he pulled a face and told me I wasn't to get at him; how did I think *he* felt about it? I got on with the tea. We drank our tea sitting on chairs at opposite ends of the table and he started again. He said it didn't matter anyway, because he hadn't really intended giving up, he only went along with it because the rest of us were so keen and he'd cleared off because he didn't want to tempt us.

'I like what I'm doing, why should I want to give up?' he said.

'And what happens when you turn blue, like Lily did?'

Tar gave me a grin and said, 'Live fast, die young, you know, Gems ...'

'You don't really think like that,' I said.

'You don't know anything about it when you're dead,' he said.

'Yeah. But no more junk for deadies ...' I teased.

It was quiet for a bit and then Tar got up to put some music on and he started talking ... how he felt better now, stronger; how he was going to have another crack in a week or so; he would have been all right but he knew Rob had some so it was going to fail anyway, but now it was different because he knew what he was up against ...

I sat there and I watched him. I wasn't even listening really. I was thinking about how much better he'd been these past few years. I'd really thought that, that he was better. But suddenly I really wanted the old Tar back. I wanted my Tar back.

I started to cry. I put my head in my hands. I said, 'You never even do anything to that sodding dandelion any more,' and I tried to squeeze back my tears.

Tar came and put his arms around me. 'I didn't mean it, Gems ... I was just saying that. I want to live and stay with you.'

I just wept.

'Dandelion,' he said.

I turned and buried my head against his stomach. 'Dandelion,' he said. 'Dandelion, dandelion, dandelion.'

'I love you,' I said. And I bloody meant it too.

'I've been waiting for you to say that all these years,' said Tar in a quiet voice. He stroked my face. I looked up at him. 'I love you too,' he said. 'I love you too. Dandelion.'

'Dandelion, dandelion, Tar.'

22
Skolly

It used to be a nice area round here. You look at the houses.
Big stone things, Victorian, Georgian, some of 'em. This
must have been a posh part of town, believe it or not. Even I
can remember when I was growing up, there was some posh
money about. And those of us who didn't have it, you'll've
heard this before, but it's true, we were all in it together.
There was a sense of community.

You just have to make the most of it, but I feel sorry for
some people. There's this old lady I know, she must be
ninety-odd, she's lived in St Paul's all her life. Now look at
it – the whole street is black. Reggae booming out all hours.
Curry everywhere. Muggings, drugs, prostitution. I mean
live and let live, all right, but she remembers the days when
all this was a good area. You never even saw a darkie when
she was a girl. I drop round there with some chocolate from
time to time and let her go on – not often, once she gets going
you can't stop her. But it is interesting.

Of course she makes it hard on herself – never goes out,
never talks to the neighbours. You can't blame her, they
probably taught you that darkies ate you when she was a kid.
She probably thinks the curry's full of old dears like her.

On the other hand she was probably a snooty old bag even
when she was young.

We had riots a while ago. Blacks, mainly. As usual. My shop

got smashed up, would you believe? And you know what they painted on the front?

'Fat Jew Bastard.'

Me ... a Jew? I ask you. I'm so Jewish, I think a bar mitzvah is a sort of biscuit. Fat ... all right. Bastard ... well, sometimes. But I'm no Jew-boy. Those Rastas are more Jewish than I am. Lost tribe of Israel – some of them believe that, I've read it. I'm Bristol-born, Bristol-bred. My dad was, and his dad before him. We go back for years. I admit my great grandfather was Jewish-ish. That's where the name comes from. I'd have changed it if I was bothered. I get a bit of stick about the name, but I never thought anyone'd smash up my shop because I had a Jewish name.

Even if I was Jewish, what have they got to get at me for? They're always going on about being picked on 'cause of their race; how do they think the Jews feel? Those darkies don't even know what persecution is. Actually, my side of the family had it easy, we were over here when everyone else was getting gassed over there, but still.

They've only been over here two generations, the West Indians. Didn't take 'em long to pick up the local prejudices, did it?

I'm going off the point. I was very upset about my shop.

Anyway, seediness. I say this because I was going down the road the other day, on my way for a pint at the Eagle, and there it was – the police car half up on the kerb, flashing lights, the ambulance blocking off the road, everything looking busy and no one in sight ...

It's always interesting when someone gets into trouble. Although this could have been more interesting if it was something else. The ambulance – it could just have been someone hurt themselves falling downstairs. Or a fight, something domestic. Now if it were armed robbery or supplying stolen goods – what you might call traditional crime – that would've been nearer home and something to tell the lads.

I did a little detour just to have a nose. I knew the house very well from years ago. On the corner, quite a nice big garden. I keep an eye on things but on the City Road there's always people moving in and out; you never know, you can't keep track of them all. I hadn't even noticed who lived there for donkey's.

I was walking down the road opposite and the door opened and these two ambulancemen came out, half carrying, half dragging this lad between them. The police car was going, flash, flash, flash. I dunno who he was, I don't remember seeing him before.

I thought – drugs. It had to be. This bloke, his head was on his chest, he was stumbling. He'd taken too much and given his mates a scare and they'd called the ambulance and now they were being done as well!

Typical.

I thought, Nah, not really my scene. I don't take drugs and I don't deal in them either, although I know some of the boys make a lot of money like that. I watched them load this lad into the back of the ambulance and I was about to head off down the Eagle when the door opened again. This time it was the cops, and they had this boy and a girl. The bloke was tall and thin with a scatty haircut. I didn't recognise him. The girl was young and pretty, or at least, she used to be. She was still young, but ... I knew her from a while back, you see ...

She used to work down the massage parlour on the Gloucester Road.

Now, don't go on at me. If you knew my missis. She's really let herself go. I mean, all right, we're both on the large size, but it's different for a bloke. Anyway, just getting the right bits in contact with each other is a matter of logistics these days and I don't think she's all that bothered the past few years. So, yes, I do have recourse to the massage parlour once in a while. If my horse comes up, or sometimes my brother comes over from Spain and we drop by before we head off on the beer. Or even on the way back, but the girls have to work for their money then.

I knew this one because ... first of all she was very young, younger than most of them. I like that. And then she was nice in the sense of having an attractive personality. That's important for me. I like to relate to a girl. Most of the girls don't like talking customers but this one liked me. At least, she gave that impression

The way it works is, you go in for an ordinary massage, see, and then you have to negotiate if you want a special – so much for this, so much more for that. You can always tell if they don't fancy you because they up the price. This one – Nicky, she called herself, not that that means anything – this one drove a very hard bargain, but in the end she'd always give me what I wanted. You know?

I'd say, 'I can't afford it, love.'

She'd say, 'Oh, well, you'll just have to have something else then.' Then halfway through she'd say, 'Oh, all right, since it's you ...' and she give it me anyway.

She didn't have the heart, see. All I had to do was look disappointed. She liked me. And then ... this is what I really liked about her ... she'd finish me off, and then I'd give her what she wanted in the first place. And she'd laugh her head off. Like we were mates. I mean, that's charming, innit? I like to think she liked me, but you don't know. Maybe she was just good at her job. I always went away after a session with Nicky feeling like a million quid.

Yeah, she was great, Nicky. We used to talk about all sorts. The other girls did you off and then wanted you straight out so they could get the next payer in, but not her. She really gave herself. She'd share her opinions with you. We used to talk politics, but not too much because we differed rather radically on that. She had some odd views on being a whore, though. Apparently, if it wasn't for people like Nicky, all the sad little blokes who didn't get it off their wives, or who hadn't got a woman or whatever, they'd get so frustrated and worked up that they'd be off committing sex crimes.

I said, 'Are you trying to tell me that if I didn't come round here once a month, I'd be out molesting little girls?'

'Oh, no, not you, not you,' she said.

I said, I should think not.

That put me off a bit, actually. She was being a bit too open there, because she let slip what she thought about the punters. I mean, I know none of the girls respects the customers. That's the trouble with whoring as a profession. As a tobacconist, you can smoke and respect your fellow smokers. As a whore, you have sex, but for some reason, they all look down on the blokes who pay for it. Fair enough, I suppose, because the blokes who pay for it look down on the girls that sell it. Well, I knew that and she knew that, but she shouldn't have let on.

She got a bit hard in the end. Some of them do. The ones that don't care can stay fairly easy about it, but the ones what do care, the ones that shouldn't be doing it, they're the ones that get hard. She got on to drugs in the end. I saw the track marks on her arm. I told Gordon, that's the owner at the parlour, I told him I didn't want Nicky after that. You have to be careful. Aids, all that stuff. Sharing needles. They get a bit sloppy when they're doing junk. Besides, I have my pride. I mean, I'm old and fat and out of breath and if I want anyone to sleep with me I have to pay for it, but I don't have to do it with a junkie. I'm not that desperate. I'd rather try it on with the missis, to be frank.

I don't know if she was still working at the parlour. I hadn't seen her for a bit, but then I'd asked not to. She looked pretty ropy. It might have been the blue lights or what was happening to her, I dunno, but she looked about forty, and she used to reckon she was seventeen and I thought she was lying upwards at the time.

Then this funny thing happened. There was this pause while the coppers opened the car door. I was staring at Nicky and the skinny-looking bloke with her was watching me watching her ... and he gave me this little nod. I thought it was for someone behind me at first; I looked over my shoulder but there was no one there, so it had to be me. I didn't know him from Adam. I thought, What's he nodding at me for? But I had seen him before, walking up and down the road. He was just one of those faces that walk past over the months and then disappear one day, and you never notice they're gone any more than you noticed they were there.

I stared hard at him. Then it clicked.

It was only David. It was only that lad I'd given to Richard a few years before. I thought, Bugger me, you've come a long way and most of it's been straight down. I remembered that time he turned down my fags and told me they turned your skin grey. I had a pack of Bensons in my pocket; if I'd had the nerve I'd have waved them at him and shouted, 'I bet you wouldn't say no now.' But there were coppers everywhere. It's not all that clever to catch the eye of the Bill when they're busy about their work. I saw the copper who was with them watching me, so I did what I always do when I see a copper watching me. I moved on.

23
Tar

WHEN YOU WANTA BE MY FRIEND
KNOCK ON MY DOOR
I WON'T OPEN IT
I KNOW
WHAT YOU'RE FOR
I KNOW EXACTLY WHAT YOU'RE FOR

Lurky

I was round at Dev's place when this friend came round and said, 'Your place is being done ...'

I went straight there. I couldn't work out why they were doing it then instead of two o'clock in the morning like they usually do, when they know everyone'll be there. But there it was, the car flashing blue. It was like a dream. I wasn't scared. I was relieved. Which was funny. I was surprised about being relieved. What it was, of course, was that at last the whole shitty mess was going to end. Only, of course, it didn't.

I walked up and down a couple of times. Lily and Rob had moved out into their own place a few months ago when the baby was born. I didn't know if Gemma was in or not but I thought she probably was. I didn't know what to do. I mean, if the ambulance was for her, there was nothing I could do but I wanted so bad to find out if it was for her. If she was okay or dead or what ... And then if she was okay I'd go in and take the rap quite happily, but if she was out it would be the most stupid thing on earth I could do.

The thing is, we had this friend staying – Col – who used to go out with Sally. He'd been away in Amsterdam for about six months and he'd come back and he was kipping on our settee. It could have been him. I just didn't know. But in the end I had to find out. I couldn't do nothing. So I went in.

The police were there in the hall. This big one, really big like an extra-size man, and this ordinary-sized one. I say ordinary, but he was a big bugger as well. They grabbed me, one on each arm, as soon as I walked in the door.

'What do you want, son?'

'Where's Gemma?'

'Never mind Gemma, what are you doing here?'

'I live here ...' They glanced at one another. 'Is she all right? Who's that ambulance for ...?' And I tried to get free and get through to the living-room door, but they just tightened hold of my arms and lifted me off the ground slightly. I might as well have tried to push my way past King Kong.

Of course they didn't tell me anything ... if she was there, how she was, anything. They dragged me to the back of the hall and searched me. All the time I was saying, 'Where's Gemma, where's Gemma?'

'Never you mind about Gemma,' they kept saying, like I was a naughty kid.

I said, 'Anything you've found, it's mine.'

There was a pause.

'And what might we find, David?' asked the big one.

'I live here, anything here is mine.'

'Do you want to make a statement?'

'Yeah.'

'Arrest him first,' said the other copper.

'Hang on,' said the big one. He went through into the front

room. He opened and closed the door quick, so's I couldn't see what was going on.

'I just want to know if she's all right,' I said.

'If who's all right?' said the copper ... as if I hadn't said Gemma ten times already.

Then the door opened and the big copper came out with a plastic bag. Our stash was in it. Maybe a quarter of an ounce of heroin, plus a little lump of hash.

'Is this yours, David?' he asked.

I had a look, it wasn't just ours in there. Some of it might have been Col's, but ...

'Yeah, that's mine, it's all mine,' I said.

'I arrest you under suspicion of being in possession of Class A drugs, and holding Class A drugs for the purpose of sale to person or persons unknown ... I must warn you ...'

I was half listening. It was awful. I kept glancing at the door where Gemma might be.

One of the coppers wandered off up the hall to have a gab in his walkie talkie. Then the door opened and two ambulancemen came out. They had Col between them. He was in a state, gauching out as they walked him along. I mean, losing consciousness, then coming round. His head kept falling and lifting up as he came round, then going back down.

'How is he?' asked the policeman standing guard over me.

'He'll live,' said one of the ambulancemen.

'And what about the other one?' asked the copper. The ambulanceman just looked at him, and then at me, and I thought the worst at once ...

'Where's Gemma, where's Gemma? Gemma, Gemma!' I yelled, and I was struggling to get through the door. The copper grabbed me and pinned me to the wall, my feet off the ground, but I carried on shouting and pushing. But then I heard her ...

'I'm all right, Tar, I'm okay ...'

Straight away this woman's voice said, 'Shut your gob!' A really hard woman's voice, she must have been a real bitch. Gemma shut up but it was done. I knew she was there and I knew she was okay. I could have wept with relief after seeing Col ...

The copper was really pissed off. He shoved me against the wall, hard. But it was his own fault. He only asked that stuff about 'How's the other one?' just to wind me up.

'You could have told me she was okay, it wouldn't have done you any harm,' I said.

'Stupid little toe rag,' sneered the copper.

Then I had an idea and I yelled out at the top of my lungs, 'The stuff's mine, Gems. Okay?'

The copper was furious. He grabbed hold of me and gave me a real shake, and the woman on the other side of the door screamed, 'Shut his fucking mouf!'

'Clever little git, aren't you,' hissed the copper, and he had a really nasty glint in his eye. He'd have loved to poke me one. I reckon the only reason he didn't was because the ambulancemen were outside the front door listening.

Soon after that they led Gemma out into the hall and took both of us into the police car. I saw the woman who spoke to her; she had a face like a white mask, horrible, vicious-looking. They marched us out to the car and, it was strange, guess who I saw watching on the pavement opposite? Skolly – the bloke who first took pity on me and put me in touch with Richard.

I felt so embarrassed. I hadn't exchanged a word with him, not even to say thanks, since I left the squat three years ago. I nearly did once. We were coming home late at night from this party and we bumped into him and some other bloke. He'd been out on the beer by the look of him, lurching down the path with his hands in his pockets. I recognised him at once. I think he was about to have a go at us for bumping into him, even though it was his fault really, but then he saw Lily in the lamplight. She was wearing her usual party gear – the string vest. It took whatever he was going to say right out of his mouth.

I was about to say hello, but Lily took one look at him and started screaming, 'Beer Monster! Beer Monster!' We all ran off as if he was something horrible, screaming, 'Beer Monster!' I remember hoping he didn't recognise me.

Down the nick the police were a lot better. The desk sergeant was quite kind, an older guy. But it didn't make any difference because I got questioned by these two thugs who arrested me. They were horrible. The big one kept coming in and shouting and snarling at me. I remember getting spit on my face from where he was leaning right over the table and yelling. I wiped it off with my finger and I thought, Cop gob, but I didn't dare say it.

Then he'd go out and the other one would come in and pretend to be all nice and friendly. He called me David and sat down next to me 'for a little chat before my friend comes back from his tea break ...' They were trying to find out names and addresses, where we bought the stuff, who from, that sort of thing. I kept my mouth shut, of course.

I knew what they were at – Mutt and Jeff. You're supposed to be so scared by the nasty one that you tell everything to the nice one. The funny thing was, the nice one was too stupid to make a good job of it. He couldn't bring himself to be nice. After all it was him who'd called me a toe rag. I kept asking for a fag and he'd say, 'In a minute, David, in a minute ...' But the fag never came and it soon became clear it wasn't coming. He couldn't help it. It was just too hard to do. They'd taught him Mutt and Jeff, but they'd forgotten to teach him how actually to be nice.

But it still worked. Funny, isn't it? I really had to hold

myself back, especially when the nice one was telling me it would go a lot better for Gemma if I told, how the Judge would be a lot more lenient if I was co-operative ... It was just lies, I knew that, but still ... He told me she'd spilt the beans and I might as well too. I almost believed him. Of course, when I got out later I found out it was all lies.

They released Gems that night. I was away for three days. They charged me and put me through the Magistrates' Court. I was remanded into the care of the Social Services for trial. I never told them anything, not a word.

**

I was out in the grounds the other day. The house itself is a dump, all shiny paint on the walls and stinking of boiled cabbage. But the grounds are beautiful – shrubs and lawns and wild places and big, big trees they must have planted a hundred or two hundred years ago. I came across this bush full of red berries and it was just blazing. And the air smelt of leaves and soil. The colour was so bright it hurt my eyes. I don't mean like coming down, when bright colours are really unpleasant. I'm clean now. It was just a blaze of red, and I felt I was looking at something for the first time in three years. I thought, All that time the smack has been between me and the world around me, like a fat cushion you can't see through or hear through or touch through. It's like three years that never were. Like I put myself in a mental hospital and I've been heavily sedated for all that time.

I guess that's about what happened.

No, it's not prison. My case doesn't come up for another three months. This is the detox centre in Weston-Super-Mare. My solicitor says that if I complete the course here in Weston, if I get a good report, if I stay clean, if I've settled down with Gemma and I get a job and all the rest of it, I stand a good chance of getting let off with a conditional discharge.

We might even get married, Gemma and me. But the solicitor says, maybe that's going a bit far, at our age.

I'm here, let's face it, because I'm too scared to go inside. I know people who've done time and they all say the same thing: it happens, you just get on with it. But I keep thinking about the screws and how hard everyone is and I couldn't cope with it, I know I couldn't cope with it.

Funny thing, it wasn't like that when I got busted. I was sitting in the cell thinking, Thank God that's over. It was out of my hands, see? I thought I'd go to a young offender institution straight away, just get put away for a couple of years. No more decisions, no more failures, no more promises and lies. No more heroin. I'd lose everything – all the gear we'd bought, Gemma, my friends, the flat, the lot. And I was pleased about it. I was thinking, What a relief, I don't have a life any more. Thank God for that.

And then the bastards let me go.

And then, of course, once I was out I started getting scared about it. The choices started up. So when the solicitor said there was a chance, I jumped at it. And it's better this way. I'm in here because I want to come off. I want to be clean. I want to take control of my life, not leaving it up to the police. Christ – the cops as therapists – who needs that?

Of all the things I've realised since I came in here, the fact that I do love Gemma is the most important to me. Imagine – I'd forgotten I was in love!

I write to her every day. I draw a little yellow dandelion on every letter. We always sign our letters, 'Dandelion, I love you.'

A lot of people here tell me I should split up with her. We drag one another down. I'm weak. I know that. That's the first thing they teach you in here. You have to remember, you're weak and you'll always be weak. Every addict is. Gemma's weak. There's no such thing as a strong addict. So we drag each other down, I can see that. But I can't give her up. She's all I've got.

A month ago I could have done it, but not now. A month ago I didn't love her. I didn't care about anyone – my parents or my friends or Gemma; I didn't feel anything any more. I thought it was me being on top of things. I thought not feeling anything was being better. It was junk. The feelings are there, all right. I was just so smacked out I couldn't feel the feelings.

Gemma's sworn she'll be clean while I'm inside. We were both off it for nearly two weeks before I came in here – well, nearly off – cut down. We want to have babies and they're going to be clean babies. Lily was still jacking up when she was pregnant. She always used to go on about being a good mother and so did everyone around her. But how can you be a good mother on smack? And jacking up when she was breast feeding. I've seen her. All the veins in her arms and behind her knees have gone where she's poked around with the needle so much, so she injects into the veins between her breasts. I've seen her sitting with the baby on the breast poking about to find a vein.

'Nice fat veins when your tits are big and milky,' she said. And no one said a word.

That's junk. You think, if you don't say the truth, the truth somehow doesn't exist. You fool yourself. If anyone suggested to Lily she was doing a bad thing to her baby she'd go mad. But she knows.

Smack makes it all distant. It doesn't matter, it's not real any more.

But it is.

Gemma says that if we can't give it up together this time, we'll have to split up. She'd do it, too. That's why it's so important that I succeed this time.

Gemma's been so strong. She's given up the parlour, she's

given up heroin. That's really hard because I've had a hell of a job in here, but she's still out there with Lily and Rob and Sal and the rest of them. She writes me twice a week. Actually, she's honest about it, she cracks up every now and then. I can understand that. I value the honesty more than anything else. When I come out we're going to move away from Bristol, get our own place. I'll have been clean for a month, she'll have only been taking a little. I know she can do it because she doesn't tell lies, like I did. I always made out I was taking practically nothing. I even believed it, even when I was doing it two, three, four times a day for weeks and weeks.

***

The first thing that happened when I came in here, they got all the new intake together and told us what was what. There were about ten of us sitting around in armchairs waiting, and this lanky-looking bloke – I thought he was one of us at first – suddenly started talking.

'No one's keeping you here. Any time you feel you've had enough, there's the door.' He nodded at the large green exit sign in the corner. 'But while you do stay here, no drugs of any kind are allowed. Not even aspirin.'

We all laughed nervously. He smiled.

'Not even hash,' he added, as if that was the ultimate in mildness. 'I like a smoke and if I have to go without it, so can you.'

Everyone shifted around in their seats and laughed more easily.

'If anyone is caught with drugs of any kind, you're out. No questions, no arguments – the door. That goes for me too. So. Anyone who doesn't feel that they can do it, you'd be better to go now. Really. Go now and you can come back another time. Wait until you get caught – you've blown it forever. If you get caught taking drugs here, you'll never come back again.'

And a couple of people actually got up and walked out. I was tempted myself but – it was a choice between that and a young offender institution.

Then came the bad bit – withdrawal, cold turkey. I never had it so bad. I suppose the truth is I always had a little bit here and there to help me through, or methadone, or something. It was awful. I nearly cracked. I would have done, if I was on my own. I was sitting in my chair moaning, I felt so bad, and everyone was saying, 'Come on, Tar, you can do it, just another few days and you'll be clean.' But all I wanted was smack. In the end I told them I couldn't go through with it and I asked them to fetch one of the counsellors to tell them I wanted to leave.

It was the lanky guy – Steve. He sat and watched me for a bit; and then he said, 'Do you want something to help you?'

'What do you mean?'

'I can't give you heroin, but I have some methadone for severe cases. I can get you a prescription.' He held out a key. 'This is the key to the medicine cabinet. You can have it in two minutes if you like.'

Methadone is the heroin substitute they give addicts to wean them off. Actually, it's worse than smack in some ways. The withdrawal symptoms are worse and it's more addictive. But heroin is illegal and methadone isn't. So ... I was gasping. I said, 'Please, yeah, anything.'

'Okay, I'll go and get it. You pack your bag.'

'What?'

'Pack your bag. If you want some you can have it, but you have to leave.' He held out the key. 'Two minutes, Tar.'

I stared at that key, and I stared at him and he smiled. 'Just ... fuck off,' I told him.

It was a near thing.

I was furious at the time but they know what they're doing. They're ever so supportive but they make you fight every step of the way. They know it's not easy. I discovered later that Steve had been an addict for fifteen years. Fifteen years, and then he got off.

So it is possible.

There's one of the counsellors here who used to be an alcoholic, a really bad one. He used to eat his own sick in the morning, so's not to waste the booze. He used to wake up, and he'd always make sure he had a bit of booze right by him so he could have a drink as soon as he woke up. So he'd drink it and his stomach would reject it at once – vomit it up. But he couldn't have that because that was all the booze he had. So he'd catch it in his hands and drink it back down ...

You wouldn't guess to look at him now; he's a perfectly ordinary-looking bloke. Anyway, he gave up for ten years, ten whole years. And then one night he decided he was past it, he could relax a little bit. So he had a drink.

'That was it – skid row. I woke up the next morning in the gutter. I knew there was only one thing would ever make me feel better again. So I did it. And I was on the booze again for four years ...'

I remember Dev and his girlfriend once deciding to give it up and they booked this holiday to the Canary Islands. And you know what? They actually met a guy *on the plane* who was a dealer and had some on him.

That's one of the things they teach you. You can never touch the stuff ever again, whatever it is, fags, booze, smack. No matter what happens to me, no matter what I do or don't do, I can never touch heroin again. Not once. Because I'm not strong enough. Because it's stronger than me. That's the important thing I always have to remember ...

They teach you things like that but most of the work here is therapy. We all sit talking to one another, about one another. You have to show everything. People listen. They don't judge you. They're not full of the bullshit you normally get from people who've never had the problem. And the other thing is – perhaps the main thing is, unlike all the addicts I know – they all really want you to get off.

We have all sorts here – speed addicts, heroin junkies, people on barbiturates, people on Valium. There's a woman here about the same age as my mum and she's been on Valium for thirty years. Imagine, stoned on Valium all that time. Her name is Nancy. Her doctor has a lot to answer for. There's a lot of women like that apparently. Actually it makes me think better of my mum. At least she found a drug that was more interesting than Valium.

Nancy has a son about my age she doesn't often see. They took him off her when he was eight. And, of course, I have a mum I don't often see. So we have something in common. We go for walks around the grounds, and she asks me what it's like being the son of an addict, and I ask her about what it's like being a mum. Actually she doesn't much remind me of Mum but it makes me feel good because I think it helps her. If her son hadn't been taken away, he might have ended up like me, you see. So somehow, I'm useful to her just by being useless, if you see what I mean.

Nancy sticks up for me. Sometimes the other people pick on me because of Gemma. I've told everyone our story, so they know that she more or less ran away because of me. She'd never have gone if I hadn't been there, so in a sense it's my fault she's a junkie. A lot of people say I ought to leave her. There's this thing about junkies supporting one another's addiction and making it harder to give up. Even Steve says couples nearly always have to separate.

But we love each other ... that can't be a bad thing, can it? How can love be bad?

Nancy says, 'If you love her, stick with her, Tar.' She split up with her husband over her addiction, and it didn't do her any good. She's in as big a mess as ever.

The point about therapy isn't that what everyone says is necessarily true. It makes you think, that's the point. It makes you challenge yourself. All that stuff about Gemma has made me really think about me and her, and the more I think about it, the more I know I love her.

There's this bloke there, Ron. He's Scottish and he's been through everything. Sometimes he gets aggressive but he's actually a very warm sort of bloke. He's been on booze, on heroin – he's even been on cough mixture. That's the first cough mixture addict I've ever met. It's funny because ... I mean, he's a weak person. We all are, that's why we're here. But he's helped a lot of people see things about themselves. He's so perceptive. And yet when people say things about him, he just can't handle it.

Anyway, it was last week. We were in therapy; it was my turn on the spot. We were talking about my mum. We often end up talking about my mum. It's the obvious thing because she's an addict same as me, and because she's a victim same as me, getting knocked around by my dad. Then suddenly Ron sat up and said, 'All right, we've been talking about your mum and how she's a victim and how she's made you a victim and all the things you have in common with your mum. Right. What about your dad? What have you got in common with your dad? What about a bit of sympathy for the old man?'

That really threw it up in the air. There was a real argument that day. I just sat there and listened to start off with. Some of the women were really offended.

'We're talking about a man that beats women, we're talking about a man that beats his own wife and son.'

'Aye, but what did she do to him? She was a dab hand at the old guilt, I bet ... I bet she knew how to wrap him round her little finger, because I'll tell you, I've met women like that before and, I tell you, they're no helpless. In fact, I'm willing to bet she was the one who wore the trousers in that house.'

'It's not the same thing!' shouted this woman. She was getting really angry. The guide kept trying to bring it back to me, but I just couldn't answer. It was true. I'd never thought about it but my mum was the boss. He used to knock me around and she used to live in fear of him coming home. But she was the boss, all right. She used to wrap me round one little finger, and she used to wrap him round the other one.

'How about it, David?' said Ron, leaning across and grinning at me. 'How would you like to go back there and give the old woman a good kicking ... just like your da? Eh? Perhaps he had the right idea ... eh?'

You should have heard the screech when he said that!

'That's no way to solve his problems.'

'I didn't say it was. I didn't say he *ought* to do it. I just asked him how he'd *like* to do it ... Right, listen ... I've hit women before now and I may even do it again.'

'Are you threatening me? Are you threatening me?'

'No, listen ... no, I'm not ... I'm saying ... ' It was getting really loud, people shouting and roaring. 'No, look, I expect sympathy, so why not Tar's dad? Why shouldn't he have a bit of sympathy? I mean, it's worth a question, is it not? I mean you don't stop being a human being if you hit a woman, do you? Or am I not allowed to ask questions? I understood it was a free therapy session ...'

This woman, her name was Sue, was getting really upset. She'd been beaten up over and over again by her husband. I felt sorry for her because she was just learning to stand up for herself and here was Ron coming out with all this.

He said I ought to ring up my dad and find out how he was and how he felt.

It completely blew my mind.

'All right, he's got the muscles, he loses it every now and then and lashes out, but why? How is *he* being abused? Hey ... here's a thought. Maybe she *wanted* him to hit her. Maybe it *suited* her ...'

It really upset some people. Including me. I was sitting next to Nancy and I looked at her to see what she thought but she just shook her head. Afterwards she said that she thought Ron was just stirring things up but I don't know. I don't know if what he said is true but it showed me one thing: I never really thought about me and Dad before. One day when all this is over I'll ring him up, go and visit him ... maybe. And my mum. But not now. It's all there. It'll wait. At the moment I need all my strength for Gemma.

I don't believe in anything any more. I don't believe in me, I don't believe in my friends, I don't believe in Gemma. But I don't mean that in a cynical way. The thing I have to remember is that I'm weak and that they're weak. I can't do it alone. If you have an addictive personality, you have to have help from outside yourself. Not a person, or an organisation necessarily. Something deeper than that. Some force outside you and stronger than you, that you can turn to when you feel weak.

I don't know what they mean when they say that, but maybe I'm getting some kind of an idea about it. That thing outside yourself is different for everyone. I know that I can't trust myself ever again. I know I can't trust Gemma either. She's stronger than me but she's still weak. But what about love?

I was looking at a letter she wrote to me the other day and those words on the bottom she writes – 'Dandelion, I love you ...' And I thought that was magic. Loving someone. It's not you and it's not them. It's not in you, it's between you.

It's bigger and stronger than you are.

That's what I have. That's all I have, when you think about it. My personality almost disappeared when I was on heroin. I'm off it now but I still don't know who I am. I only know that I'm weak, and Gemma's weak, and that I love Gemma. And I know that she loves me.

Dandelion, dandelion. That's what I believe in: It's the only thing can help me now.

Steve said to me, 'When you go home you'll know in the first day whether you're going to get through the week.'

'I will,' I said.

I've said that before. This time I know I've got nothing to be confident about.

24
Sally

It was gonna be a wedding party, it was gonna be a honeymoon, the way Gemma was. She was jumping up and down, and kissing him and hugging him. He was blushing. He'd definitely changed, definitely. He looked so much better. I was pretty cynical about the whole exercise, but you've gotta keep an open mind or nothing ever changes.

Later on, he started going on about all that stuff they'd taught him – how he couldn't do it on his own, how he needed help from outside himself, wherever that is. Lily was really sneery. She said, 'Brainwashed. Yeah, what a drag. They took him off one drug and they put him on another. They done a good job on you, mate ...'

Well, she was right, but she didn't have to say it. Maybe he needs brainwashing. Poor old Tar. I gave her a nudge and I said, 'Leave him alone, he's doing all right.'

'Yeah, they put you in prison all right. They locked you up inside your own head and then they gave you the key and how do you get out of that jail? They made you your own jailer, it's cheaper for 'em that way ...'

I was pissed off with her, she was being really nasty. He needed that stuff. He just sat there drinking a glass of fizzy wine and said, 'You can think what you want, Lily. You're on smack and I'm not.' She hated that. Later on she went into the bathroom and came back with all these broken up little bits of soap and started trying to push them in his ear and up his nose.

'Get off, Lil!' He was getting annoyed now.

'That's to keep your brain clean,' she told him. You had to laugh. Poor Tar! Lily's a bit of a missionary. She doesn't like any other religion but her own.

Gemma was her old self that day. Bouncing about. She wanted to show the world how pleased she was to get her hands on him again. She was all over him.

It was a bit different the day before, I went round to help her get the party ready. She was doing rice salad and she looked really awful. I didn't say anything. You know, your boyfriend's coming out of detox and someone walks in and says, 'Christ, you look ugly this afternoon ...' I had a bit with me, because I thought she might need something to steady her up and I offered her some, but she said no. She was making a big thing about not doing any, but we all knew she was cracking up every now and then. The thing is, people say that your friends stop you getting off but you're gonna pack it in when the time is right. If you push it at the wrong time you only wear yourself out and make it worse.

But I didn't say anything. I got a knife and helped her cut up the peppers.

I was watching her. I kept my mouth shut as long as I could but finally she hangs down her head and starts weeping. I put my arm round her. 'What's up, Gems?' I said.

Out it all came. 'I've really let Tar down, I've really blown it for him. I made all these promises and ...' And she cracks up all over the rice salad.

I was really surprised because, you know, she'd been doing so well. She'd turned over a new life. She'd stopped doing jumps at the parlour, saving herself for Tar. She'd cut right down on the smack.

'I've been doing more smack, I did some today and he's been keeping himself clean and look at me ...'

Off she went.

'How much have you been doing?' I said.

'I did some again today, I was feeling so rotten ...'

'And when did you do it before?'

She shrugged and wiped her eyes. 'Day before yesterday.'

I mean, she used to do stuff every day. Twice a day. Three times. She used to do more than me. And now she'd cut right down, just taking a little bit when she was feeling low, and here she was blaming herself and turning the brilliant effort she'd made into a mess, just because she wasn't bloody Superwoman.

'But Tar hasn't done any,' she wailed.

'Well, of course he hasn't, he's been surrounded by all these people paid to make sure he stays clean. Where he was you'd have to be strong as hell to *take* the stuff,' I told her. 'You've done it all on your own, you're doing really, really well.'

'But he's been clean and I haven't and I don't think I'm strong enough to keep off it and I do love him, I love him so much, Sal, and I'm just going to drag him down ...'

'Listen ...' I gave her a squeeze. 'You're really lucky. I wish I felt like that about someone. You don't know how lucky you are, Gems ...'

She smiled at me through her tears.

'You're going to be all right.'

'I ought to go away. I've been thinking if I was strong I ought to go away and leave him because maybe he'd stand a better chance without me.'

I started getting a bit irritated with her then. I told her, 'You're mad, you don't leave someone because you love them. You're mad ...' I started laughing, and she started laughing a bit through her tears, because it was so stupid.

We did a little one together. She was worried about it but you can't turn yourself into Superwoman. She did a chase, so

Tar wouldn't see any marks on her. She hasn't done a needle for weeks. That's brilliant. She was falling to bits, what sort of homecoming would that be for him?

I told her, she can't be strong for everyone all the time, she had to learn to take some strength off him. I told her, he'd been taking strength from her for a long time. Maybe now it was her turn. If that place where he'd been was any good, he'd come up with enough strength for the pair of them.

I was scared that when the party came she wouldn't be able to cope with it, but she was brilliant. Gemma knows how to rise to the occasion. She was bubbling. Tar was as cool as a cucumber, although looking back maybe he was a little freaked.

Later on I noticed Rob was missing, and I knew what that was likely to mean so I went upstairs and found him, sure enough, doing one in the bedroom. And guess who was there with him?

Well ... that didn't last long, did it? I was pretty annoyed with Tar about it, I can tell you. Gemma had tried so hard and she'd done so well. He was saying how it was a party, he was just having a hit because it was a big day and he was feeling a bit freaked out with all those people. I thought, Maybe it didn't mean anything. But of course I knew exactly what it did mean.

I sat on the bed and shot up. We sat about talking about nothing and then, Lily came in ...

She just stood there looking at Tar and nodding, going, 'Yeah ... yeah ...' He just smiled wryly. You could see there was a performance on its way. Then she starts going round the room looking behind the wardrobe and in the drawers and under the bed and she says, 'You know what? I can't find God anywhere.' God, of course, was what she thought Tar was on about when he talked about something outside himself helping him.

'He didn't hang around long, then, did he?' she told Tar.

'It's not a problem to me, Lily. I'm sorry if it bothers you,' he said, smiling at her like he was drinking milk.

I lay back on the bed and closed my eyes. I just couldn't be bothered. I'd have said something, but he didn't look as though he cared either. I don't suppose he did; he hadn't used for over a month. Lucky bastard, you could see by the look on his face. He felt good. Even so Lily stood there staring at him until he began to wriggle about in his chair.

'Gemma did some,' he said at last.

'Oh, that's all right then,' Lily said. Then she started on at Rob. 'You prat!' she said.

'He asked me, what was I supposed to do?' said Rob.

'Oh, leave him alone, Lily, for God's sake, it's supposed to be a party,' I said.

'Look at him, he's practically gauching out ...'

'I only had a chase, I didn't use a needle,' he said.

I said, 'You're making too much of it, Lily. It's his party.'

'It doesn't mean I haven't given up,' said Tar.

I said, 'Oh, God,' because that was asking for it.

Lily was right in. 'Oh, yeah, you take the stuff but you've still given up, sure ...'

'... this is a party. Anyway, Gemma did some tonight. She told me. She asked me if it was okay.'

'And you said yes.'

He smiled. I thought, You crafty git. Of course Gemma could have some. Because then so could he ...

Well, you know, that's junk. We're all the same. There's always a reason when you want to do some.

Then he said, 'Don't tell her, will you, Lily? It won't do her any good, you won't be doing her any favours.'

Lily sneered. 'Yeah, you want me to play your game. How are you gonna feel about this tomorrow?'

'I expect I'll think I fancied some heroin, Lily.'

She flounced around the room a bit then snapped at Rob. He'd been sitting quietly. He knows not to put his head over the edge when Lily's off. He'd been doing her a works and now he handed it over to her. Lily sat on the edge of the bed and started digging about for a vein behind her knees.

'You've really buggered it up for both of you,' she told Tar.

I'd just about heard enough. I got up and stamped out to the door.

'What's up with you?' she snapped.

I turned round at the door and said, 'You, lecturing him about junk with a needle stuck up your arse, that's what,' and I slammed the door and walked out. Lily came running to the door and leaned over the bannisters screaming at me,

'You fucking slag! Are you calling me a junkie? Are you calling me a hypocrite?'

I just ignored her and walked on down. I didn't even look round. I knew she wasn't going to come for me. She still had her works loaded up in the bedroom behind her and she wasn't likely to leave that behind, not in a room with two junkies in it.

I got to the bottom of the stairs imagining I was one of those starlets in an old fifties film where they descend the grand stairway in a ballgown, and all the heads turn. All the heads were turning, of course, but not because I was looking beautiful. I stepped off the last stair and I thought, So she isn't a junkie? Hasn't the penny dropped for that girl yet?

25
Richard

HELP ME HELP ME HELP ME HELP ME
THROW ME A LINE AND I'LL SPIN IT BACK
HELP ME HELP ME HELP ME HELP ME
BUT WHAT I REEEEEEALLY NEEEED'S THE CASH
Lurky

I said, 'Are you clean?'

'Sort of.'

'I don't want any needles in the house.'

'I'm not that bad,' he said. He sounded slightly offended. I didn't ask any further than that. I thought it was just a visit. We made arrangements for the weekend, then I put the phone down.

I was living with Sandra at the time. I'd had a great time in Australia and South-East Asia. Bicycling is the only way to travel. I used to go down regularly to the New Forest when mountain bikes first came on the market and I knew at once I'd seen the future of cycling. South-East Asia was only the first step. I'm going to do India next.

I'd often thought of Tar when I was over there. He'd have loved every second of it. I used to think of the last time I'd seen him and what he'd said to me, 'I don't have to run away to Asia to have a good time, Richard.'

I was sitting on this fallen statue in Thailand at the edge of a ruined temple in the jungle. I'd slept on the beach, had a swim and cycled through the jungle for fifteen miles. There were huge butterflies everywhere, big as birds. I thought, I know where I'd rather be ...

Then when I got back I went to live in Birmingham for a bit. I had friends in Birmingham, but it's a city I'd never lived in before. That's where I met Sandra. She was living in the same house as my friends and we started to have an *affaire du coeur*. Unfortunately I'm not very good at that sort of thing. Then she got a place in college at Reading. Reading! I must have been mad! I went and interviewed at a bike shop there and they offered me the job.

That's life. I came back thinking I'd earn enough money to get off to India fairly quickly. Instead I ended up with Sandra in a flat in Woodley. The worst of it was, Sandra liked it.

I keep falling in love but it always makes me unhappy, I've no idea why. When I told Sandra about Tar she was very disapproving. I tried to tell her what a lovely person he was, what a hard time he'd had as a child, all that. It wasn't as though she's unsympathetic, actually, but only profession-ally. Her course was for working with handicapped kids. She was doing work experience with some very badly handicapped kids and it had a very high burn-out rate. By the weekend the last thing she wanted was work at home.

'Junkies are bad news,' she announced. I suppose after dealing with people with those sorts of problems, addiction looked a bit self-induced.

I told her what he'd said.

'What's "sort of" supposed to mean?' she wanted to know.

I had a good idea.

Tar was his usual shifty self. I mean, that's usual for him since he got on to smack. He'd lost that open look he used to have about him quite early on, after about six months of leaving the squat, I'd say. It was funny. I hadn't actually liked him for years. I loved him when he first turned up. He had this way of trying to hide everything but it all came shining through anyway.

The heroin covered that up soon enough but I kept getting little glimpses. He'd look shyly at me out of the corner of his eye, or a slow smile would spread over his face and I'd think the old Tar was still in there somewhere.

The evening started off not too bad. He told me about the bust. I thought it was very noble of him to go in when the place was crawling with pigs and take the rap. And he talked about the detox centre. I think he got a lot from it but Sandra wasn't impressed.

'Obviously you didn't get enough from it,' she said. It wasn't very comfortable. She went up to bed early on but I stayed up with Tar rapping. He had a lot to say about junk and getting off it. It all sounded very sensible to me. I thought he was okay.

I went up to bed about an hour later and Sandra was furious.

'I want him out of the house first thing in the morning,' she said. I couldn't believe it.

'Why?'

'He's just bombed out of his head, that's all.'

'No, he told me he's been clean for a month ...'

'He says! Didn't you see his eyes?'

'He wasn't ... was he?' And even as I said that I knew it was true. He'd been getting more and more dopey and his pupils had been getting smaller and smaller. I'd been smoking so I hadn't really noticed, but looking back he was bombed out of sight. If it wasn't heroin it was something very similar.

'His pupils were like pinheads,' said Sandra in disgust.

'I'll have a word with him,' I promised at last. 'But don't boot him out. He's a friend of mine. Please.' She snorted and rolled over in the duvet. But she didn't make me chuck him out.

We were planning on going for a walk along the river the next day, but first Sandra and I had a few chores to do. We tended to spend Saturday morning doing things like the laundry, ironing. Sandra was being a pain. We put that sort of thing off when her friends came visiting. I got sent to the supermarket. Tar came along with me, and I noticed he was a bit fidgety in the car on the way out. He seemed distracted but at least he wasn't out of it. Then at Safeway's he bought some Paracetamol.

'Not feeling well?' I said.

'A bit 'fluey,' said Tar. The number of times I've heard him and his friends talk about being 'a bit 'fluey'.

'Oh, yes?' I said.

'Really.' He looked me in the face. 'I really have got a bit of 'flu, really,' he insisted seriously. He swallowed a mouthful of Paracetamol.

I didn't say anything. He was so convincing but Sandra had burst the bubble. I thought, Well, if he doesn't want to admit it, that's his business. Actually that's not true. What I was really thinking was, oh dear, more trouble. Because if Sandra found out he was coming down ... oh dear.

Sandra and I hadn't been getting on well for weeks. Ever since we moved to Reading, actually. We split up a few months later. Not a very good atmosphere for poor Tar to come off heroin in.

I was hoping when we got out in the fresh air by the water he'd feel better, but we went back home. Sandra still had loads to do. I was getting annoyed about it. From what I could gather she'd been on the phone to her mum all morning, she didn't seem to have done anything at all while we'd been out. I suggested Tar and I go on our own, but no, she wouldn't have that either. So we had to hang about while she got the ironing board out. I could see it was going to take ages, so I went to load the washing machine in the kitchen to try and speed things up.

I was thinking about having a word with her and telling her that I thought he was coming down and that we ought to be helping him, when suddenly there was Tar behind me pulling his coat on.

'Where are you off to?' I asked.

'I'm going back.'

'What for?'

Tar shrugged. His eyes drifted across the floor. 'I need to go back,' he said. 'Can you lend me the bus fare? I've left myself with no money.'

'Oh ...' I felt I was letting him down. 'Is it Sandra?'

'No, it's nothing to do with her, I don't blame her at all, I just have to get back ...'

'Why?'

Tar looked away from me, at the fridge, at the wall opposite. 'I'm coming down, I'm doing cold turkey, but I can't go through with it. I want to go back and get some heroin,' he said. And he looked at me and shrugged.

I said, 'Why didn't you say?'

'I just thought I'd give it a go and it'd happen, but I'm not making it. I have to go back.'

'But you said you'd been clean for a month.'

'I didn't want to tell you I was coming down. Look.' He spread his hands open. 'Can't you lend me the money? I'll only hitch home if you don't.'

'What were you on last night?'

'That was downers. I took some barbs along to help me through the first night, but they're gone now. I can't do it, Richard, I'm sorry, I can't do it. Not this time.'

I started trying to talk him out of it, telling him to think of

Gemma, telling him how well he was doing, which we both knew was a pack of lies. He hadn't even made it through one day and, in fact, I was appalled at how bad he was. I was still going on at him when Sandra came in.

She stood and looked at us, Tar in his coat.

'What's going on?' she said.

'Tar wants to go back. He's been trying to come off it on this visit.'

Sandra just snorted. She turned her back and went to the washing machine and began to go through the clothes I'd loaded.

'I'd better go,' said Tar, and he made for the door.

'Wait ...'

I could have killed her. He was coming to see me because he thought I might be able to help him, he was my friend. He was still just a kid! If she decided she didn't want to help, I might as well give him the money now, except I'd have an argument on my hands about that as well.

He got to the door when Sandra came back in. 'How long have you been off it?' said Sandra.

Tar turned at the door to look at her. 'Just one day,' he said.

'What about last night?' she said.

'That was barbiturates,' I said quickly. 'He took some to help him get over the first night but they're gone now.'

Sandra snorted softly.

Tar said, 'You're right, I'm just a junkie. I'm just a junkie and I just want to get back and get on with ...'

And as he said this his face began to crumple up. He began to cry. As he started to cry he turned and ran out of the room.

I was shocked. He'd looked so cool. I stared at Sandra. She looked at me and suddenly, she ran out after him. He was at the door fumbling with the lock and Sandra threw herself on him and she grabbed his shoulder and spun him round, tall bloke though he was, and fixed him with a hug. She just wrapped her arms round him so hard he couldn't move and hugged him and hugged him. I stood and watched his face over her shoulder. It was terrible. He cried and cried, he couldn't stop. All the strength fell out of him. When she let him go he sank to his knees and then lay down on his side, his face in his hands, and he cried and he cried and he cried.

'I'm just a junkie, I'm just a junkie, I'm just a junkie,' he said, over and over and over. Sandra lay down next to him and put her arms around him. I got down too and lay half on top of him.

'I'm just a junkie, I'm just a junkie,' he said. He tried to get up but we held him down. I put my arms around him. I was crying too. Tar lay there underneath us both and wept.

Sandra was brilliant. Once she realised what was going on, she was right there. After a bit when the tears began to subside she said, 'I've got some strong painkillers upstairs, would that help?' Tar nodded. I mentioned the Paracetamol, and he said he'd had two. Sandra and I glanced at each other; he was in such a state we were scared he could do anything, so we made him hand over the packet and sure enough, he'd just had two. So Sandra went and got her painkillers. She'd had them prescribed for her periods, which had been really bad ever since she'd had a coil fitted.

Then we discussed what to do – me and Sandra, that is. Tar just sat there and watched us. Whether we should get to a doctor and try to get him on a methadone script, whether we should give him some money and pack him away on holiday somewhere. I have to hand it to Sandra – she'd have given over her life savings to save him once she came round to his side.

The trouble was, Tar wouldn't have any of it. The tears had stopped, but he was as stubborn as a mule. He was going back to get some heroin. That was all. He wouldn't agree to anything else. When she asked him if he wanted to go on holiday to Spain or somewhere, on us, he just said if we gave him any money he'd go straight back to Bristol and spend it on heroin, so it would be better for us not to.

All he wanted us to do was lend him the bus fare. In the end we decided to put off any big decisions and just go for that walk. At least he might feel better by the river. We could go to a pub and get a few drinks down him. But time was getting on and we decided we'd better have some lunch first.

We went to get it ready. I was in a right mess. I was appalled at what had happened. But one thing – he was himself again. He'd come back, all open and helpless, and I suppose that's what won Sandra round in the end. But it was so sad, because it was being himself that he found so difficult to cope with.

We chopped vegetables and talked about what to do. Sandra, bless her, wanted him to stay as long as he needed to. I remember standing there beaming to myself with pleasure and thinking, It's the first time I've done this for weeks.

But when we went through with the food he was gone.

We ran round the house but his bag was gone from his room. I ran out on to the road but I couldn't see him. I went one way, Sandra went another, but he was nowhere. So we ran back into the house, grabbed our keys and made for the car.

'He can't be at the bus station, he hasn't got any money,' I said.

Sandra said, 'We'd better check my purse and your wallet.' I just looked at her, but she was right, he was desperate enough. We ran back in and Sandra spent ten minutes looking for her purse, but she found it in the end. The money was all there.

'He must be hitching.'

We jumped into her old Renault and headed off towards the motorway junction.

We got to the roundabout – no one there. We stopped and got out of the car to see if he'd spotted us and hidden on the slip road, but he was definitely not there.

Then I realised: 'The other roundabout ...'

There are two in Reading.

'But that's miles away.'

'Yes, but that's where he got dropped off when he came, that's where I picked him up. He might not even know about this one.'

So off we went again. We got on to the motorway and drove up to the next turn off. We drove around that round-about, but he wasn't there either. We got off the roundabout and drove back in towards town.

He was walking down the road towards the junction. He didn't try and hide. We pulled up, jumped out and ran towards him. Tar put down his bag and waited for us.

'Got you!' I grinned. He smiled back wanly. I think he was pleased to see us.

Well, we argued and argued all over again. Tar wasn't interested. All he was willing to talk about was whether we were going to lend him the bus fare or whether he was going to hitch. It went on for ten minutes or more, but gradually it began to sink in on me – there was nothing we could say or do. He'd already given up in his mind.

'But you can do it, other people do it,' Sandra kept saying.

'It's no worse than a dose of 'flu,' I reminded him.

'And I can't even cope with that,' said Tar.

I sort of understood. That was how worthless he felt. It was poison and you knew it was poison. Maybe it was just like the 'flu, maybe it was even easy to stop, but he couldn't do even that.

'I'm going back to Bristol to get some heroin. You can't stop me. All you can do to help me is lend me the money to get back on the bus.'

'We're not lending you anything,' said Sandra.

Tar must have seen in my face what I was thinking. 'Tell her,' he said.

And I just shrugged. The thing was, if he hitched back it would be so miserable. It was a lousy day, cold, damp, he wasn't dressed for it. But he'd freeze and get sodden for the sake of heroin, and what would that achieve? He'd just feel even more worthless and useless than if he caught the bus, because then at least he wouldn't have to suffer for it.

I tried to explain to Sandra, but she was more or less convinced anyway. He was so sure of himself, if you see what I mean.

'I can't give up for you,' Sandra said. 'Or I would.' I rummaged in my pockets for the money. He was looking miles better all of a sudden, and I could have kicked him for it.

Then we drove him to the bus station.

'You did the right thing,' said Tar. And we both glanced at each other because it was like he'd pulled the wool over our eyes, because he was so pleased with himself. Maybe. Or maybe he was just glad that he didn't have to hitch after all.

We went with him to the station to wave him off. Sandra said, 'Come back soon, any time you want to try again.'

'Any time at all,' I said firmly.

'Any time at all,' she agreed.

Tar nodded his thanks and moved towards the bus. We stopped him to give him a goodbye hug and he waited while we did that. Then he climbed on board and the bus drove him off.

26
Gemma

OH HOW COULD YOU EV-ER LET ME DOWN
NOW HOW COULD YOU EV-ER LET ME DOWN
THESE PROMISES (AH AHHHHHHHHHHHH)
WERE MADE FOR US
(O - O - OH O - O OH OOOOOHHHHHHHHHHHHHHHHH)

The Buzzcocks

I had a problem. Maybe I had a problem. I was waiting to see
if I did when someone started pounding on the door and
yelling. I leaped up and spilt tea down my front and scalded
myself.

I thought, Police! But it was a woman doing the yelling.

It was a complete accident I was at home at all. I should
have been at the parlour but I just couldn't face it that day.
This time it wasn't the junk. My period was late. My period
was late and my boobs felt sore and ...

That was absolutely the very last thing on this planet I
wanted and now a monster was knocking on my door.

I walked very quietly down the hall as if I wasn't in.

Bang bang bangbangbababababang ...

I knew it wasn't the police because it was so desperate.
Then I heard the breathing. It was ragged breath. I mean,
almost choking. Then, again – BANG BANG BANG – and
the voice– 'Please please please ... '

I ripped the door open and Lily fell on to me. She had

Sunny in one arm. Lily slammed the door behind her, moaning and weeping.

'What happened, Lily, are you all right?'

She couldn't talk. She could hardly walk. She had one hand on her throat. She gestured with that hand and I saw that her throat was red. She was only wearing her dressing-gown.

'God ...'

I dragged her in and plonked her on the settee. I took Sunny off her. He was screaming his head off. Lily leaned over the side of the settee and threw up.

I got the story slowly. It was a punter. He came up and he got her to undress and then he asked her to ... something she didn't want to do. When she said no, he grabbed her and shook her. Lily tried to scream to alert Rob, who always waited downstairs with a baseball bat in case there was any trouble, but the guy clapped his hand over her mouth. He shoved her over the bed and grabbed a pair of her old tights – her floor was always littered with clothes – and he put them round her neck and pulled them tight, really tight. He really pulled them tight.

He kept half strangling her and then letting go, just enough for her to know he could kill her, really kill her, if she didn't do what he wanted. She couldn't scream. He let loose just enough for her to get a breath and then he'd squeeze tight again. He was doing these things to her while she was being strangled. At one point she got her hand under the tights and flipped over on to her back and kicked him off. He turned her over and he bent her arm right up her back until she thought he was going to break it. Then he got the tights back on again and carried on with what he was doing, all the time tightening the tights around her neck.

When he'd finished he let her go and she tore the tights off and tried to scream. Her throat was wrecked, but she made some sort of noise. The bloke did his clothes back up and walked out of the bedroom and downstairs. Lily heard Rob shout, but a minute later the door went bang. Then Rob ran upstairs. She was trying to tell him not to call the ambulance because they'd bring the police along with them, but she couldn't speak. Rob just stared at her. His head was bleeding. Then he ran back down.

Lily got up and tried to get downstairs. She got halfway down the stairs when Rob reappeared.

'Go back up,' he said. 'The police are coming.'

Lily tried to say, 'You stupid idiot,' because he'd rung them up and the house was full of needles, weighing scales, heroin, everything. But she still couldn't speak. She carried on downstairs. Sunny was on the floor screaming his head off. She managed to pick him up with one arm. Rob tried to stand in front of her and block her way, but she just pushed past him. She was still naked so she grabbed a gown from a chair and ran out and came straight round to our place.

While she was telling me all this two things happened. One was, we heard the police come. The sirens. I kept expecting Rob to turn up but he never did. He went round and hid at Dev's. The other was, I had this pregnancy test on the table. It was one of those ones that shows you a little ring at the bottom of the tube if you're pregnant.

That's what I was waiting for. You have to wait so many hours. I was sitting next to Lily comforting her, but Sunny was screaming so I had to get up and make him a bottle. This little test tube was in the way. I had a quick glance and it seemed okay, you know? There was no ring, everything was fine, I wasn't pregnant.

I thought, that's something, anyway, and I reached out to move it and as my hand went towards it I had another glimpse and this time there was the little ring at the bottom of the tube. A perfect little ring, saying you got it. I don't know why I saw two different things; it must have been the angle, the light, I don't know. But it was too late to stop my hand. I grabbed the tube and everything in it went up in a little puff. The ring was gone as soon as I'd seen it and I had no idea which glimpse was the real one and which one I'd imagined ...

I heard my mum saying, bad things always come in threes.

Rob turned up later and they had a terrible argument. She was furious with him for calling the pigs, even though she'd almost been strangled. Obviously they couldn't go back to their place because the police'd be watching out for them ... they were both scared even to go out of the house. We put them up in our bedroom and they were screaming at each other all night – Lily croaking away because of her throat and bursting into tears. One of them started to trash the place. Me and Tar just sat in the kitchen and listened to it; we didn't dare go in. The baby was 'mazing, quiet as a mouse the whole time, although I heard him crying at night a couple of times.

It got quiet later on. Me and Tar made up some cushions in the spare room and kipped down there. I said to him, 'What're we gonna do?'

He was lying there looking at me in the dark. He said, 'They can't stay here.'

'Why not?'

'The police are looking for them. We'll only get done. Anyway, Rob'll be wanting to carry on dealing and we can't have two dealers in one house.'

I thought, You bastard, they did everything for us and now all he can worry about is his business. I shifted about a bit, then I said, 'Maybe we ought to move out and let them stay here.'

'What for?' He sounded surprised.

'You know what a mess Lily's in.' It was true. Lily was worse than any of us. She'd got hooked in Manchester, now she'd got addicted again here. 'She can't cope with getting a new place,' I said. 'She should stay here. We can go. We could move right out. We could get out of here ...'

Tar shook his head. 'I'm not giving up my place for them, why should I?' he said.

'I mean, we could get right away. You know?'

There was a pause and then he said, 'Not yet, Gems. I'm not ready for that yet.'

I didn't say anything. I thought about that little ring at the bottom of the test tube. I thought, When did Tar turn into a shit and when did I fall in love with him?

He leaned across and kissed me. 'Dandelion, I love you,' he said.

'I love you,' I said. He pulled a smile, I pulled a smile, not real ones. Then he turned over and went to sleep.

I didn't tell him about me being pregnant. I knew what he'd say. He'd want me to have it. He keeps saying we should have a baby like Rob and Lily. It's stupid. We're both junkies. But the really awful thing is – I want to have it, too. I knew that when I caught that glimpse of the little ring in the bottom of the tube. I wasn't frightened or upset by it, you see. I was pleased.

I want to have Tar's baby. Now that really is stupid, isn't it?

I don't know why I've started to love him so much. It always used to be the other way round, him loving me more. I don't understand myself, because he's a bastard now, really. He lies, he cheats. He pinches my money. Just helps himself out of my purse. He nicks our stash. He takes the smack and goes away and doesn't come back till he's finished it. Then he tells me he loves me. His eyes sort of swivel about. I don't know if it's true. I don't think he knows what's true any more. I always used to think that when I fell in love, I'd fall for some bastard with an earring. Well, now I have.

I lay in bed and I thought for a long, long time. About Tar. About Lily and Rob and Sunny. You look in that baby's eyes – he's *full* of it – junk, I mean. He must get it through the milk. She even rubs a few grains on his gums if he's playing up. He's a junkie, he's been a junkie all his little life, he was a junkie before he was even born.

What was scaring me was, that little blob of jelly inside me seemed like the only thing worth anything I had in the whole world.

Much later I heard Lily moving around in the sitting room, so I got up, too. She was wandering around with the baby on her arm looking for something in the drawers.

'Hi.'

She looked at me. She looked awful. 'Yeah.' Sunny was snuffling on her arm, half moaning. 'He won't sleep, I'm looking for his dodee,' she said. She yawned and smiled at me sleepily.

'Let me hold him for a bit.' She let me take the baby off her. She doesn't often let me hold Sunny, she clings on to him. I touched the folds of white cloth around his face. He was so sweet. Holding babies always makes me feel broody.

'I wanna have one,' I said.

'Yeah, you will one day, Gems, you deserve it.'

Lily sat down. I put the baby on the settee next to her and made a cup of tea. The lights were on a dimmer switch, very low. It was cosy. The embers were still in the fire. I made a pot of tea and we sat and drank it.

'How's your neck?'

'It hurts.' Lily smiled. I smiled back at her. She looked really motherly and warm in her gown. Sunny was making gurgling noises. I took advantage of Lily being okay about it and had another hold. He ponged.

'I think he's filled his nappy,' I said.

Lily yawned. 'I'll finish my tea first,' she said. 'He might' – and she tipped back her head in a great big yawn – 'he might do some more ...'

'I'll do it,' I offered.

'Nah, I'll do it.'

Lily sipped her tea and began to doze. She was so tired, I thought I'd change Sunny for her anyway.

I took him over to the mat by the fire and undid his nappy. It was a mess. He really did some monsters in there, that baby. He bent his legs back the way babies do and gurgled and cooed and held his feet and tried to eat them. I wiped him clean. Then I let him try and suck my nose.

There was a voice behind me. 'You didn't have to do that, Gems.'

I cried, 'Ah!' Lily had crept up behind me to see what I was doing. She scared the life out of me. There was something strange in her voice. I spun round. She was staring at my hands on her baby.

'You fell asleep,' I said.

She brushed past me and picked up Sunny. She looked at me as if she didn't know who I was or what I was doing there and said, 'No one's ever gonna take my baby off me.'

I was just shocked. I said, 'I never said that, I never said that.' It never occurred to me. She was looking at me like I was some kind of monster come to steal her baby away. And I felt as guilty as hell because now she'd said it it was obvious that she thought it should be taken off her.

'No one's ever gonna,' she said, and she turned away with the baby. She sounded like she was going to cry.

The whole room was buzzing in my ears. I don't know why it was so powerful. I think it was because the mask slipped. I thought, My God, she's completely out of her depth. And we both knew it, we both knew she'd shown something she never ever showed to anyone, because suddenly she gave me this little glance over her shoulder. Her face was so scared. She was like a baby herself she was so scared. Then she cradled her head against Sunny, and rubbed her cheek into him and kissed him and loved him.

'He's a lovely baby, Gems,' she said. She tried to smile at me. She was just trying to be normal, but it wasn't normal. She stood there staring at me, trying to keep her face straight, and as I watched, her eyes filled with tears. Her mouth opened and I knew what she was going to say. She was going to say, 'Help me.' Don't ask me why but I just knew. I could see her reaching for the words, but she couldn't do it. I reached out to hold her but she just shook her head, a stiff little shake.

There was a horrible few seconds in which I thought she was going to break down and cry. But Lily turned away and went back to the kitchen. She walked around the room a few times. She sat down on the settee. I couldn't move. I didn't know what to do. I thought she might suddenly jump up and ... and stab me or something. I was sure she was going to be angry the next second.

Then Lily tipped back her head and yawned, a big, big yawn. I didn't believe that yawn; it wasn't real. She turned and smiled that big Lily smile at me, like she was herself again.

'I've had it, Gems, I'm going to bed.'

'Okay, Lil.'

She got up and she had to walk past me on her way to the door. I had to force myself not to move back away from her. She looked at me and she said, 'It'll be all right, Gems.'

'I know, Lily.'

'Night.'

'Night.'

I watched her as she left the room. She turned at the door and gave me a big warm smile, and that scared little look again. Then she went out. I sat back down on the rug and drank my tea. I listened to her getting into bed. I waited a long time.

That baby was all she had. He'd always been such a good baby, so quiet.

I thought to myself, I've followed you everywhere you've gone. I've followed you everywhere but I'm not following you here ...

After a while I went down the hall and got my big coat on. I went ever so quietly down the corridor and let myself out of the front door. It was late, two, three o'clock. It was cold but I was scared to get dressed in case Lily came or Tar woke up. I went very quickly round the corner because I didn't believe Lily was asleep. I got to the telephone booth and I dialled 999 and asked for the police.

When I'd finished I said to the woman, 'Will you go round straight away?'

'They'll have to get a warrant first, it'll be a few hours ...'

'Goodbye.'

'Just a minute, Miss ...'

I put the phone down.

It was a real drag that it was going to take so long. I'd been planning on going back and waiting for the music to start with the rest of them, but I just couldn't stay round there waiting for hours.

I had nowhere to go.

I began to walk up the road. A car pulled up by me – someone kerb crawling. I just shook my head and walked on. I was only in my nightie and my coat and my shoes. I carried on walking for a while and I began to cry, trying to think what on earth I was going to do next ...

27
Vonny

Wednesdays we play badminton.

I moved to Clifton when I got my place at college. Now I pay rent and everything. Boring really, but you need a good base when you're doing something like that, and you could never tell how long a squat was going to last. I took my course at college seriously and I didn't want the hassle of having to move every few months.

John's an art student. After badminton we usually go for a few drinks. He gets through his grant in about the first month, so if I want to go out with him I have to buy the drinks, which irritates me no end. He gets the same as me, why should I pay for him? He says his appetites are bigger, which is true – he drinks more than me. Maybe he should apply for an extra-large drinks allowance.

Normally we stay at my place because it's so much nicer, but on Wednesday we usually go to his because mine's a bus ride away and his is just round the corner from the Sports Centre. I usually stay there and go straight into college the next day. So I don't get home till Thursday afternoon.

I've got a garden flat that I share with a girl called Sandy, but she was away that week. Willy lives a few doors up from me. We call her Willy because she has two kids and she used to yell, 'Are the children all in bed?' out of the front door when she wants them to come in and go to bed, like Wee Willy Winkie.

She came round to see me an hour or so after I got back.

'There was a girl sitting on your doorstep yesterday morning. A punky type – one of the scabby ones. She was there for hours.'

I'm a bit of a punky type, as Willy calls it, although never one of the scabby ones. I couldn't work it out because I don't know anyone like that any more, not since I left St Paul's.

'She was there for ages. I think she only had pyjamas on under her coat, she must have been freezing. She was there first thing in the morning, God knows how long she'd been there. I went out about ten o'clock to see what was going on and I told her you wouldn't be back till this evening. She looked awful.'

'Didn't she tell you her name?'

'No. She knew you, though.' Willy looked suspiciously at me. 'Who was it then?' she asked.

I scratched my ear. 'I can't think ... What did she look like?'

Willy started to describe her, but that didn't help either. I just suddenly realised ...

'Gemma!'

I hadn't seen her for ages. It got worse and worse round there, full of brain-dead zombies. I used to go round and nag her quite regularly. She was boasting about it all the time – being on the game, using needles. She thought it was all a big gas. I kept on going for a bit after Richard moved out of Bristol, but then I stopped.

I thought she must be in trouble. I mean, she'd been in trouble for years, but now she'd realised it at last.

I drove straight round to her place but I couldn't get an answer. I looked through the windows and there was no one there. I got back home, fiddled about. I was worried about her – scared, really. She was in such bad trouble for so long and she never even knew it. I like Gemma. She had a lot going for her, but she was just such a lousy judge of character.

It was six o'clock in the evening before I discovered the note. She must have pushed it through my letterbox, but there's a little piece of carpet I use as a mat and sometimes it rucks up and letters get stuck underneath it.

'I can't wait any longer, I'm going to the hospital to try and get them to admit me. Gemma.'

I'd told her so many times I'd always be there if she needed me, and she'd just laughed at me. But she remembered in the end. I ran out and jumped in the car and drove straight there.

She looked like death. I sat on the bed and listened to her story, and I kept thinking, she's eighteen and I'm twenty-four, but she's so much older than me. She's an addict, she's fallen in love, she's slept with dozens of men, she's pregnant. She was only eighteen but I felt like I was sitting there listening to an old, old woman telling me what had happened to her when she was still young.

The police had been round to interview her but Tar, bless him, had taken the rap again even though he must have known she'd called the cops ... and even though it would mean youth custody for him this time.

The hospital was keen to get rid of her. She was just taking up a bed as far as they were concerned. She'd only got in because she was getting these violent stomach cramps. She said she always got them when she was coming down but to be honest, I think she'd exaggerated it so they'd give her a bed. So she was just lying there waiting to be chucked out with nowhere to go.

Poor Gemma! Of course I could take her into my house. I would have done but ...

'Give me your parents' number, Gemma. Let's try that first.'

'I can't.'

The number of times I'd asked her. The number of times she'd said that. I didn't know if I was doing the right thing.

'It's out of your hands, Gemma. Just say the number.'

She covered her face with her hands. '0232 ...' she began. She remembered after all those years.

The phone rang three times. A woman picked it up and said, 'Hello.'

I said, 'Mrs Brogan?'

'Yes.'

I took a deep breath and said it. 'It's about your daughter, Gemma.'

28
Emily Brogan

Three and a half years.

I wanted to catch the train. It would be quicker but Grel insisted on driving. I suppose the driving took his mind off things. I thought it'd be unsafe, but in the event he was as good as gold. I sat there and thought about all the things I'd missed – the things Gemma had missed – growing up, going to school, exams, boyfriends in the living room, parties ...

I'd looked forward to all of it. Having a daughter was like living my own childhood over again and I'd missed out on so much. We all had. I was furious with her because of that. And because ... You see, after all those years, you try to tell yourself you'll probably never see her again until you're an old woman. And then this happens and the wounds are all as fresh and raw as they were when she first left. She was eighteen years old and in trouble but she was still a child to me.

How could she do that to us?

I kept remembering what that girl had told me. 'She's in hospital. No, she's not hurt.'

'But why?' I kept saying. 'Why's she in hospital?' I assumed she was having a baby.

And then at last, 'She's a heroin addict. She's having severe withdrawal symptoms, apparently.'

Three and a half years. She could have died. She still could.

* * *

We got to the hospital and asked for Gemma Brogan. They made us wait and there was a doctor who wanted to discuss her case with us before we saw her. He told us she was pregnant, after all. As well as. He gave me to understand there wasn't a lot of sympathy for someone with her problem.

'Hospital beds are for people who are sick,' he said. In other words, she was going to be booted out. He clearly expected us to take care of her.

We walked towards the ward. Grel said, 'A baby. She's been taking that stuff with a baby ...' He sounded furious. We walked a bit further. He said, 'I suppose she'll expect us to bail her out.'

I couldn't believe my ears. I just stopped and stared at him. She was our child. I was so angry with him, I was prepared to have a row right there in public, standing in the middle of the corridor. But when I turned on him, I saw that he wasn't furious at all. He looked at me with big wet eyes – that's how he cries, his eyes just get wet, and his hands hanging by his side and his face as grey as winter rain. He looked like his whole world had been blown up.

I suppose we let Gemma down in many ways. But she let us down too. She destroyed our lives. The way Grel and I were with each other after she went. We blamed each other. The bitter, bitter arguments we'd had about what we'd said and done and what she'd said and done. It nearly wrecked our marriage. Perhaps it did wreck it. Perhaps we're just together because we have nothing better to do.

But at least we are still together ...

I took his arm and squeezed it. God knows, we're none of us perfect. And he, God bless him, he hung his head and closed his eyes for a moment and a tear trickled down his cheek. Then we hurried on. I can take anything but Grel crying. It always makes me blub and I wanted to save any tears I had for Gemma.

At the ward I did a very selfish thing. I said to Grel, 'I want to see her alone.' I don't defend it. He had as much right as me. I suppose I wanted that precious moment all to myself.

He just shook his head. I nearly said, 'I'm a mother,' but I bit it back just in time. Then we walked in ...

My first thought was, My God, she looks like my mother. Despite everything I still thought of her as a fourteen-year-old girl. But she looked like my mother, my own mother. An old woman.

I went to sit next to her and put my hand on her hand. I wanted to make it as normal as possible for her sake, talk about home and ask her what she'd done, although how on earth we could talk about what she'd done in those years I don't know. I didn't want to cry, I knew I shouldn't but I thought of all the things I'd missed and I couldn't help it, I couldn't get even a word of what I'd planned on saying out. I just started to weep. I tried but I couldn't speak at all so I laid my head on her breast and I wept and I wept and I wept ...

She was crying too. I knew it was all right when she started to cry. The tears said everything for us.

Then she said, 'I want to come home, Mum, can I come home, Mum, please ...?' I nodded my head and tried to say yes, yes, and we just held one another and cried.

29
Tar

You keep your head down and you get on with it. That's how you do your time. If you suck up to the screws you get trouble from the other lads. If you suck up to the other lads the screws think you're becoming a hard man and start putting you down. It's bad enough being locked up all day without the screws screaming at you.

I think I'm going to get through it. I'm steady. Just this past week I've been thinking like that. Maybe it can be an opportunity. Before that I was *so* depressed and before that I was ill, of course.

The first thing was coming down off the methadone. I'd been on a script for over a year. They put me on twenty-five mil and I'd come down a few mil a week, but of course I was using all the time as well. Well, not all the time. A lot of the time I was selling the methadone to buy smack; you get plenty of methadone users, too. Then I'd have a binge and tell the doc to put me back up to twenty-five or thirty. But in the last weeks before my case came up I was doing quite well. It was something to focus on, I suppose. I was thinking: don't use needles, stick to chases if you have to, do your best not to take any at all. And I did all right considering I'd been in such a huge mess in the months leading up to it. I managed to get by without any junk at all in the last week, and that's not bad because you can imagine how tempting it was – the last fling, make myself feel better, you know ...

So coming down was the first thing and it was *awful*. Coming off methadone is worse than coming off junk. It really makes you feel bad. They're crazy, because that's what they give you to come off heroin – something that's even more addictive and worse to come off. The only reason they give it to you is because you don't get the same hit. It's not fun. It's medicine so it can't be nice. It's bonkers, really.

I spent a few hours rolling around groaning in my cell and they let me go to the pharmacy. I was in a horrendous mess – sweating this horrid yellow juice that stung and aching, and my teeth with this toothache that kept jumping from tooth to tooth.

I explained to the nurse what I needed and she just laughed at me.

'We don't have methadone in here, David.' Stupid git that I am, my heart actually leapt. I thought, Yeah, they're going to give me a diamorphine script – that's the real stuff. You don't get it any purer than the hospital gets it.

'But I need something ...'

'You'll live,' she said.

I waited a few seconds as it began to dawn on me that the heartless bitch was going to give me nothing. My teeth started screaming in horror.

'You don't understand –'

'I don't suppose I do. But I do know we don't give methadone to heroin users in a young offender institution.'

I said, 'Some Valium.'

'Sorry.'

'Something,' I croaked. She pulled a face and went to the medical cabinet and broke off a couple of tabs which she handed to me.

'Two Paracetamol?' I said. I couldn't believe it. I thought, Doesn't she know anything?

I tried to be patient and explain to her. 'Two Paracetamol

won't do anything to me. I'm a big user, I need something a little bit stronger ...' I smiled encouragingly at her, which wasn't easy when your bones are trying to break themselves up in your body. She'd just about had enough.

'I've got a lot of people to see ...'

I stood there staring at my miserable two tabs of headache pills until the screw pushed me back outside.

I was horrified. Two Paracetamol! It was monstrous. It had to be against the Geneva Convention or something. I mean, locking you up, I could understand that, maybe even electrodes up the bum. But giving me just *two* Paracetamol in the middle of methadone comedown was inhuman.

'You don't understand,' I said to the screw as he slammed the door in my face. The thud of it went right through my spine; I thought it was going to snap in twenty different places.

'Have a nice time,' he told me. And they just left me there.

I'd have escaped. I'd have committed murder. I broke the Paracetamol into four halves and took a half then and saved the rest for later. When that's all you have to get you through, you might as well go for the placebo effect. I even ground one of them up and snorted it, but that wasn't much good either.

That's the way it works. You'll eat shit or go in the ring for ten rounds with Mike Tyson – slave, hero, rent boy, pimp, master of the universe – you'll do whatever you have to do to get your next hit.

Looking back – some of the things we were doing. Rob was cottaging – you know? Selling sex to homos in the public toilets. Lily went mad when she found out, it totally did her head in. It was all right her doing it at home, but him doing it with men – she just went ape, running around screaming and crying. Me, I was nicking stuff. Not from the shops; I'd lost the bottle for that ages before. From Gemma, from Rob, from Lily. Anyone. I'd turn up late at a friend's house, stay late, ask if I could stay and then get up in the night and sneak about opening drawers and digging around in cupboards and coat pockets.

Gemma was the only one who seemed to be getting better. She stopped doing jumps at the parlour. She was a heavy user, though, She was using as much as me, I reckon, and I was using a lot. And then, of course, she broke out. Trust Gemma.

There was all hell that night when the pigs turned up. Everyone knew, somehow. Lily was screaming at me, 'Bitch! Bitch! Bitch!' as if Gemma was sort of a part of me. Actually I had a pretty good idea it was going to happen. I didn't know about the baby till much later, but Gemma had been going on about Lily using and having a baby. I think that really shocked her. I heard her going out of the front door that night and I knew all her clothes were in the bedroom, so it had to be something pretty weird. And she didn't come back.

I lay there and I thought, Is this it? I just lay there. I thought I'd find out soon enough.

They hauled us all in. Me and Rob took the rap, or tried to. Lily tried to implicate Gemma but it didn't wash.

'It's that bitch who rang you up – she did, didn't she? It's all hers, we're just living here ...' Standing there in the middle of the floor in her short nightie with her beautiful legs all covered in needle bruises ... yeah.

They're both in care now. I'm the only one who got a custodial sentence. Lily and Rob didn't even see the light of day, they never even got bail because they were considered to be so much at risk. Lily went with the baby into one detox centre, Rob went into another. Then straight into separate rehab centres. And there they are now, eight months later. Gemma says they'll be moving into halfway houses in a few months. I don't suppose either of us'll ever see them again.

Actually the comedown could have been worse. Like the nurse said, there was nowhere I could go and score. Well, that's not strictly true. You can get any kind of drug in prison, it's a user's paradise, but of course I didn't know that at the time. The thing was, I didn't have that awful feeling – all I have to do ...

Then I was depressed. I never was so depressed. Not much to say about that except I got through it. That's one thing about being inside, you get through it, whatever it is, because you don't have any choice. Gemma came in to visit me and I didn't tell her how I was feeling. I just said I was keeping my head down, getting on with it, doing the things you do.

And then – like I say, I thought, Maybe it's not so bad. Somehow my head popped up above water. I was getting through it. Look at it, after all – I've been clean for over three months now, for the first time in years. I might not have done it myself out of choice, but I am clean and that's the important thing. It's something to build on. I got a reasonable sentence. It was my second conviction, they could have given me a lot longer than eighteen months. With any luck I can be out in nine; that's a third gone already. The other day one of the screws said to me as I was going past, 'You're doing well, David ... keep it up.' He smiled and nodded at me.

And I thought, Yeah ... I am. I'm doing well. I was pretty pleased with myself. I'd been ill, I'd been depressed, now I'm doing all right. Some of the screws are okay. You get some horrific bastards, of course, but some are okay. And I was doing all right.

I told Gemma. She must have seen how proud I was because she laughed and said, 'Hostage syndrome.'

'What's that?'

'Loving your jailer,' she told me, and I just smiled. She was right, I was proud I'd pleased a screw. It's a bummer really, you feel grateful to them just for being human. But it helps and anything that helps is important.

Gems is as big as a house! She got bigger and bigger every time she came in and now she's about ready to pop. Next time she comes in she'll bring the baby with her. It's due in about a week. Last time she was sitting in her chair beaming away and patting her huge tum. We sit at these little tables, and I put my hand on it so I could feel it kicking.

'He's gonna be a footy fan, I reckon.'

And she leaned back in her chair and slapped her big tum and pushed up her big tits and said, 'And it's all yours, boy ... it's all yours. You come out clean and it's all there waiting for you.'

Like I say, I keep my head down and my nose clean. I just think ... it's all there. All I've got to do is time.

30
Gemma

SO WHAT'S SO INTERESTING 'BOUT YOU-O
WHERE'S THE DAMAGE, WHERE'S THE FUN?
THINK OF ALL THE THINGS WE DONE
BUT WE'LL NEVER DO 'EM NO MORE-O
O NEVER DO NO MORE-O

Lurky

I'm in my sitting room writing this.

It's a windy day, the house is draughty. I've got the gas fire on full and I can see the flames move when the wind gusts outside. When I look out nothing's moving, even though the wind is so strong. In Bristol I could always see the trees swaying in the wind. I can see the sea from here. I mean, I could if it wasn't so dark. The waves must be lashing up full of foam. I can't see it but I can smell it, even in the house.

Bloody Minely again. I like being near the sea, though.

The baby's on the settee. She's not asleep, I just fed her. She has this toy my mum gave her – you wind it up and it plays a tune and casts pretty lights on the ceiling for her to watch. It's dim in here; I'm probably doing my eyes in writing this. I can hear her cooing at the pretty lights. Her name's Oona and I love her to bits. She saved my life, really.

Tar's in bed, asleep.

He came this afternoon. They let him out at seven this morning. I was going to pick him up in the car, but it's miles and miles to Meadowfield and he said no, because they give them a pass for the train. So I met him at the station at Gravenham instead.

It was great, it was great. He was pale and grey from being locked up so long, but he was his old self – Tar, my Tar. He was shy. He got off the train and stood there with his little bag smiling at me as I walked up the station towards him. Then he saw Oona and he smiled even more. You could almost hear the skin stretching at the sides of his mouth.

I was going to do the ol' 'Wow! you're the greatest, wow wow wow!' trick on him that I did when I went to Bristol that time, but I thought better of it. I was talking to Sally on the phone. She's off junk now, she's on a methadone script but I don't know if she'll hold out. And she said, 'Don't come on too strong, remember he's been inside.' My mum said the same thing. So I didn't go mad, I just ran up and I gave him a big, long, slow, hard hug. I squeezed him so hard, and I buried my face in his neck and then I went, 'Whooo!' I couldn't help it, I felt so *glad*. Then I gave him the baby. And he was beaming away like ... like Tar on a good day, holding his baby girl.

Ah, Tar. And he was clean. He'd been off junk for over a month before he went inside on a methadone script, and he was off that in Meadowfield, so he was as clean as a whistle. And I was *so* pleased to see him.

I had a bit of a party back at the house for him. None of the old crowd – I didn't want any of that. I invited Richard and Vonny, that's all – and a few old schoolfriends and some people I've met since. Nice food, loads to drink, a bit of hash going round. Music. We had an hour or two at home just to get him acclimatised, then people started turning up. Everyone was making a fuss of him. He was like – like Sally said – you know, you've spent all that time without ever opening a door, being locked up all the time, the screws watching you, all those hard cases, and then suddenly there you are, you can go where you want and do what you want and it's all a bit of a shock.

Richard was funny. He had a tee-shirt on with a dandelion on it he'd had screened from one of Tar's pictures, and those green boots Tar'd painted flowers on all that time ago – all cracked and faded now.

'How was the holiday camp?' he said, and he beamed at the door over Tar's shoulder.

It felt good. There were some of his old friends there as well. I'd been keeping my eyes open for people. I had Barry who put us up in his dad's garage and a few others – some of the beach crowd, people from school. Afterwards, we went for a walk on the seafront with Oona, and Richard took us out for a meal. I was feeling a bit jittery by then but I put it down to all the excitement and not seeing him for so long. I thought it was maybe because I was a bit fishy about the junk. I'd said he had to be clean before he came to live with us and he was, but only by being locked up. But ... you gotta give him a chance. He knew – first whiff of junk – out you go.

In the evening we went out for a few drinks with Richard and Vonny, while this friend of mine babysat. Down my local. It was a Wednesday night so it was quiet. Tar looked exhausted, totally exhausted.

Vonny said, 'Do you want to go back?'

'I'm all right.'

Richard said, 'I'm feeling a bit tired myself,' and got up, which was his way of giving Tar a way out.

I put Richard and Vonny in the baby's room. Well, she doesn't sleep there yet, she sleeps in her cot next to my bed. Then we went to bed.

I felt really weird about it. I mean, I hadn't done it for so long. We both hopped into bed starkers – it was all very exciting. Then he kissed me and stroked me and touched me and I just went ... aaaaaaaaaaaaaaaahhhhhhhhhhhhhhhhhh ...

It was *horrible*. I just ... I *did not* want to be there with him. I didn't want him to touch me or lie on top of me or next to me, I didn't want to be anywhere near him. It was awful. I couldn't believe it. I'd been looking forward to him for so long and missing him and loving him and then as soon as he touches me I feel like I can't stand him touching me.

I must have stiffened up. He said, 'Are you all right?'

'Yeah, I'm all right, I'm all right, I'm all right,' I said. I tried to relax and get into it and that was horrible too because I had to put on an act. I mean, I've done that before ... But this was Tar.

I didn't know what to do. I mean, I'd been waiting there; the house, Oona, me, all safe and waiting for him, no more junk, nice little family, everything's going to be great. And he's my Tar and he's taken the rap for me twice, and he's been through all this shit ... the detox, youth custody, all for me, and he'd probably never even have become a junkie if it wasn't for me – and then ... bang!

We did it in the end. It wasn't easy. I was so shocked I was as dry as yer dad's handkerchief, but I managed to concentrate and get down to it, and it was all right in the end. I told him I was just nervous. I don't know if he believed me.

I waited until he looked like he was asleep, then I picked up Oona and crept out of the room. I just had to have a little space and try to think. What does it mean? What on earth does it mean?

I was sitting out there for ages. I must have drunk about a gallon of tea. Then to make it even worse, he came out to see if I was okay. He couldn't sleep either. I tried to make out I was just upset and nervous. It seemed reasonable enough. He sat next to me and we had a cuddle. I just tried to think of him as my Tar, my little boy who'd had a really hard time and needed to be comforted, and that made it all right.

***

I told my mum about it. She was good. It's been quite a shock to find I can talk to my mum. Dad's ... well, I don't think anyone manages to talk to him about that sort of thing, not even Mum. But Mum's not bad. She said, 'Give it six months.' She knows we've been through all this stuff together; she'd like to see us split up, I expect. But she lets me make my own mind up. Tar's the father – I suppose that makes a big difference in her book.

Six months. I really, really hope it gets better. It's just not fair, is it? I end up with the life: he ends up with nothing. It ought to work, oughtn't it? It ought to work.

He's doing really well. He wants to go to art college, but he needs to get the O-levels and A-levels first. He's going to start at the Tech College, but that doesn't begin till the autumn and it's only May, so he's doing night school in the meantime. And he's got a little job behind the bar – off the cards or they'd take it off the Social. He does two nights and I do two nights. Well, just because you want to be clean doesn't mean you have to turn into something out of *Neighbours*, does it? And he's a great mate but ...

It's just gone. Where'd it go? Funny thing, I was going to give him the elbow just before I met Lily and Rob. Funny thing. I just feel so bad about it.

I was on the phone to Sal the other day. She keeps wanting to come and visit but I put her off; it's too early. She's not clean, she's on methadone but she slips up from time to time. She's got this new boyfriend, Mick, and they're going to go to Amsterdam together and live over there for a while. Yeah, she's bound to stay clean over there in the Drug Capital of

Europe, as my dad likes to call it. To be fair to Sally, she doesn't make much of a pretence that she's going straight. But she'll be all right, if anyone is. Sal's one of those people who can go on for ever.

I envy her. I'd like to go but I know what'd happen. Me, I don't even dare go back to Bristol for a visit. So I'm stuck here in sodding Minely for the rest of my natural. Well, for a bit anyway.

But she said a lot of interesting things, Sal. She said, maybe it was some sort of comeback for being on the game. You know, maybe it put me off sex. That's an interesting one. I try to think it's that. I asked her, What about you?

'Oh, no, oh no,' she said. 'You know me ...'

I can't tell because I never slept with anyone while Tar was away. But I don't think so. I mean, it's not the thought that turns me off. Just, not with Tar any more ...

And she said, 'You've got to give it a chance, Gems.' Everyone says that. And she said this: 'You've gotta do what you feel in the end.' That's what my mum says, too. And that's what everyone says. But I don't wanna do what I feel. I wanna do all right by Tar.

I just feel so sick about it, it's so unfair. He could do with a break, Tar, and I thought – I suppose I always thought – that I was the break. And then I think, what good have I ever done for him? He'd never have got in with Lily and Rob and junk if it wasn't for me; he'd have stuck at the squat with Vonny and Richard.

Actually my mum disagrees with that. She says he'd have found his way there on his own in the end. Maybe ... he was a bigger junkie than I was. I don't mean he took more; I was up there with the best of them while I did it. But when I came here, I did my cold turkey and that was it. I just didn't want to know; I didn't want to go near the stuff ever again. But Tar ... he'd hitchhike halfway round the country to score. In fact he did, several times. So maybe my mum's right. But it's still not fair, is it?

He loves Oona *so* much.

Give it six months. I just wish ...

I just wish he didn't want to sleep with me.

31
Tar's Dad

It wasn't a love story.

That seems a hard thing to say, but one of the things you learn is to look facts straight in the eye. Not necessarily without flinching.

For example ... I'm a sad old man. You try it, at the age of fifty-five. Your only child hates you, your wife hates you, your colleagues – ex-colleagues – despise you. All for good reasons. Everything you worked for is gone and there you are. It doesn't feel like standing at the threshold of a new dawn, I can tell you. I don't feel sorry for myself ... well, that's not true, of course I feel bloody sorry for myself. I mean to say, I know that it's my fault.

Jane and I, that was a love story. We fell in love when we were young – deeply, deeply in love. It went wrong later on. You can say all sorts of things about why – she wasn't who I thought she was, I don't suppose I was what she thought I was. In the end though there's only one answer – booze, booze and booze. I like a drink, I used to say. Not any more. Bit late in the day. The funny thing about it is that we both ended up on the bottle. Isn't that odd? Neither of us was at it to start with, it just seemed to happen. Makes you wonder.

When David came back to Minely, I was scared silly. But I hoped. My son, after all. It was hard because he saw through me a long time before I saw through myself. Your son, your little boy who thinks you're the whole world and you have to stand in front of him and say, 'Here I am, I ballsed it up for you. Will you have a relationship with me? I don't blame you if you don't ...'

'You shouldn't have left her,' he told me.

'David, I couldn't even look after myself, let alone your bloody mother.'

It all fell to bits pretty quickly after he left. I thought I was holding the whole thing together. Apparently he thought it was him. People hang on to situations. You think you *are* the situation. Then when the whole bloody thing falls apart ... you are still there.

But there wasn't any reason to hold it together after he left us. No matter how hard things got I always thought, I have to stay here for the boy, I have to keep going for his sake, I can't leave David here at the mercy of his mother. He didn't make it any easier, though. Interfering all the time. Trying to take care of her. Doing the housework for her. Taking away her self-respect – taking away the only things she had to keep her going. It's the worst thing you can do for an alcoholic. Your self-respect is low enough to start off with. How she must have felt about herself, having her son doing her job for her! I tried to tell him: 'Your mother has a problem, David, we have to help her get on top of it ...' But he just carried on, trying to run her life for her.

I suppose what I should have done was to say, 'Your father has a problem, I need help.' But the need for self-deception in a situation of dependency is quite staggering. I never even knew I was an alcoholic until everything had already gone.

For example. I'd come back and the whole house would stink of gin and perfume. 'You stink of alcohol,' I'd yell.

'YOU stink of alcohol!' she'd shriek back. But I knew she was lying. Funny, isn't it? There was no way she could smell me because I was too clever for her ... ha ha ha! I drank vodka and wore after shave. She was only saying that to get off the fact that she'd been on the gin all day.

I must have stunk like a skunk.

I used to hit them. I expect you knew. No hiding place, eh? I wish he could forgive me but it's asking a lot. No, I haven't and never will ask for forgiveness from my son. But if he offered it, that'd be different. I'd accept in all humility.

Jane lives in the old place; I don't see her very often but when I do, there's this smell long-term alcoholics have. A sort of warm urinous smell, tinged with a bit of spirit. And they don't know it. You splash on the Tasker after shave or the perfume and you think, Aren't I clever, ha ha ha.

I lost my job about a year after David left home. I wonder how I got away with it for so long. The smell, apart from anything. That humiliates me to this day – the thought that I smelt. My final humiliation came about during a meeting of Heads of Department. I fell asleep in my chair, dozed off. Not a unique experience. I woke up with someone shaking my arm – it was Tamla Williams. 'Wake up, Mr Lawson ... I think you've had a bit of an accident ...'

It took a moment to dawn. The smell. Then the warmth on my lap turning cold.

I said, 'Excuse me,' and I got up and walked out. I picked up a copy of the school magazine from the table and held it in front of me and I walked as fast as I could to the car, saying to myself, 'This is a dream. This is a dream. This is a dream.'

The bastards. They could have just tiptoed out of the room and left me to wake up on my own and clean up and sneak away. At least then I might have been able to fool myself it hadn't happened in public. Come to think about it, I wonder how often they *did* do that? There was this time ... no. No. It doesn't bear thinking about.

I just tried to shut off about it, but you can't help

imagining it all ... them sitting around thinking, The poor old sod's dozed off again, sad, isn't it? Then the smell, the looking around, the realisation as someone sees the drips coming off the edge of the chair on to the carpet. The embarrassment rushing round the table. Then watching me rise, just in order to show everyone the great wet patch spreading over the front of my trousers. I can't even remember what they were, but I have been known to pray that they weren't the pale moleskins. Please God!

I'll think of it on my deathbed, I know I will. Maybe it'll be my last thought on earth.

The news spreading round the staffroom. Mr Lawson wet his pants at a staff meeting.

David Hollins, the Head, was very nice about it. I'd been at the school twenty years. 'We can't go on like this, Charles.' Phrases like that. 'I'm putting you on indefinite leave.' And, 'Not fair on the kids ...'

Wife, son, job, bang. And what's left, you ask? Ah. A corny answer to that one, but the truth. God's left.

Sorry. I'm not one of your evangelical types. I'm not out to convert anyone. I was always a believer, I don't want anyone to think that God is a replacement for the bottle. I always prayed. I pray more these days. I go to church. I think to myself, At least I have my faith. Now, David, he really has nothing. Not that he ever had a job to lose. But he's lost his wife, or the equivalent, and his daughter. At nineteen that's a slightly different proposition. He has his daughter to gain. Maybe I have my son to gain.

I did try to convert him. I said, 'What else is there that's outside yourself and big enough and strong enough to help you with addiction if it isn't God?'

'Faith, hope and charity,' he said with a smirk. I *think* he was being sarcastic.

The thing about me and David is, we have so much in

common. There's so much we could talk about. But he isn't really interested. I think he'd despise any insights I could give him. All he really wants to talk about is me being a bastard ... hitting her, hitting him.

I suppose he's outraged that I should even try. The thing is, I have a point of view. Murderers, psychopaths, angels – everyone has a point of view. You don't have to agree with it but if you're going to have some sort of a relationship with them, you have to understand it. But perhaps he doesn't want a relationship with me.

We saw quite a bit of each other when he first came back. I was living in a bedsit down the road, a reformed character, so he must have thought he ought to give me a chance. He used to come round and let me hold my granddaughter. I was very grateful. I still see her ... Gemma comes round from time to time. I take her for walks in the park and feed the ducks and push her on the swing ...

'Hello, clouds!' I shout.

'Hewo, cwouds,' she yodels.

'Hello, sky!'

'... skwy ...'

'Hello, birds!'

'Hewo ...'

'Hello, God!'

I wonder if her father would approve?

He didn't talk to me very much about his own private life, only mine, so I had to piece together what happened later on. Basically, it didn't work. He came out of prison and she didn't want to know. That's why I say it wasn't a love story. Jane and I met each other and fell in love without the aid of any artificial stimulants ... and we stayed in love. I think we still are despite the anger and the failures and the violence and the booze. It's not possible for us to live together, of course, that's the tragedy of it. But we loved ... we love. I do anyway. But David and Gemma were on drugs the day they met. The beach crowd. Not heroin, I daresay. But drugs are drugs, aren't they?

I accused him of that and he rolled his eyes and said, 'Just a bit of smoke – that's nothing.'

'Is it?'

'It's better for you than fags,' he said, and we said it together:

'I couldn't do without my smokes ...' I say that often enough. We had a laugh about it.

Anyway, it didn't work, that's the point. He wanted it, she didn't. I don't like Gemma very much. I blame her. I blame myself – but I blame her too. Apparently, it went on for months. She asked him to go; he wouldn't go ... it was his child too, why should he go, that sort of thing. In the end she moved back into her parents' house and told him she wasn't coming back. He hung on for a week, then he gave in and moved out of the flat so she could come back. Obviously he couldn't sit there leaving her and the child stranded with those awful parents.

I offered to put him up. He could have stayed with his mother, there was enough space there. But no, he went and stayed with friends. And apparently – I never heard about this for ages afterwards – apparently he got very angry about it all, very bitter. He started going round there late at night and shouting outside the door until she let him in. Shouting. Drunk. Disturbing the child. Making a nuisance of himself.

How very familiar.

And one day, to cut a long story short, he went round there pissed up, and he did the dirty. Oh yes. He knocked her down and kicked her around the room. She wasn't that hurt, not black eyes or fat lips. But that's not the point. The point is, he hit her.

He didn't tell me about that, of course. Gemma came

round after he'd left Minely and I got most of it off her then. I'd hardly seen anything of him for ages; I didn't even know he'd gone.

I waited a long time for him to get in touch with me. I wanted to talk to him about it; I mean, I wanted him to talk to me. I thought, O-ho, what have you got to say for yourself now, mister? I hoped he might turn to me then, at last. Not for advice as such. But I thought by that time our similarities would have been too strong for him to ignore. It would have been nice to share a common weakness. Actually, I did gloat. He'd spent so much time telling me what a bastard I was and now ... ho ho ho.

Well, I know I'm not being fair. It's different, it was just once. He went round and apologised the next day. Maybe I make too much of it – anyone can lose their temper, especially after all he'd been through. I bet it gave him a fright. I bet he thought he was turning into the old man – the bogeyman!

But we've both lost our relationships, we've both lost our children. We've both been addicted to something or other. I know the shapes of our lives were different. I was a respectable teacher with a mortgage and a family living inside the law and he was a junkie living in a squat outside the law. But still, you'd have thought – certainly hoped – that there was something in me he might relate to. But he went away and never got in touch. There was a postcard from Hereford some time later. Apparently he had friends there; he was going to do his A-levels at college. Had a girlfriend. Sounded happy enough. Gemma says so. They're friends these days. More than me and Jane are.

'He's really well, he's got a lovely girlfriend. No, he's great, he's clean, we get on really well,' she says. He comes to see her and Oona from time to time. He takes Oona away on holiday so Gemma has some time off. It sounds all very worked out. He never comes to see me even though he's in Minely from time to time. I'm patient. One day I hope there'll be a phone call or a knock at the door. He's a good boy, a good person. It's his instinct to help. I believe he's capable of great love and affection. I know I'll never receive these things from him but I like to think I was instrumental – when he was little, before things went wrong – in nurturing them in him.

One day, my boy, all this will be yours. As they say. All my goods and shackles, such as they are. There's no one else. The other thing you leave your children is your life – the example of it. One day, my boy ...

And so, in your absence, David, I raise my glass to you – a cup of tea, actually – and I say, Here's to you. Good luck! Make the most of it.

And don't end up like me.

32
Tar

EVER FALLEN IN LOVE WITH SOMEONE
EVER FALLEN IN LOVE
IN LOVE WITH SOMEONE
EVER FALLEN IN LOVE
WITH SOMEONE YOU SHOULDN'T FALL IN LOVE
WIIIIIIIIIIIIIIIIIIIIIIIIIIIIIIIIIIITH?

The Buzzcocks

It was a love story. Me, Gemma and junk. I thought it was going to last forever. It was the biggest adventure of my life, you know. Gemma's something special, isn't she? And so's junk.

I liked being in love. It's like giving part of yourself away. Love is forever! Yeah, well, I don't believe that any more. It's something that happens to you, like anything else. It starts and then it stops. Being an addict ... now *that* lasts for ever. Like they said in the detox centre, once an addict, always an addict. You don't dare to take the stuff again no matter how safe you feel. Which is a pity really, because heroin is instant love. To love another person you have to feel safe, you have to be ready for it; it's not easy. But with heroin all you have to do is push down the plunger – and hey presto! And it's so real.

But I don't want to talk about that old stuff. You've got to keep positive. The future's looking pretty good to me. I'm

moving on. I've got a new girlfriend now. She's called Carol
and she's a lot better for me than Gemma was. She's got both
feet on the ground. Gemma was all over the place, wasn't
she? I thought she knew it all. When you're in the state I was
in, even someone like Gemma looks sorted.

I met Carol round at a mate's place and we got on just like
that. I moved into her place a few months later. It's a big
house; we share it with a few other people. It's good. I'm
clean, I've got a great girlfriend. I'm working ... me with a
job! Yeah, in a warehouse. You know, stacking shelves, that
sort of thing. I'm not doing college this year. I got my O-levels
in Minely. I got good grades. I enrolled at the Tech here in
Hereford, but I'm going to leave the A-levels for this year.
College is waiting for me, I know I'll go there one day, when
I'm ready for it. Me and Carol live a nice quiet life and that's
just what I need for now.

I see Gemma every few months ... because of Oona. Me
and Gems, I expect we'd have stayed in touch anyway.
Although it's a bit like the past when I see her ... you know;
there's some bad memories. Splitting up. I don't really want
to talk about that, it's over now. Oona – she's the future.
She's a reason to stay clean – and Carol, of course. And me.
But Oona's lovely. I bring her here for the holidays. It gives
Gemma a break. It makes me and Carol ever so broody,
having her here.

I said to Carol, 'Doesn't it make you want to have one?'

And she said, 'No.'

That's Carol! She's knows me. She's got her head screwed
on. She knows better than to have babies with me. She makes
me laugh, Carol.

I don't spend much time with Gemma when I go to
Minely. It's all right talking to her on the telephone or seeing
her down the pub, but when I see her with Oona it does hurt.
That's my place. I want to be in on it but Gemma won't let

me. That makes me angry and I don't want to be angry with Gemma. What for?

It's over, that's the point. Me and Gemma. All that's left is these tiny little pills – five mil of methadone, the tail end of everything. Carol knows all about the past. I told her everything. She's knows I'm on a script. Five mil is nothing, I can't even feel it. I don't need it, not in the sense of being addicted. It's nice to know it's there, that's all, and it's coming down a little bit every week.

I know myself a lot better now. I know I can't make it on my own, I need help. There's a lot of junk in Hereford. Well, there is everywhere, but there are some familiar faces round here. Quite a few people from Bristol end up here for some reason. I could go and score now if I wanted. You can't avoid it.

It's amazing how the stuff seeks you out. About three months after I came here, I'd just been with Carol for a few weeks, I got talking to this bloke at a party and he said, 'Do you want some?' Funny thing was, I didn't know him and he didn't know me but he just seemed to know. I shook my head and said no, and he went upstairs with someone else.

That was it for me – the thought that they were up there with junk and I was down here without it ...

I went and got Carol and I said, 'We've got to go.'

'What for?'

'I've just got to go.'

She could see I was in a mess. She got her coat and we went, even though it was a good party. We walked round the block and she said, 'Okay, what is it?' So I told her.

She already knew about the smack, about Gemma and everything. She said, 'You're not as clean as you said you were, are you? You've been ambushed.'

Carol's really good. I don't know how I'd have coped if it wasn't for her. I'd have been back on junk for sure. After getting offered some at that party I started getting these terrible cravings, like I hadn't had for over a year. It was knowing it was there, see? It was the first time since before I was inside that I knew I could walk out of the door, walk down the road and score. I couldn't stop thinking about it. I went to see the doctor and told him about it, but he wouldn't give me any methadone because I hadn't done any junk So I went away and had a think about it. I knew I wasn't going to make it without help. The next day I went back and told him I'd lied, I had done some. Which was true, actually, although that was another time. It was on a visit to Bristol. It wasn't important, it was like a holiday romance, you know? You forget it all when you get back home. I didn't worry about it because I was in control. So I used that, told a few fibs, told him it was just the other week when in fact it was over two months back. But it worked. I got my script. All in a good cause, getting me clean again.

I'm coming off really slowly. A little bit at a time. I wanted to come off it really fast, get it over with. I was impatient to get on with it, but the doc said that's not a good way to do it. You have to do it real slow, so that you barely notice.

It's going to be okay. I'm doing all the right things. It would have been pretty surprising for someone with my history if I hadn't had a couple of setbacks when you think what's happened lately. The thing to avoid is those ambushes. Sometimes I take a handful of methadone – you know, as a drug. I don't tell Carol about that, though! Wow, I wouldn't dare. You have to be careful with Carol: she's great, she doesn't take any stick. But she's never been on it, so she doesn't really understand. You can't talk to her about it.

I'm doing my best, that's what's important. I try to be positive about it. I'm doing the right things. I'm not pulling the wool over my eyes. It isn't all easy going, I can admit that. I've slipped up a couple of times. I don't dare tell Carol about that, either. And I certainly don't tell Gemma. She might stop me seeing Oona if she knows I'm using. She has no right to do that. I'm her dad, I've got a right to see her ... and she's got a right to see me.

With my history you can't rush it. It's so easy to think, Oh God, here I am, I'm back on methadone, I slipped up again, I'm just a junkie. Once you get a low opinion of yourself, you've had it. You have to think, the methadone is going down, I'm seeing the doctor once a week, I've not got a junk habit. I'm doing the right things. And I think – it's a bit like the carrot on a stick, you know? – that maybe if I get off, I'll get back with Gemma again.

I know, I know. She didn't chuck me because I was using ... I was as clean as a whistle at the time, more or less. But you have to hope. Like the doctor says, you have to be positive before you can get anywhere.

READ MORE IN PENGUIN

For people of all ages, Penguin represents quality and variety – the very best in publishing today around the world.

For complete information about books available from Penguin – including Puffin – and how to order them, contact us at the appropriate address below. Please note that for copyright reasons the selection of books varies from country to country.

On the worldwide web: www.puffin.co.uk

In the United Kingdom: Please write to *Dept. EP, Penguin Books Ltd, Bath Road, Harmondsworth, West Drayton, Middlesex UB7 0DA*

In the United States: Please write to *Consumer Sales, Penguin USA, P.O. Box 999, Dept. 17109, Bergenfield, New Jersey 07621-0120*. VISA and MasterCard holders call 1-800-253-6476 to order Penguin titles

In Canada: Please write to *Penguin Books Canada Ltd, 10 Alcorn Avenue, Suite 300, Toronto, Ontario M4V 3B2*

In Australia: Please write to *Penguin Books Australia Ltd, P.O. Box 257, Ringwood, Victoria 3134*

In New Zealand: Please write to *Penguin Books (NZ) Ltd, Private Bag 102902, North Shore Mail Centre, Auckland 10*

In India: Please write to *Penguin Books India Pvt Ltd, 706 Eros Apartments, 56 Nehru Place, New Delhi 110 019*

In the Netherlands: Please write to *Penguin Books Netherlands bv, Postbus 3507, NL-1001 AH Amsterdam*

In Germany: Please write to *Penguin Books Deutschland GmbH, Metzlerstrasse 26, 60594 Frankfurt am Main*

In Spain: Please write to *Penguin Books S. A., Bravo Murillo 19, 1° B, 28015 Madrid*

In Italy: Please write to *Penguin Italia s.r.l., Via Felice Casati 20, I–20124 Milano*

In France: Please write to *Penguin France S. A., 17 rue Lejeune, F–31000 Toulouse*

In Japan: Please write to *Penguin Books Japan, Ishikiribashi Building, 2–5–4, Suido, Bunkyo-ku, Tokyo 112*

In South Africa: Please write to *Longman Penguin Southern Africa (Pty) Ltd, Private Bag X08, Bertsham 2013*